SHE HAD TO FIGURE OUT A WAY to get out of going into her dark, deserted basement with Adam Lawrence, murder suspect . . .

"Adam, I can't go into the basement with you," Georgette blurted. "I'm scared of the dark."

"Surely there must be a light fixture in the basement."

"That doesn't make a bit of difference. I'm also scared of places that are dark most of the time."

Adam stalked closer, his body movements fluid and wondrous. He planted his left hand against the wall beside her head, his tanned fingers a scant inch away from her dark hair. She suppressed a gasp.

"That doesn't make sense," he said. "Most any place on earth is dark almost half the time."

"What are you trying to do, make me paranoid?"

He planted his other hand, surrounding her with 180-plus pounds of thoroughly virile male. His face descended toward hers. She clamped her eyelids shut, figuring that whether he choked her or kissed her, she was correctly prepared.

"I am certain," he said softly, "that no one can make you into anything other than what you are, nor should anyone try . . ."

Books by Carol Budd

Scarlet Scandals
White Lies

Published by POCKET BOOKS

SCARLET SCANDALS

Carol Budd

POCKET BOOKS

New York   London   Toronto   Sydney   Tokyo   Singapore

This book is a work of fiction. Names, characters, places and incidents are either the product of the author's imagination or are used fictitiously. Any resemblance to actual events or locales or persons, living or dead, is entirely coincidental.

An *Original* Publication of POCKET BOOKS

 POCKET BOOKS, a division of Simon & Schuster Inc. 1230 Avenue of the Americas, New York, NY 10020

ISBN: 0-671-67901-5

First Pocket Books printing August 1990

10 9 8 7 6 5 4 3 2 1

For my parents
Joseph Pellegrini and Jeanette Marchbanks Pellegrini
with love and admiration.

My thanks to Patti Barricklow, Maria Greene, Terry Mills,
and David—always.

San Francisco is a mad city inhabited by perfectly insane people whose women are of remarkable beauty.

—*Rudyard Kipling*

SCARLET SCANDALS

Exclusive to San Francisco Lifestyle and
Leisure Magazine

SIN REVISITED

by

STU BAKER

*Hidden in the vicinity of Russian Hill and Pacific Heights
but claimed by neither of these fashionable areas of the
city is a short, dead-end lane whose ivy-laden sign
proclaims it Scarlet Street. Named for the Gold Rush Era
bordello that was its founding structure, nineteenth-
century Scarlet Street served as magnet and haven for
assorted blackguards, rakes, and scoundrels. Zeb Hoagsworth, a crusading evangelist of the period, once
charged that, "Every reprobate in the city has come into
something not his own behind the lowered shades of
Scarlet Street."*

*After the earthquake and fire of 1906 swept the area
clean, Zeb Hoagsworth claimed the street for the righteous and decent. The sinners were banished, and from
the ashes of evil rose crisply painted homes banked by
rows of brilliant azaleas and spreading oaks. But because
secrecy is as imperative for the righteous as for the
sinner, the shades on the windows of Scarlet Street
remained tightly shut. Speculative gossip flourished until
the 1920s when these stiff-corseted, natty eccentrics*

found their domain invaded by the nouveau riche: notorious ladies who pranced about without under- garments and infamous gentlemen who gambled, drank, and debauched, and didn't give a damn who knew it. Mating ensued with rapacious abandon, and the results of these couplings proved explosive. Over the years their descendants have animated Scarlet Street with a dizzy- ing array of nefarious festivities, titillating tête-à-têtes, outrageous frauds, and now, once again, murder. . . .

Chapter
1

Georgette Richards studied her reflection through a veil of curls that cascaded from the top of her head down to her toes and then some. She looked, she decided, like a blond sheepdog. A quick shake of her shoulders did part the wall of hair but only in areas pornographers would appreciate.

With an "Arrrgh," she threw off the heavy wig, and Lady Godiva's garb joined the other rejects piled high on her bed. As Cleopatra, she'd resembled a white-draped fireplug sporting an asp. Helen of Troy's robes camouflaged her so well, she might as well hostess her upcoming pre-Halloween housewarming party from inside the Trojan horse. And for George's diminutive endowments to shore up Lillie Langtry's décolletage would have required a feat of suspension rivaling the Golden Gate Bridge.

Muttering, she snatched up the last costume and, with arms held high, let the fabric slide to her waist. "Joan of Arc would have been perfect but oh, no, I had to let Marfa use her own judgment.

"Some judgment," she puffed, punching her hands through the armholes. She bent over. With one hand

3

stretching the zipper, the other tugging at the tab, she jumped, landed flat-footed, and the zipper whined upward.

"I swear if it's the last thing I do . . ." Another jump snapped the zipper closed like the jaws of an alligator, encasing four-feet-eleven-and-three-quarter inches and ninety-five pounds of Georgette Richards into a riot of polka-dotted tulle.

She spun, confronting her image in the mirror. Ruffles sprouted from her shoulders, brushing the tips of her earlobes. The bodice fit like a second skin, stark white with large blue dots. She pushed down on the skirt, but several dozen layers of white net crinoline bounced back resiliently, standing out like a tutu. Clenching her hands into fists, George smashed at it again. It was a miniskirt for the toddler set. "And after all the help I've given Marfa—to be reduced to this!"

Determined to get good and angry, she plopped the huge picture hat on her head and secured it under her chin with a floppy bow. She grabbed up the final prop, a long stick with a curved end, and surveyed herself once again.

"Blast it," she said, pounding the tip of the shepherd's crook against the floor. "Little Bo Peep fits."

She marched toward the telephone, glad that it was eleven-thirty, glad that to answer Marfa would have to climb out of her bathtub and break all her precious little French soap bubbles and miss the opening moments of "The Tonight Show." Actually, it was the announcer Marfa liked. She claimed to be attracted to men who appreciated a good beer and liked Clydesdales, a fact that she attributed to a summer spent in Germany. George knew better. Marfa appreciated a few good beers and liked sharing them with men built like Clydesdales.

"I don't want to hear any more of your explanations!" George yelled the second Marfa started to speak. "Patent-leather flats with buckles and ankle socks in front of three hundred people wasn't enough. Now this!"

"Ah, I see that they delivered the costumes. But I'm here in the dripping nude and I really must—"

"Don't you dare hang up on me!"

"George, really," she pleaded, the first chords of the talk show theme song reverberating in the background.

"You never hesitate to call *me* when you're in the midst of one of your Roman tragedies, and I always help you which is more than I can say— Who filled in for you last week when one of your models had the cramps?"

"She really did and you looked adora— I mean wonderful."

"You didn't bother to tell me it was her *first* period, or that she was only eleven years old, or that I, a perfectly normal woman who just happens to be petite, was the only one you could think of who could fit into that frothy little preteen peach Easter frock!"

"But you have the spirit of eternal youth, the glow and radiance of the freshest flower."

"Marfa, I'm thirty-three years old. First thing you know, my petals will start dropping—everything will start dropping. At this rate I'm going to end up wilting on the vine!"

"Little Bo Peep is perfect. Trust me."

"Ha!" George slammed down the receiver. The polka-dotted skirt bounced perkily. As she watched it bob, tears welled up in her eyes. Marfa had known all along which costume would fit. "You, you . . ." she sniffed, glancing at the pile of rejects that were the proof positive of Marfa's foresight, "you *asp.*"

Downstairs the doorbell pealed. "Oh, for heaven's sake," she grumbled, closing her bedroom window. Quickly, she dabbed her eyes with a streamer of the bow. After one last sniff, she straightened her back and squared her shoulders then stormed past packing crates and haphazardly arranged furniture. She flounced down the stairs in full regalia and pulled open the stained-glass and oak front door.

A slender man leaned against the door frame. Dirt smudged his sweatshirt and jeans. He rolled his head against the wood, his face shadows in the weak light.

She squinted into the darkness. The faint odor of liquor flavored the cool night air. "Well, who in the world are you?"

"I'm sorry to disturb you but I . . ." He pushed himself

away from the doorjamb and took an unsteady step toward her. The light from the foyer chandelier shone on the angles and planes of his face, and she recognized him. What was her neighbor's gardener doing here?

His eyes scanned her. With exaggerated slowness, he blinked once and opened his eyes wide. His lips parted as if to speak. Then, quite suddenly, all expression drained from his face. With a deep sigh, he crumpled on the foyer rug.

She successfully dodged his falling body while maintaining a firm hold on both her picture hat and shepherd's crook. She goggled down at the man. She dearly wanted to point out that his soil-crusted attire was staining an Oriental rug whose cost alone could have easily supported a family of four for a year, but for only the second time in her life, she was absolutely speechless.

The long-awaited event had finally happened. A man had fallen at her feet, a handsome, earthy man whom she had openly admired for nearly two days as he tilled the soil, sweat gleaming on his flexing biceps, denim clinging to his narrow hips. The fact that he'd appeared a trifle disoriented before his collapse did little to dampen her joy. Or, at this auspicious moment, did she choose to dwell on the fact that in the two days since he had been neighbor Fiona Breathwaite's gardener his only tangible impact on Fiona's postage-stamp yard consisted of the near destruction of her beloved camellias by drowning.

Suddenly, the heady realization struck. Her gaze darted from the prostrate man, to her cutesy polka-dotted dress and back to the man. She began to sputter. "And to think that all this time, I mean that for all these years, I thought you men wanted black lace, a red feather boa, maybe a standing rib roast when all along you really wanted a Little Bo Peep show."

She frowned. Could Marfa possibly be right? Could a woman who dated behemoths whose middle names were usually "the" actually know what knocks men out?

She shook her head. "No, it can't be. It's not possible."

George gently prodded the man's shoulder with the tip of

her shepherd's crook. "I don't have to stand for this. Wake up and get out. You're confusing me."

Still, the man remained motionless. Cautiously, George leaned over him and sniffed. "I should have listened to my nose right from the beginning. Demon rum."

Crouching down next to him, she studied the half of his face that was visible. Although his nose was slightly crimped where it pressed into the rug, his profile was strong and masculine. Smile lines radiated from the corner of his eye, and one curved beside his mouth. His hair was the color of chocolate, semisweet with silvery swirls at the temples. She laid the shepherd's crook down beside him, arranging it parallel to his body. He was about five feet nine or ten, in other words, the perfect height for her. He was also gorgeous —and a fraud.

She tugged at his arm. "Okay, get up, you fake. The game's over. I bit, you won, match point, touchdown, ha, ha."

A tiny moan issued from the prostrate man. His head lolled against the rug. Exasperated, she pushed at his shoulder. The man sprawled flat and muttered several unintelligible phrases.

George rolled back on her heels and implored the heavens. "Why me? Why do all the degenerates land on my doorstep?"

Her glance cut to the man, and though she was determined to be furious, her gaze lingered. "Fiona did hire you and what with her away at her gin night . . . I mean she would expect me to help her employee in his hour of need. Wouldn't she?"

In the final analysis she found herself swayed by a deeply ingrained lesson more lasting than any she'd gleaned during years of expensive private schooling. When she was a teenager, she had hunkered beneath a silk sheet with a flashlight and a package of frosted animal cookies and consumed the forbidden novel, *Candy*, cover to cover, three times.

With a shrug of her shoulders, George closed the front

door. You don't, she reasoned, throw out a perfectly wonderful-looking gardener, even if he is unconscious.

As the Chinese Chippendale clock chimed seven, the man sprawled on the sofa groaned. George bounded out of a wing chair, skirted the antique chow-legged table, and rushed to his side.

Last night Dr. Pelton had said that he might be groggy when he came to and for her not to worry. "Remember the television show 'Wild Kingdom'?" the doctor had asked, successfully launching a fifteen-minute dissertation on anesthesia. She'd ended up practically pushing him out the door, then slumped against a packing crate, feeling guilty. After all he had dropped his sea cucumber experiment to rush over and check on the man who, true to Dr. Pelton's predictions, was struggling awake.

What an unscrupulous thief this gardener was, taking advantage of Fiona's trust just so he could rob her the minute she stepped out for the evening. Luckily Fiona's burglar trap had stopped him.

Fiona had been so careful to avoid even the slightest breath of scandal. There was no telling how the Jack Smith campaign people might manipulate an incident like this until it proved embarrassing for Marvin. Fiona would be devastated; she wanted so badly for her son to win the race for city supervisor. Unless . . .

What if this bogus gardener really worked for the Jack Smith campaign? Smith was certainly low enough to try to get to Marvin Breathwaite through his mother. After all, lots of people around the city claimed that during the last election it was really Smith who planted the *Fred's of Fresno* oversize body parts catalogue in his opponent's trash.

Oh, dear, George prayed, please let the gardener only be a criminal.

His lower jaw worked as though he were grinding his teeth. After several more moments of languid chewing movements and some mild facial calisthenics, his eyelids eased back. He rolled his head against the floral cushion and blinked, trying to drive away his sleepiness.

Actually, he looked sort of sweet, the type of man who read books with his feet propped up in front of a fire and took the time to stop while jogging to pet a dog. With a twinge of remorse, George raised the shepherd's crook high over her head. "One false move and I'll bean you."

His eyes widened, but only slightly as they fixed on the shepherd's crook. George supposed he was used to being threatened, given his real profession. After all, criminals were supposed to have nerves of steel.

Calmly, he scrutinized her, roaming over her polka-dotted dress, which she hadn't had the opportunity to change, then upward to her face which he studied without expression. "Where am I?"

Each word was enunciated very precisely and with a hint of a British accent. He sounded nice, but she quickly reminded herself that Jack the Ripper had been English.

"San Francisco," she answered.

He winced, a cleft appearing between his dark brows.

"That's in California," she added for clarity, "northern California. And not far from San Quentin, by the way."

He pondered the information, his gaze never wavering. "Miss Peep, whoever or whatever you are, I suggest that you lower your pole and," he raised up as far as possible given his present circumstance and added softly, *"untie me."*

"Absolutely not!" George tossed her head in the direction of his hands which, like his feet, were bound together and secured to the spindly sofa legs with granny knots. "It took me the better part of an hour and every tieback from my new living room curtains to make sure you wouldn't get away. Why on earth would I let you go now?"

"Because kidnapping is a federal offense."

"Of all the nerve," George fumed, pacing, her short skirt swishing. "How can you say that after I watched over you all night, even called Dr. Pelton when I could just as well have thrown you out and let you freeze under a rosebush which, come to think of it, is probably exactly what you deserve."

The man opened his mouth.

"And don't even think of calling me Miss Peep again,"

she said, pointing to the shepherd's crook. "My name is Georgette Richards."

"Thank you for that useful piece of information. Now I'll know who to press charges against."

"We'll see who gets pressed with charges . . . taking advantage of Fiona's trust, getting mud all over my rug. And don't think for a minute that you're going to waltz out of here without paying me for the cleaning. Last night I had a moment of weakness. I don't normally take in drunken criminals, you know."

His expression was bland. "Tell me, Miss Richards, how does one define normal in your universe?"

"I would never even consider trying. Like most people, I hardly ever give normal things a second thought. But that's totally beside the point, isn't it?"

"That's true," he observed dryly. "Now, let me understand this. You tied me up because you were afraid I would leave without paying your cleaning bill which you feel amounts to a criminal offense."

"Of course not. I could have taken the money out of your wallet." George laid aside the crook, pulled his wallet from her décolletage, and tapped the wallet slowly against her other hand. "What I don't understand is why you looked so shocked when I told you this was San Francisco when according to your driver's license you live here. The fact you live in Pacific Heights puzzled me because that takes money. But later when I pieced it all . . . is Adam Lawrence your real name or is it an alias?"

"Miss Richards—"

"Everyone calls me George, that is, everyone except stuffed shirts. *They* call me Miss Richards." After a pause, she added, "Call me Miss Richards."

The oddest expression crossed the man's face, and George tilted her head toward him. The wallet slipped from her fingers and thunked against the carpet, but she failed to bend to retrieve it. At that instant she glimpsed a sadness in this man, so clear that his emotion was nearly tangible. The revelation struck her as a sudden illumination, as jolting as stripping away a blindfold in brilliant sunlight. The pain forced her eyes closed, and when she opened them, his handsome features were merely intent. She took a deep breath and exhaled, relieved.

"In the interest of clearing this matter up," Adam began, "I'd like to propose a compromise. I will make one factual statement and you will respond in kind."

Still a bit shaken, she replied softly, "I always try to be kind."

"You misunderstood me. I tell you one truth and you tell me another—a simple exchange of facts, one at a time."

"Oh, oh, yes." George lifted her arms and let them fall to her sides. "As long as we're in the parlor, we might as well play games."

"Last night I had one brandy, therefore I was not drunk."

"I *know* that."

He frowned. "Then what made you say I was drunk?"

"I didn't say you were drunk. I said I didn't take in drunks; there's a difference."

"But the implication—"

"That was rude, you know. You were the one who insisted on rules, and look, you've already broken them. You interrupted me before I even got a chance to play."

With a groan, the man pinched his eyelids shut.

"Are you all right?" she asked.

Suddenly, his breathing became slow and deliberate. Then for an agonizing moment, he remained utterly motionless. He swallowed and began to pant. "Pills . . ."

George dropped to her knees. Her hand flew to his forehead. "Tell me what's wrong. Talk to me, please. Oh dear, Dr. Pelton said 'Wild Kingdom.' What would Marlin Perkins do?"

"Must . . . have to . . . untie . . ."

"Ooooh." George dived under the sofa, crawled to the leg and started picking at the knots that secured his bindings. "Hold on. I promise to get you . . . Ouch!" Reflex caused her to jerk back. She banged her head against the sofa springs, then shot her finger into her mouth to ease the sharp pain of her broken nail. A knife would free him quickly but, oh dear, the cording was rare and beautiful. . . .

"Stop thinking like an interior designer! What are ruined tiebacks compared to a man's life?"

She hurried into the kitchen and grabbed a butcher knife. It was long and unwieldy, the kind she always visualized between the teeth of a marauding pirate. Stainless steel flashing, she swept into the living room and descended on the bound man.

As she rounded the end of the sofa, she spied a telltale movement of his head. His eyes had snapped shut an instant too late. He'd been watching the kitchen door!

"Why you miserable fake!"

He twisted his head away and moaned theatrically.

"Save your acting for the prison musicals!"

The doorbell chimed.

The man's head shot up. "Help, please. Help me!"

"I don't believe this morning," George grumbled, searching the room for something soft and small enough. Settling on a neatly tied stack of potpourri-filled sachets, she snatched them up, and ignoring the man's stunned expression, shoved them into his mouth. "Don't you dare bite down. They're genuine Irish linen."

George scurried into the foyer, wondering at society's rampant disregard for proper manners. People seemed simply to drop in and always at the most inconvenient moments. Why was calling ahead too much to ask?

She swung open the front door, then recoiled, startled. "Ooooh, Mark. Good morning." She pasted on what she hoped was an innocent smile and glided her gaze up the long length of business suit to his tanned face. He was staring at the butcher knife in her hand. "Oh, I was just slicing bread, you know, that whole grain, organic bread that gets bruised by mechanical slicers." She slipped the knife into the folds behind her skirt and began to rock on her toes, trying to ignore the nagging feeling that the proverbial jig was up. Only fools tried to hoodwink Mark Ryerson.

He smiled far too widely for her liking. "I know miniskirts are back but I haven't seen one like that on anyone over the age of five."

"Ugh, it's a costume, for Halloween, for my pre-

12

Halloween party this Saturday the fourteenth. You know I expect you and Shannon to come."

Mark leaned in and looked toward the living room. "I thought I heard someone calling for help."

"Oh, that. Well, you see—it's the television. The news. Why don't we talk outside, it's such a pretty morning." She pushed at his towering frame.

"It's foggy, George."

"Yes, and isn't it beautiful?" she caroled, stepping out onto the porch and slamming the door behind her. "That's what I love about this city. I hardly ever need to use moisturizer."

She knew he wasn't buying any of her explanations. Worse still, he must realize that she knew it. But Mark, always the gentleman, would avoid embarrassing her. He was a catch in a million. When it came to love, her cousin Shannon had monopolized all the luck in the family. Darn her.

Mark shuffled his feet. "I'm almost sorry I'm going to have to miss the explanation for all this intrigue, but I only have time to drop these plans off. Shannon isn't going to make it into the office today."

George grabbed his arm. "She is perfectly all right, isn't she?"

"Only tired. Last night she said that the babies are going to be born big enough to walk out of the hospital under their own steam. She's counting the days."

"She ought to remember that a lot of women are miserable for nine months and don't get two babies out of it."

Mark laid a consoling hand on her shoulder. "Okay, tell me what's wrong."

"Nothing, really, I mean nothing but . . ."

"You're worried about Shannon, and you shouldn't be. The doctor says she's doing great."

George nervously pleated the stiff fabric of her skirt. "Mark, what would you think of a man who mumbles the word *debenture* over and over in his sleep?"

"A man with a warped sense of timing."

"Be serious."

"A debenture is a type of bond."

"Like a bail bond?"

"More like an I.O.U."

"But does it have anything to do with criminals?"

"Not usually." He leaned down and added in a confidential tone, "Then again, he might be into some sort of insider trading scheme. Tell you what, next time he falls asleep, ask him if he has any stock tips. You pass them along, and I'll let you know."

George socked him in the arm. "You never take anything I say seriously."

"All right, okay. The guy might be into investments, banking, whatever. I really wish I could sort through all this but I can't, not right now. Tonight's good. You could come for dinner."

"I know you and Shannon want to be alone together while you still can. Anyway, I still have a lot of unpacking and getting settled to do, and I might as well get it over with while our schedule is light. I won't be able to put our clients off forever."

"Okay." Mark turned toward Scarlet Street and paused, surveying his surroundings with eyes that could wither large moguls with a single glance. "I sure don't understand why you moved here. This place is ghoulish."

George was forced to agree though she refused to admit that buying this house had probably been a giant mistake. The cool wind seemed colder, the fog denser, the nights darker here, and her new neighbors positively reveled in this pall of gloomy winter that enveloped Scarlet Street. Their huge, dismal homes seemed snared within thickets of gnarled oak branches and dying leaves. George hugged herself and shivered. "Too bad you didn't see it on a sunny day before the leaves turned. The trees were a gorgeous green and over there," she said, pointing toward the next yard, "is a beautiful pond with a waterfall." She omitted even a tactful mention of what she'd heard Hangtown Harry Frye actually did in the pond, weather permitting.

She added thoughtfully, "Not ghoulish, but maybe a little weird."

Sirens whined in the distance. "If you say so," Mark muttered as he left.

After Mark's sedan disappeared around the corner, the wail of the sirens grew increasingly louder. Moments later, a fire engine swerved around the corner with a police squad car bearing down on its bumper, red light whirling.

George's mouth went dry. They were heading for her house!

The gardener had gotten loose and called the police.

George lunged for the door and tore it open. "You ingrate!" she yelled, plunging into the house, her knife held high. "Miss Breathwaite is going to kill us!"

Chapter 2

Adam Lawrence moaned. Until this morning, the concept of being tied to a silk-covered sofa at the mercy of a very attractive, costumed young lady held considerable intrigue. Reality certainly kicked the hell out of a man's fantasies.

The number of his body parts in pain was fast approaching a triple digit figure. He could almost forget the stabbing pain in his shoulder and the aching in his joints and muscles but whatever was in those little cloth bags had made him nauseous. Shortly after they had been rudely shoved between his lips, he'd pushed them out with his tongue. Still the wretched taste blanketed his mouth and trickled down his throat. Anything producing a flavor worse than borscht might be poisonous.

Consequently, the fact that Miss Richards was rushing toward him brandishing a knife and screaming about murder, held only marginal interest. Instead, he contemplated the irony of his situation. After thirty-nine years of carefully designed living, fate had conspired to doom him for his first-ever impulsive action. Only two days after making his madcap dash into an enticing, unknown lifestyle, he was facing imminent mutilation at the hands of Little Bo Peep.

Amazingly, Georgette Richards swerved course and weaved between the packing crates toward the bay windows at the front of the house. She parted the curtains with the blade of the knife and peeked through the narrow slit, affording Adam a rather nice view of her costume's ruffled panties. He hadn't given Halloween costumes a thought in over three decades—yet another whimsical thing he'd overlooked far too long.

Judging from the sirens outside, it appeared that he might get a chance to correct the error of his former ways, yet it was strange the police were arriving at all. No matter how much he'd wished otherwise in the past half hour, telepathy never eclipsed the effectiveness of direct dial.

The small woman whirled around. "I don't understand how they got here."

Adam shrugged. "Habit, perhaps. As you can see, I am a bit indisposed at the moment."

"Fiona . . . Oh, dear, the headlines. What will everyone say?"

"Gardener held hostage by Bo Peep," he suggested.

"How dare you lie there and quip at a time like this." Glaring fiercely, she marched toward him. "Fiona is going to be heartbroken. Marvin will never forgive her for this."

"What has Fiona done that this Marvin-whoever-he-is can't forgive her for?"

"Hiring you, that's what."

Adam closed his eyes, vowing never to ask this woman another question. She spewed riddles with the alacrity of a sphinx.

Summoning his repertoire of positive persuasion techniques (previously reserved only for heads of major corporations and maître d's), he assumed what he knew to be a commanding expression and adjusted his tone of voice to match. She had taxed his tolerance to the limit. "Miss Richards, call Fiona, immediately."

She frowned at him. "I can't, not with the police outside."

"It must be obvious to you that if they were coming here they would have rung the bell by now."

"Yes, yes, that's true."

"I have been as patient as any mortal man can be expected to be only because Fiona mentioned how fond she is of you. But since this er . . ." Charade, farce, and lunacy jumped into his mind as apt descriptions, but the unabashed intensity of Miss Richards's stare suddenly had him tempering his words. "This situation has already extended beyond the realm of er . . ." Sanity somehow seemed too harsh. "What I mean is that normal people . . ."

He released a defeated sigh. "No, actually I mean that . . . "Normally when an incident like this happens, well, the employer must be contacted."

"But last night was Fiona's—"

"Dial the number and place the receiver against my ear. I'll do the talking."

"All right," she said. "But I certainly wouldn't want to be in your shoes. Last night was her *gin* night."

"Yes, gin. She mentioned that she and her friends get together every two weeks for some sort of meeting."

"They reminisce. Have you ever heard a song like 'What Do You Do With a Drunken Sailor?'"

Adam lifted a brow. "Dial," he demanded.

Ten minutes later, Fiona Breathwaite entered the living room, her strides slightly stilted in contrast to her customary gliding walk. She pressed two fingers against her forehead as though to balance the cloth ice bag resting on the opposite side. Her carrot red bun was skewed; wisps of hair curled around her face. Her trim body was clad in loose-fitting warm-ups, her feet, strangely enough, in high heels. Listing slightly, she squinted down at Adam through a bloodshot eye. "Untie him," she commanded, lowering herself into the wing chair across from him.

Georgette Richards sputtered. "You're going to trust him without even listening to my side? You can't mean that!"

"I don't trust any man. They're devious. But since you failed to immobilize the truly dangerous part of his anatomy, you might as well release him."

Miss Richards threw both of her hands in the air which Adam had already catalogued as one of her trademark gestures. Pointing an accusing finger, she shouted, "Knowing you were out for the evening, this man tried to break into your house and sprang your burglar trap. He was shot with your tranquilizer gun. Dr. Pelton removed the dart."

"My God," Adam gasped.

"My head," Fiona groaned.

"Dr. Pelton rushed right over from the aquarium—"

Adam strained against his bonds and bellowed, "You called an ichthyologist! You let a fish doctor operate on my arm!"

Georgette inched backward. "Uh, fish are only his hobby."

"You let a *fake* fish doctor operate on me!" he raged.

Georgette spun around and implored Fiona, "Oh, don't you see? It wasn't until after Dr. Pelton left that I put it all together, that this man must be a felonious gardener, or maybe even in cahoots with the Jack Smith campaign, a conspirator, a spy! Then, I didn't dare call the police, not after what you promised Marvin."

Fiona scowled. "Oh, Marvin."

"Who the hell is Marvin?" Adam roared.

"One of her sons. The oldest one?"

Fiona's brows knit. An instant later she began counting on her fingers.

Oh, God. They're crazy, absolutely crazy.

"Anyway, Marvin is running for public office, city supervisor, and Fiona promised him that she'd behave, no scandals until the election is over. By the way, his specialties are ears, noses, and throats."

"Marvin's?" Adam asked through clenched teeth, wishing he could have found the inner strength to resist.

"Lips, chests, and buns," Fiona said. "Those are Marvin's specialties. Truly his father's son, but without the verve. What verve!" Blushing, she readjusted her ice bag to cover her forehead. "Pelton's the ENT man. But, George, didn't the doctor insist on reporting the incident to the police?"

"I told Dr. Pelton that I shot him myself, by accident."

Adam gaped at her, incredulous. "And he believed you?"

"He took out my tonsils."

Adam and Fiona stared together.

"He's known me since I was three years old."

"George," Fiona began, "I think you had better cut this man free. He appears pained. I'm certain that he isn't involved with Jack Smith. Besides, I really don't think he meant to break into my house. He lives there. True, it is the basement apartment, but I also happen to know that material possessions hold little appeal for him. Why else would he quit his job as one of the highest . . ."

Adam's gathered eyebrows succeeded in stopping her cold.

"Really," Georgette said thoughtfully. "That explains a lot, especially his old address in Pacific Heights but—"

"Oh, well," Fiona continued merrily. "Better left to another time. Anyway, George, you were a dear to keep him for me."

"But, Fiona—"

Fiona made a sweeping motion with a finely manicured hand. "Now take your knife there and start sawing."

"Carefully," Adam demanded, and Georgette Richards did, thank God. As she kneeled beside him, she rewarded Adam with one long, appraising look. At a distance she was pretty; up close she was lovely. In addition to the creamy skin, and the full, alluring mouth, she possessed the most magnificent and arresting pair of eyes he had ever seen. Vivid turquoise, they blazed within a halo of long lashes and slender, arching brows. Their glittering brilliance radiated life, energy, joy. She flipped her shoulder-length dark hair away from her forehead. About her, the air held the subtle fragrance of a spring breeze.

He wondered how anyone could call this completely feminine woman George.

"While we're on the subject, Adam," Fiona said, "just exactly how did you happen to spring my burglar trap last night?"

He cleared his throat. He should have seen that one

coming. Damn, this was embarrassing. "I was trying to figure out how to drain off the water that's standing on your camellias."

"Oh, yes. The area you flooded yesterday afternoon. I remember it well. Very well, in fact. Half of my yard resembled a catfish farm. Now, tell me the truth. It wouldn't be wise for you to alienate me now. If you forced me to fire you, I couldn't in all honesty give you a good reference."

Adam sat up and rubbed his wrists. He glared pointedly at Fiona who quickly began resettling herself, her hands smoothing her sweatpants.

"Never mind, Adam. Let's leave it that you had an irresistible impulse to climb into my bedroom window and run your fingers over my lingerie. Yes, I think I like that explanation. Anyway, bothering with the truth can be a tedious nuisance."

"Not to me." Adam stood, stretched, and tucked his shirttail into his jeans. "Why don't you explain to me what a burglar trap is and why you have one?"

"Oh, it's Dwight. You know, Dwight Phillips, the financier."

"Across the street," Georgette mumbled absently as she examined the severed ends of her tiebacks.

"After burglars broke into this house a few months ago, conked Dr. Emerson on the head, and killed the old grouch, Dwight insisted on tinkering up a trip wire and attaching it to an old tranquilizer gun of my father's. Half the time I forget to turn on that electronic alarm system, and that low window on the dark side of the house is practically a butler-delivered invitation. He put the trap there."

Sighing, George tossed the ruined tiebacks on the sofa. "Would you like some coffee or something?" She stood close to him, pleasantly close. She raised her hand, her fingertips venturing to within an inch of the bandaged wound on his arm. "I am sorry."

He reached to capture her hand, surprising himself. It was the first genuinely spontaneous gesture he could remember making toward a woman in a very long time.

Wild barking and scuffling sounds emanated from the front porch. "What on earth could that be!" Fiona exclaimed.

Who cares, Adam thought, Georgette's hand small and warm within his own. Her smile added a magnificent glow to her face and evoked a tightening feeling in his stomach.

Adam tried his best to ignore the scratching and crying outside, but Georgette's sudden look of alarm forced his attention toward the foyer.

When Fiona opened the door, a large furry animal leaped at her chest.

"Mr. Moto!" Georgette screamed.

Fiona spun away from the black and brown hulk, lost her balance and swerved into the path of a young, uniformed policeman who was plunging after the dog. The policeman slammed into Fiona. The ice bag sailed skyward. The policeman grabbed her by the arms in an apparent attempt to steady them both. But they toppled over, the policeman landing on his back with Fiona sprawled spread-eagled on top of him.

"Grab that dog!" the policeman yelled.

Mr. Moto raced around the room, vaulting at random over the furniture and bobbing between the packing crates.

"Close the door!" Adam shouted at Georgette, his plan of action already decided. The dog darted toward the center of the room, tongue extended and flying. Adam waved his arms, herding him back toward the perimeter. Repeatedly, Adam forced him back until the dog ran in a circular pattern, hugging the walls.

"Take over," he called, motioning Georgette. She rushed to Adam's side. "Distract him."

"Mr. Moto! Mr. Moto!" she chanted as Adam slipped behind a packing crate that stood close to one wall. Grasping his plan, Georgette chased Mr. Moto, forcing him toward the narrow passage where Adam waited, hidden. Catching one final glimpse, he gauged the speed of the hurtling animal, timed his move, and scooped up the dog.

Mr. Moto squirmed, driving his strong legs, attempting leaps without traction, paws flailing in midair. He sucked oxygen in labored wheezes. Adam clamped down with his good arm and held on tight.

The policeman helped Fiona up. "Tell me, do they teach that step at the academy?" she asked dryly.

"Sorry, ma'am, but the dog escaped and came over here. I was in pursuit." He punctuated his statement with a smirk, as if taking credit for the capture.

Fiona scowled. "That wasn't pursuit; that was a disaster."

"Poor Mr. Moto," Georgette soothed and succeeded in stilling the dog's thrashing. "He doesn't normally act like this. What have you done to upset him?"

The officer stared at Georgette and her costume, paying particular attention, Adam noted, to her legs. "Found his master this morning, dead."

"Hangtown Harry, dead?"

"Yes, miss, if you mean Harry Frye."

Fiona gasped.

"He's one of your neighbors?" Adam asked.

Georgette nodded, then stopped, her brows gathering over troubled eyes. "Murdered?"

"Looks like it, miss. But how did you know?"

Chapter
3

Humming off-key, Georgette Richards drew a knife across a stack of sliced bread in one deft stroke. She trimmed the other three sides, swept the crusts into a silver Revere bowl for Mr. Moto, and positioned a new stack of bread on the cutting board. Pausing, she glanced at Fiona who peered out of her kitchen window at the gloomy morning.

"Yesterday a man is murdered and by ten in the morning the weather is glorious. Now today we get the rain." Fiona let go of the cord, and the venetian blinds crashed down against the sill. "It seems to me that this whole thing ought to be better synchronized. Then again Harry was on a collision course with a padded cell. One could hardly expect him to get the timing right."

"Butter knife?"

"Second drawer on your left."

George yawned as she dug through the jumble of utensils. What she wouldn't give for a few hours sleep. "I wonder," she said, yawning again, "if chicken salad sandwiches and ham roll-ups are considered proper refreshments for 'circling the wagons'?"

"Servants," Fiona grumbled, snatching up a pair of silver polishing gloves and donning them with the ceremony of a surgeon. After a quick stretch of her fingers, she began a brisk massage of a magnificent thirteen candle candelabra. "Last night I began to doubt my judgment in calling this neighborhood meeting," she puffed between strokes. "Natasha and the others may want to 'circle the wagons' with us, but the question is do we want to circle with *them?"*

George considered the truth of that statement. Yesterday's events had served as a perfect showcase for her new neighbors' eccentricities. When the ambulance arrived to bear Hangtown Harry's body to the morgue, Agnes Clodfelter had hyperventilated while Natasha Velour scratched notes for her new novel. Estelle Capricorn had mumbled a chant to the ancient dead, Dwight Phillips had maintained a stoic silence, and Elmo Burroughs had nipped repeatedly from an engraved flask. Marshall Hoagsworth, Jr. had glared down at all of them from a window on the third floor of his decaying mansion.

"Do you think Marshall Hoagsworth, Jr. will come?" George asked.

Fiona removed the gloves with a shrug. "Probably not. He's been a virtual recluse for years which, of course, is unusual in someone so young. Few people realize that he's only in his late fifties and still quite handsome. His mother, Ina, lives with him; neither of them socializes." She fidgeted off to a cupboard and pulled out a bottle of clear liquor. George struggled to read the label; it was unusual and unrecognizable.

"Yes," Fiona continued, holding the bottle close to her chest and unscrewing the cap, "Marshall, Jr. bears a strong physical resemblance to his father."

George noticed that fresh color highlighted Fiona's cheeks as she swept across the room to an exquisite portable bar set with a Georgian silver punch bowl and matching cups. Holding the bottle high, she poured the liquid into the punch bowl. "This ought to loosen a few tongues. Everclear, 190 proof grain alcohol—the secret of my infamous punch and the best friend a hostess ever had. My family hasn't

25

given a dull party since my forebearers were expelled from the temperance union during the twenties."

"Is this one of those scandals that the people around here talk about as if I ought to know every detail right down to the last whispered secret when it all happened years before I was born?"

Fiona shook the bottle to free the last few drops. "Over the years Scarlet Street has had quite a few, I'm afraid. Actually, most everyone around here is rather used to them."

"I guess that has its advantages. No one probably batted an eye when your relatives were expelled."

"As a matter of fact, it wasn't quite that way." Fiona guided the bar near the refrigerator, opened the black glass door, and put the end of a hose into the punch bowl. She manipulated the hand pump on one of the two metal containers to begin the flow of chilled fruit concentrate and stirred the mixture as the bowl filled. Just when George thought that Fiona would never resume her story, she continued, "It was a terrible scandal, and because it centered around the temperance union and her parents, my mother was horrified to an extreme that can only be achieved by fundamentalist librarians or the average teenage girl.

"She tried to escape the disapproving gestures by marrying the first fop who came along and ended up doing more whimpering than roaring through the rest of the twenties. Two days after their wedding, my father steamed off to Africa where he spent the next eight years hiking through the jungles in khaki shorts and a pith helmet."

"He was the big game hunter?" George asked, thinking of this house and its bizarre decor.

"He shot wild animals and stuffed them as a substitute. Allegedly his most important pistol didn't fire too well or too often which is likely the reason I'm an only child with a lot of dead carcasses for sale."

"It sounds like a horrible—"

"Mistake would be an understatement. Mother's choice

was disastrous, but then again, women often make all the wrong choices where men are concerned."

"Some always do," George muttered, thinking of herself.

"Mistakes are one thing. But I've always felt that it's damned foolish to allow a man to make you miserable without it being worthwhile in some way. There can be compensations—wealth, position, travel, excitement. Instead my mother had complete misery, carefully tended to appear noble."

"Why didn't she divorce him?"

Fiona laughed. It was hollow and melancholy. "My mother couldn't bear a scandalous divorce with court appearances and newspaper coverage; not headlines such as 'socialite charges mental cruelty; husband counters wife spoiled, unreasonable.' Mother was completely paralyzed because she valued people's impressions of her more than she valued herself. She wasted her whole life worrying what people were thinking of her when they were quite probably hardly thinking of her at all."

Fiona closed the refrigerator and wheeled the bar into the center of the room. "Punch?"

"Yes, thank you," sounded a smooth, cultured, and resoundingly male voice. Adam Lawrence.

George whirled to face him. "You certainly know how to sneak up on a person. Are you sure you don't have burglary somewhere in your background?"

"You have a propensity for fanciful interpretation of my every action. And no," he said firmly, "I was not a burglar."

She studied him intently. His broad shoulders were militarily straight beneath a tightly woven maroon sweater. The collar of his white shirt was open, spotless, and starched; his navy slacks creased, his black loafers shined. He was no gardener, and George decided it was high time to take aim at his charade and shoot. "I need some professional advice. I'd love to plant azaleas, but I'm not sure what kind of soil they need."

"The brown kind."

"But I've heard that they need special fertilizer."

Adam lifted his shoulders. "Camellias are more my specialty."

Fiona harrumphed.

"You might as well admit it, Adam Lawrence, you're no gardener. So what are you, really?"

"Thirsty," he said casually. With a nod, he accepted a cup of punch from Fiona.

"I'd guess that you're a business-and-finance type, but what I don't understand is why I haven't seen you before. Heaven and half the country knows my father has arranged for me to meet or go out with every important . . . I've got it! You were in business, but you were unsuccessful."

Adam slowly shook his head.

"Old money? Daddy says they lack motivation."

Again, Adam shook his head.

Exasperated, she tossed up her hands. "Why won't you tell me?"

He inched his gray eyes over her body, over her sun yellow challis dress and down to her rainbow-colored heels. "I like the way you're dressed."

"What's that supposed to mean?"

"Most people would have chosen dark colors for today."

She sensed brewing male trickery and chose to feign nonchalance. According to part two of *Ditch the Jerk and Snag the Man of Your Dreams,* that approach always worked well in awkward situations. She was certain, however, that the author had never faced fifteen years of chicanery by men whose romantic fantasy was getting into *her* trust funds. "Oh, really. Why do you say that?"

"Because lately I've been taking note of things I used to overlook. And it just struck me that there's a definite correlation between clothing selection and the weather. On gloomy days people tend to wear dark colors, and I bet the reverse is also true—at least for most people. You don't fit that pattern."

"I see," George said. This was certainly a new twist on the old game. Adam Lawrence, obviously impersonating a gardener, certainly hiding his past, was probably paying her an honest, if oblique compliment. He was a walking contra-diction. "Who are you, really?"

He smiled, a bit smugly, she thought. "My name is Adam Christian Lawrence and my former profession is irrelevant. Excuse me," he said, setting aside his now empty punch cup. He hefted two stacks of china luncheon plates and disap-peared into the hallway.

George trained narrowed eyes on Fiona who shook her head. "Not on your life."

"Infuriating," George muttered, gathering two platters to carry into the dining room.

"Irresistible," Fiona corrected, wheeling the bar behind her.

Walking into the great room of Fiona's house was, George decided, like entering a drafty medieval castle owned by a prideful warrior who cared nothing for comfort. Only an occasional Persian rug or antique tapestry broke the cold monotony of tile flooring and stonelike walls. Clearly the room had been designed and decorated expressly to house the animal trophies that stood grouped in alcoves like displays in a museum of natural history.

After they carted and arranged the feast across the length of a massive spool-legged dining table, Fiona excused her-self to retouch her makeup, leaving Adam alone with George. "I need to ask you for a favor," he said immediate-ly, his tone low and confidential.

He stood next to her, in front of the salmon canapés, close enough for the spicy scent of his after-shave to drift into the air she breathed. She raised her eyes level with the V of his sweater then upward to his hair that curled slightly along the smooth skin of his neck. He'd missed his regular cut, she'd bet; the dark hair was still short enough to appear neat but too long now to look corporate. His neck was tight and corded, his chin strong, face long. And he had the most intriguing scar at the base of his neck, one that invited exploration. *Oh, God, he's so good-looking.* She asked, "What kind of favor?"

"It's rather embarrassing, but I know you can help me

remedy this situation." He shrugged, his attention still fixed on the sandwiches and, in that instant, she wondered if he was hungry for more than seafood.

"I can?" she asked with studied slowness. Her stomach squeezed the way it did when the roller coaster hit the crest of the track.

He laughed awkwardly. "We can be back before the watercress wilts."

She fumed, "Is that supposed to be some kind of joke?"

"Well, I thought that line was kind of clever."

"Clever? Clever?"

"And it's true. It won't take long to get the pump, provided you know where it is."

"Pump? Pump? What pump?"

"Didn't Fiona mention the water pump I need to borrow from you to get the water out of her basement? I guess not. If you'll recall, when I dug the hole for her new tree, I inadvertently piled dirt in the area that provides drainage for the camellias I was watering. Early this morning when I went to dismantle that burglar trap, I found water standing in the basement, obviously from—"

Strangling a curse, she blurted, "Stop. Stop. We'll go, later, after the party. Just don't say anything else, please."

But she thought she heard him mutter, "Touchy," as he disappeared to answer the door chime.

George crossed the cavernous mahogany-paneled room to greet the first guest, Agnes Clodfelter, who arrived, slumped and wringing a lace hanky in her arthritic hands. Above her hung the head of a male moose and in a nearby alcove two rams faced each other, heads lowered for the charge. Price tags dangled from their horns.

"It's ghastly, positively ghastly." Miss Clodfelter twittered.

George grimaced. "I agree. Fiona really ought to consider having an auction, or maybe even a garage sale. All this death around her—it's enough to give a person nightmares."

"Oh, yes. I can't sleep for thinking of it, not a wink. Murder, here. Right here on our little street."

"Actually it probably happened in Africa, or possibly Tibet," George mumbled absently, wondering how the rams' glass eyes could appear so wild and obsessed.

"It must be an outsider, a vandal, a hoodlum. Perhaps someone from Oakland. It must be. Everyone here loved Harry, especially his omelets. I'll never crack another egg without thinking of him."

"Oh, now I understand," George said, tearing her attention from the gruesome trophies. "You mean Harry."

Agnes Clodfelter waved her hanky, fluttering it over the sagging skin of her throat. "What else could I mean? What else could anyone think of at a time like this!"

"Lunch," answered Estelle Capricorn, joining them. Her earrings, a golden cascade of half-moons, stars, and astrological signs, tinkled as she smoothed her outrageous mane of blond hair. She splayed her fingers and held her hands palm out framing her unnaturally taut face. George figured her age at between fifty and sixty-five, depending on the skill of her plastic surgeon. "Certainly, I will miss Hangtown Harry and his Hangtown Fry. He was a deep and spiritual man. He had the gift and was so generous, giving himself up to the voices of those tormented souls still restless and searching for riches even now, over one hundred years after the Gold Rush."

Miss Clodfelter added wistfully, "I'll always remember those summer afternoons, Harry crouched by the fish pond with his gold pan, chatting away with Emperor Norton as if the old fraud truly believed he was there to listen."

"But he was, Agnes, at least for those of us who have the vision and desire to join in oneness with the orgiastic rhythms of the cosmos. Harry's omelets were a glowing example of his visionary prowess. They were his statement, his way of defining the unity of life on earth blending the egg, representing the essence of life on the land, the oysters, the sea . . ."

"And the bacon, the ham in us all," Adam suggested. "You're speaking of the Hangtown Fry which originated in Placerville during the Gold Rush. Doubtless it accounts for his nickname, though Mr. Frye certainly did not devise that

31

delicacy. What amazes me is how you sound exactly the way you do on the radio, Estelle. However, I can't say I'm among the ranks of your loyal listeners. I'm seldom awake at two in the morning."

"Oh, Adam, the gardener," cooed Estelle, plainly ignoring his sarcasm. She thrust out her chin and lowered her eyelids. Her green eye shadow glittered in the dim light. "I'm having a gathering at my house this evening before the broadcast. Will you come?"

"No, I don't believe I will. But thank you."

Dipping a shoulder, Estelle altered her pose and sidled closer to Adam.

George crossed her arms. Estelle Capricorn could give Little Egypt writhing lessons.

"You really should consider it."

Fiona pushed a cup of punch between them and into Estelle's hand. "Another fertility rite?"

"Everyone knows that *I* am an astrologer and medium, not a . . ."

"Witch?" George said sweetly.

"Oh, dear!" Miss Clodfelter gasped, her breathing rapid and loud, as though her ribs chafed her lungs. "This constant turmoil . . ."

George wrapped an arm around Miss Clodfelter's slim waist and guided her to a chair. "Here, sit down and try to relax."

Agnes collapsed, dragging in air in halting little wheezes. Even in distress, she was very much a lady, her hanky poised against her cheek, her knees clutched tightly together beneath her black silk dress.

Fiona appeared bearing punch. "Drink this down, Aggie."

The older woman obeyed immediately, draining the glass in surprisingly few swallows. She finished with a barely audible "Aaaah."

"Better, Aggie?"

"Why, yes." She coughed softly into starched, mono-grammed white linen. "Much. But I would like another glass." She added another delicate cough.

"Just a moment."

"George," Fiona whispered, drawing her aside.

George glanced over her shoulder at the now smiling woman. "How could Miss Clodfelter drink that strong stuff so fast?"

"Aggie is a teetotaler."

"But . . ."

"Never mind that now. That young policeman Troy Hasselbush is here. You know, the one who chased Mr. Moto yesterday."

George groaned. "Why did you invite him?"

"Information. He knows all about Hangtown Harry's death, and we must find out what's going on. Everything Estelle said about Harry is absolutely true. Harry claimed to have regular conversations with dead people and got his nickname from cooking up the Hangtown Fry. He was obsessed with the Gold Rush. But that's just the point. His eccentricities were quite endearing; he was sweet and harmless. Why on earth would anyone kill him? Unless, just maybe, they killed the wrong person. Look around you—and these are only half of them. We have potential victims galore. Suppose whoever killed him actually meant to kill one of us instead?"

"Are you implying that the murderer suffers from blindness, absentmindedness, or simply a bad sense of direction?"

"I don't know, but maybe you can find out. I'm convinced that Troy will cooperate fully with you." Fiona lifted her eyebrows.

"But I don't like the way he looks at me. It's so . . . so . . ."

"Lustful. The man obviously adored your Little Bo Peep suit, and when he heard you'd had Adam tied to the sofa for hours on end, he was positively captivated—and wants to be." She winked. "I don't care what kind of oath he took to the police department. Duty and honor lose out to hormones every time."

George heaved a long sigh, understanding at once what Fiona had *not* said: that Marvin's campaign for city supervisor was in the final, crucial stages, and that he and Jack Smith were locked into a close race, one that Marvin, running as "the law and order candidate" might lose. A lengthy murder investigation involving his own mother might deliver Smith the precise tool he needed. Fiona Breathwaite would be heartbroken and San Francisco would be stuck with a rotten supervisor—again.

"A murderer is stalking Scarlet Street. We need you."

George squared her shoulders and threw back her head, imagining herself as Ingrid Bergman in *Notorious,* strong, beautiful, and tall, sacrificing herself to save her country. She scowled at Fiona. "You're expecting an awful lot from a naturalized resident."

"We need you, George. Please go talk to him. See what you can find out."

"Those are probably the exact words Cary said to Ingrid right before Claude poisoned her."

Fiona clapped her hands silently. "I've got it! 'Days of Our Lies,' 1972."

Fiona's comment was a gift, and George seized the opportunity for reparation. She rolled her eyes theatrically. "Well, I'm shocked. The year was 1972, but it was definitely 'As the World Spurns.'" When George left her, Fiona was clearly reflecting over countless years of daytime skullduggery, illegitimate babies, and timely resurrections. And George's conscience was perfectly fine. Reviewing a cavalcade of unrelenting distress was the least Fiona deserved for forcing a perfectly sane, upright woman like herself to confront Troy Hasselbush.

Rounding the end of the table, she nearly collided with Dwight Phillips. If she was twenty years older, she would have definitely used Dwight as a pleasant excuse to abort her mission entirely. Nearing sixty-five, he stood straight-backed, trim, and distinguished. Though he resembled Abraham Lincoln too much to be called handsome, he managed to be intense and congenial simultaneously and was undoubtedly among the most wealthy and eligible bachelors in the city.

"Good morning, Georgette," he said softly. "I hope you slept well, despite what happened yesterday."

"Well, er . . . oh, fine, I guess," she lied. No matter how hard she had tried to convince herself to sleep like a baby, other objects associated with those old clichés like logs, stones, and rocks came to mind, too, transforming invariably into sinister clubs and bone-splintering lethal weapons. Even cuddling the fuzzy Mr. Moto hadn't done much to help her sleep, and the dog had snored blissfully through the entire night.

"Elmo." Dwight tapped the shoulder of the shorter man next to him who appeared engrossed with filling his punch cup to the rim. He submerged the ladle, added a few more drops, then shuffled around to face them. "I believe you met Miss Richards yesterday."

Elmo said nothing. The contrast between the two men was powerful: Dwight, a man consumed with maintaining his body, and Elmo, one who simply consumed. Dressed in rumpled old clothes, Elmo Burroughs could come to her upcoming Halloween party as a derelict. Burroughs rasped, "You bought Doctor Emerson's house, didn't you?"

"Yes."

"Emerson was murdered too, just like Harry."

"Yes . . . I mean no. That was months ago and completely different. As far as I know the police have finished their investigation. They definitely said that the doctor was conked on the head by burglars who were after drugs."

"Dead's dead, and marching right down the block. Emerson, Harry, it's my place next, don't you see? Even that hairy mongrel couldn't save him. What'da I do? What'da I do?" His upper body shook as if gripped by palsy.

"Excuse us," Dwight said. "Elmo's quite sensitive, but he'll be fine." He freed the punch cup and guided the hunched man toward the kitchen leaving her with nothing left but to confront Troy Hasselbush.

The young policeman spotted George's approach. His

smile was ruined by the fact that he obviously knew it was stunning; he grinned too broadly and for two beats too long. My, my, George thought, but how he filled out a uniform.

"Hi," he drawled.

George sighed. Though "and good-bye" was poised on her lips, she asked, "How are you, Troy?"

"Great."

"How is the case progressing?"

"Case?"

"Hangtown Harry." She made a stabbing motion at her stomach. Troy's only deposit of cellulite was apparently between his ears. "The man who was found murdered yesterday."

"Oh, Harry Frye. But he didn't get it in the gut. He was stabbed in the back."

"Uh huh, literally stabbed in the back. I wonder if that means something. The killer might not have seen his face. Maybe Fiona is . . . But who would a murderer expect to be in Harry's house except Harry?" She broke off, suddenly aware that Troy had stepped closer. He ogled her the way a hawk eyes a tasty-looking young rabbit.

He glanced quickly from side to side then leaned down and said in a low voice, "When would you like to come to my place and see my tattoos?"

"Ugh . . . you've really put me on the spot. I promised my father not to look at any tattoos in odd numbered decades."

Troy grinned again. "We can pretend that I'm your daddy. I'd give you permission."

She swallowed hard. Where was Fiona and her infamous punch now when George really needed it? "You see I've never had much imagination, and you don't look a bit like my father. It just won't work, Troy."

"Then we can do what you did with that other guy. You can put on your little outfit and tie me up."

The only person paying attention was Adam, viewing them from across the mammoth room, his expression placid. Easy for him. "There's something special between Adam and me—call it lust, call it passion. Whatever, he

36

kindles a flame in me that he alone can douse. I simply can't imagine doing Bo Peep and bondage with anyone else."

"I can make you hot, babe, believe me."

George crossed her arms, impassive.

"Besides, you don't want to be with that Adam Lawrence anymore. He's all messed up in this murder thing. Hell, the detective on the case thinks he did it."

Chapter
4

George took her turn at ogling Troy Hasselbush. How dare he call Adam Lawrence a suspect!

The policeman's eyelids lowered, his smugness showing. She instantly tagged glib and gross as the footnote to his incredible statement. The man clearly enjoyed dispensing shock and heaven only knew what else.

She spotted Adam, relieving her eyes from having to regard the odious Troy. Standing near the dining table, Adam munched on one of her chicken salad sandwiches and nodded intermittently at the wildly gesticulating Estelle.

Oh dear Lord, she thought, and a deluge of memories assaulted her mind, leading with a wild, roaring torrent of tiny details of a previous evening, of costumes, doorbells, darts, tiebacks, and knives . . . of Adam Lawrence, Hangtown Harry, and murder.

"Ugh, what about—"

"Don't interrupt me, Troy. I'm thinking."

She dismissed the evening of night-before-last's murder as too complicated to deal with at present and focused her study on Adam and his peculiar behavior. Having successfully made his escape across the room to one of the alcoves, he scrutinized a trio of stuffed antelopes: father, mother, and child. He gazed with obvious dismay at the young antelope, then turned his attention to the magnificent male. He pressed his thumb against his forehead then stretched his pinkie along one of the antlers, using his two fingers like the legs of a caliper. Adam continued his measurement by moving his hand higher, meticulously positioning the ball of his thumb where the tip of his pinkie had been before and stretching his hand toward the tip of the antler. Completing his measurement, he backed away with an angry shake of his head.

Watching him, witnessing his display of frustration over life sacrificed for vanity and egotism, her heart of hearts longed to proclaim him innocent. But oh, how that same heart had misjudged men in the past.

Even thinking too much about men was useless, an exercise in frustration. Hearts and smarts, she knew, caused trouble for Georgette Richards. She had solved the smart part early. When people expected her to be dumb, she played dumb. When people wanted her to do or be something she didn't want to be, she pretended ignorance. It worked beautifully. Then thirteen years ago, she discovered that the same technique worked in matters of the heart. She pretended to turn off the feelings associated with that troublesome organ—at least spiritually and only as far as men were concerned—and found it easy, almost as natural as breathing. After all, she had pretended in one way or another all her life.

Michael had too, and all it ever took was one thought of him, one reminder of his smooth, efficient, and cunning seduction, to effectively end any thoughts of romantic self-determination for her, past or present. Michael had tricked her so effortlessly! At least the endless parade of suitors her father sent were certain to be mercenary drudges after her father's corporate mentorship, a hard leather chair in the boardroom, and the Richards's assets whose digits made the aspirants pant to put a gold ring on one of hers. Men like them were everywhere. Though Troy was after something different, he was still the same, still trying to trick his way to the treats. He was superficial, shallow, and therefore harmless. She understood him so well.

She smiled at him benevolently and meant it. "I don't believe it, Troy. I don't believe Adam is a murderer." He appeared crestfallen at her proclamation, meaning as it did that she was refusing to view his tattoos now or ever. Yet lust was his downfall, and she needed to string him along to gain some added information. George cocked her head and gazed into those lizard green eyes so far above her. "No, I don't believe it—not yet, at least. So why don't you whisper something in my ear to make me change my mind."

Troy beamed lasciviously. His attention was neither tempting nor pleasant so she rationalized her charade. Unlike the notorious Ingrid, she didn't have to marry the villain, just charm the pants off him, and thank heavens, only figuratively.

He stooped to her ear. "The detective, he thinks that whole burglar trap–tranquilizer gun thing is a big sham put on by Lawrence just to make everyone think he was wasted and wandering in the dark when the whole thing happened."

George mulled over his latest revelation. If the police thought that Harry was killed before Adam rang her doorbell, that meant the murder took place sometime between Helen of Troy and Little Bo Peep while she was in her bedroom—*right next to the window that overlooked Harry's house.* "Do you actually mean that Harry was killed not long before eleven-thirty?"

Troy's face went blank.

"I mean that's about the time he rang my doorbell."

Troy chuckled. "Who, Harry?"

"No, of course not. Adam rang my doorbell."

"Guess Harry was killed before that then."

"Why do you say that?"

"Because Lawrence killed him, and he didn't go out that night after eleven-thirty, did he?"

Troy's eyes gleamed greenly, the shade similar to slime in a swimming pool. Twin pools of slime might fit nicely in Natasha Velour's latest novel. She'd said that in her next book she would dare to be raunchy. "Adam Lawrence definitely did not leave my house after he arrived."

"Kept him busy all night, huh?"

"Certainly," George responded impatiently. "I wouldn't dream of leaving a guest alone. It's impolite." In an effort to recover the mood, she added, "Of course, the entire evening *was* extraordinarily complicated in ways that I could never explain." She dropped her eyelids demurely and added a few coy blinks. "Why do you think Adam Lawrence did it?"

"Babe," he said huskily, slipping his hand around her waist. "If you don't know, then he didn't give you what you deserve." He leaned very close to her ear and began an impression of an obscene telephone caller complete with full anatomical detail.

George recoiled, her patience gone. "Not sex, you fool! The murder!"

Heads turned, including Adam's. Condemnation registered on his face. Or was it disappointment? Whatever, George hadn't felt so embarrassed since she raised her hand in Catholic school and asked the nun who taught the second grade to define a word spray painted underneath the bleachers at the high school. Later that evening, her father had muttered that it meant women who preferred women, but it wasn't until George was a teenager that she figured out why the nun had given her an extended regimen of prayer and crossed herself every time she passed George's desk.

Furious, she pushed Troy into a hallway. Though it was midday the corridor was bathed in shadows. Tribal shields were mounted on the walls like sconces and reluctantly allowed the meager light behind them to filter over the mahogany panels. George longed for two secret panels, one she could shove Troy into and the other for her to flee through. Arms akimbo, she drew up to her full height and faced him. "I want to know just exactly what you do know besides how to insult a woman in appallingly graphic detail."

"About what?"

"About the murder!"

"Nothing I'd tell you."

"Which is exactly nothing at all, I'd bet. You don't know anything, do you? You made that up about Adam. He's no murderer! You did it just because you thought I might go to bed with you which is totally ludicrous in the first place because I didn't even——"

He snarled, "I didn't make anything up. Bet your friend Lawrence didn't tell you that he knew Harry Frye, did he?"

"You'd say anything——"

"No reason to. You're too short for me anyway. And too pudgy in the legs."

"Pudgy in the legs," she fumed. "My legs are perfect!"

"Yeah, but I bet they aren't in shape."

"If it's hard you're after, then go get a piece of a rock!"

"This is quite a surprise," a cultured voice interjected. "Somehow I didn't think you two would be discussing insurance."

George whirled to address Adam. "We were discussing the only cellulite in this hallway, which happens to be between his ears."

Troy muttered an obscenity, but was smart enough to do it under his breath. George considered kicking him in the shin anyway, then remembered herself or, more importantly, her Bruno Magli shoes. Revenge wasn't sufficient motivation to imperil a pair of three-inch heels that were comfortable, even if she had gotten them on sale.

Adam stepped forward, shoulders square. "I think you ought to leave now, Officer."

Troy skulked away. Seconds later she heard the front door slam.

"What was that all about?" Adam asked.

"Troy is only a filthy-minded lizard."

"In principle I absolutely agree with your viewpoint. However, that exchange was hardly wise. The next time you're tempted to insult him, remind yourself that he does carry a gun."

"I only fired the last salvo, anyway . . ." George finished the sentence to herself, her head lowered: the last salvo for both of us. She bit lightly on her index finger. If Adam didn't kill Harry, then who did? She must have been in her room at the exact time of the murder; why didn't she hear something? Her routine had been the same with each costume: Put it on behind the screen then walk across the room to the mirror that was right next to the open window. She'd had a front row seat for a murder and seen nothing. But had the murderer seen her?

"Shall we take advantage of this short lull between fiascoes and go get the pump?"

George's head popped up. "Pump? Pump? Oh, that. The pump. The pump! Oh, my heavens, the pump!" George plastered herself against the wall, wishing again that a secret panel would swallow her and spit her out in her own house behind all the deadbolt locks and the new security system she planned to have installed the instant she could get home and call the tradesmen. But right now, before all the deadbolts, she had to figure out a way to get out of going into her dark, deserted basement with Adam Lawrence, murder suspect.

Chapter
5

George blurted, "Adam, I can't go to the basement with you. I'm scared of the dark."

"Surely there must be a light fixture in the basement."

"That doesn't make a bit of difference. I'm also scared of places that are dark most of the time." She asked herself if she was truly scared of Adam Lawrence and thought, no, though her current position did remind her of a woman's typical role in a knife throwing act, standing straight backed against a wall, not daring to move or even breathe. He stalked closer, his body movements fluid and wondrous. In a language without words, he transmitted confidence, determination, and—holy heavens—his attraction to her!

He extended his left arm and planted his hand against the wall beside her head, his tanned fingers a scant inch away from her dark hair. She suppressed a gasp. The first knife had been thrown.

He said, "That doesn't make sense. Most any place on earth is dark almost half the time."

"Dark? Oh, right, of course. We were talking . . ." Impatience tightened Adam's expression. She thought a moment then shot back, "You should be ashamed of yourself, bringing up a thing like that, dark half the time. I won't sleep for a week. What are you trying to do, make me paranoid?"

He planted his other hand, surrounding her with 180-plus pounds of thoroughly virile male. His face descended toward hers. She clamped her eyelids shut figuring that whether he choked or kissed her, that she, at least, was correctly prepared. "I am certain," he said softly, "that no one can make you into anything other than what you are, nor should anyone try."

"Well, I'm glad that's settled. Now you understand my position on the basement."

"Perfectly. If you're too scared to go into the basement, I'll go alone. That's not a problem. All I ask is that you unlock the door."

When she sensed him pushing away from the wall, George's eyes flew open. "You mean that after all that, you aren't even going to kiss me?"

"I wasn't planning to, no."

"Well, why not?"

Again he stepped close. "If that's your condition for loaning me the pump, I'll be only too happy to oblige."

"Oh, no." She stopped him by pressing her hand firmly against the center of his chest. Beneath the softness of his sweater, his chest felt delightfully tight and warm. "You can give me a thank-you kiss when you return my pump. Maybe by then I'll know for sure whether or not you . . . ugh." She couldn't just blurt out Troy Hasselbush's unfounded suspicions so she continued on in forced singsong, "Oh, never mind."

"I think we should arrange for a deposit though, purely as a show of good faith."

"You mean sort of like putting money in an escrow account?"

"I guess you could put it that way."

"I knew it!" Straightening herself, she raised her chin regally. "You may be handsome and have a certain savoir faire, but you are definitely a business-and-finance type and a stuffed shirt."

"Handsome and adaptable though," he mumbled, pulling down the corners of his mouth. "I guess that's progress."

George swallowed and asked in what she hoped was a natural tone, "Did you ever meet Hangtown Harry?"

"I sure did, a couple of years ago."

"Oh."

"I didn't kill him though."

"I know that!" she said with what she thought was the perfect amount of impatience.

George scoured the counters for pencil and paper. Fiona's kitchen was cluttered with remnants of food and drink yet deserted of people. The now boisterous chatter of the neighbors still drifted from the adjacent dining room. Adam had suggested that they "circumvent the inevitable explanations for their departure" by taking one of the numerous passages that snaked through the house, and George had agreed. In addition to being a medium, Estelle Capricorn was a notorious scandalmonger; if she saw George leaving with Adam, half the city and Harlan Richards would know about it by morning. But George had to leave Fiona a note.

Exasperated, she asked, "Do you have a pen?"

"No, but here's a loaf of bread. You could always leave a trail of crumbs."

"They'd melt in the rain." Brows knit, she scanned the room. "You could help me search, you know."

"You haven't tried the refrigerator yet, I'll check there."

"Some detective you are."

"You'd be surprised." The seal on the refrigerator released with a *whoosh*. "Is a pencil all right?"

"What?"

Adam stood beside the open door of the industrial-size refrigerator, sporting a thoroughly smug expression. He held a short pencil between his thumb and forefinger.

"Where did you find that?" She scrutinized the massive interior, nearly barren except for a varied collection of condiments aligned on lazy Susans, plastic tubs marked caviar, shrimp, hearts of palm, and chicken salad, several metal containers of punch concentrate, and one cut-crystal pitcher labeled Nonalcoholic.

"In the butter keeper with the grocery list."

She hadn't spotted that. She snatched the pencil away. "Think you're observant, don't you?"

His lips moved as though teasing around a smile. "I'm many things you don't know or appreciate."

"If you told me the truth for a change, I might."

"How about dinner tonight, eight o'clock, your place?"

"Why on earth should I cook for you?"

"Put it this way. All I have to offer tonight is either what I can manage to heat on a hot plate in my one-room basement apartment or a bus trip to the nearest McDonald's and that only if you promise not to order more than one Big Mac."

She thought how strange that statement sounded coming from a man wearing a cashmere sweater and slacks of impeccable cut. Yes, he was stuffy, but he was also intelligent and sophisticated. Men like Adam Lawrence didn't entertain their ladies at McDonald's. Men like Adam Lawrence weren't typically gardeners either. "Do you know who my father is?"

He nodded. "Harlan Richards."

"He usually arranges who I go out with, and just looking at you, he would think you were a reasonable candidate. *He's* the one who likes stuffed shirts. Except the men he chooses often pick me up in a Ferrari or if they're older, a Bentley, or if they want to look like sincere overachievers, maybe an economy car—but always with a telephone. They might take me to dinner at L'Etoile or Kan's or Le Club then out dancing. After that, they might suggest Irish coffee at the Buena Vista."

"I see. It makes my next question an obvious one. How much are you willing to sacrifice for your curiosity?"

She stared into his eyes. They were gray but with enough blue that his tailor had undoubtedly suggested colors that enhanced the blueness, yet Adam, judging from his present attire, stubbornly clung to the conservative maroon and navy. She added inflexible to his growing list of drawbacks

47

meaning it was either the hot plate, McDonald's, her cooking, or continued suspense. "Eight-thirty, my house. Be on time."

George scrawled her note to Fiona. *Gone to my house with baffling, stubborn gardener to get pump out of basement. 12:30 P.M. Your fault. George.* "Now," she said, her gaze panning the room, "I need to put it out of sight of the gossips but where Fiona . . ."

Adam reopened the refrigerator and raised the crystal pitcher filled with punch. George slipped the note underneath, thinking that maybe Adam wasn't as stodgy as he appeared.

Cramped together between a dripping hedge and the cement foundation of George's house, Adam patiently held the umbrella over her head while she fumbled with the keys. "Isn't there an inside entrance?" he muttered.

"Not that I know of." She tried the fourth key, one of at least fifteen on a rusty chain. "The realtor promised to mark these but . . ." Number five was another reject. "As you can see . . ." Number six refused to enter the lock at all. Out of the corner of her eye, she could see that Adam was looking over the row of wire-reinforced frosted windows that ran the length of the side of the house. The basement windows and door were disguised from view from the street and from Hangtown Harry's house by the seven-foot hedge, dense and in need of trimming. From where she stood, George could barely make out the police line, drooping from the rain and strung like a macabre garland around the perimeter of Harry's property.

"Eureka!" George exclaimed. The aged tumblers released their responsibility with a metallic sigh, but the wooden door, swollen from the rain, refused to open.

"Hold this," Adam said, thrusting the umbrella into her hand. He put his shoulder and his weight against the peeling wood. The door scraped open a foot and jammed again. He groped along the inside for the light switch, flipped it back and forth without result, then clicked on his flashlight. "You're not coming?"

"How do you know the pump is down there anyway?"

"Fiona said Dr. Emerson lent it to her once before. The pump should be around. I don't imagine there's much call for a portable water pump where he is now."

"But the realtor didn't tell me anything about any water. I didn't even know where the basement door was until ten minutes ago. What if she didn't leave the pump?"

"I'll give you a report," he promised and disappeared into the gloom.

George huddled under the umbrella, sorry that she hadn't kicked Troy Hasselbush after all, now that her beautiful shoes were wet anyway. Deciding to banish any thoughts of her cold feet, she lowered the umbrella and surveyed Harry's desolate house. A high iron fence surrounded the house, pond, and narrow lawns where Harry's prized Akita, Mr. Moto, had roamed. Beyond the black spikes of the iron gate and beneath a half-tunnel of striped awning, tiled steps rose to the magnificent front door. Harry claimed it had been dispatched from Italy by the late Joshua Abraham Norton himself before he lost his shirt, his door, and possibly his mind, trying to corner the rice market in 1853. He declared himself Emperor of the United States and Protector of Mexico. But not even the spirit of the emperor had protected Hangtown Harry Frye from his murderer.

She conjured up the image of the killer stealing through that house, stalking Harry with the skill of a mountain lion, steps silent as snowfall. She could almost see the dim circle of the desk lamp as Harry rose with difficulty, weary from long hours of reading a chilling Gold Rush history of Placerville and the men whose necks had broken in the nooses of "Hangtown."

She visualized Harry pausing, hunched over his desk, his back completely vulnerable. Behind him, gleaming steel hung suspended against the dark night. The knife blade hovered the length of a heartbeat, then sliced the air, plunging into the stooped old man, sending blood . . .

A blast of wind flung icy wetness into her face. A hand closed over her shoulder. Screaming, George jumped, spun, and brandished the umbrella like a samurai's long sword.

"Miss me?" Adam inquired calmly, holding a dusty piece of machinery. He shifted the sharp tip of the umbrella away from his nose. "So far I've been held at crook-point and umbrella-point. There seems to be no end to your ingenuity."

"And no end to you sneaking up on me! Merciful heavens!"

"Here," Adam said, holding out his free hand. She gave him the umbrella, and almost before she knew it, his arm circled her snugly and they were heading back toward Fiona Breathwaite's house through the rain. "You're shaking," he murmured. "What you need is a glass of punch. That brew is so strong it's bound to tranquilize you a bit. It did me."

But the awful image of Harry's last moments on earth lingered in George's mind. She might have been babbling at Marfa when it happened, ragging her friend over her own frustrations when that poor, innocent man had dragged in his last breath. George shivered, and not only because of her wet feet. Murder had a way of putting complaints into perspective.

They were mounting the first of the two steps leading to Fiona's kitchen when a scream pierced the silence.

For an instant, they hesitated. Dread drove a sudden pit in her stomach. Dear God, what now?

Adam tossed the umbrella aside and swung the pump onto the porch. "Stay back," he yelled.

"Not on your life!" She jumped the last stair to the porch.

Adam ripped open the screen door and bounded through the kitchen, George following him. Bursting into the living room, they halted at the horror-stricken stares of the neighbors.

Agnes Clodfelter was slumped in a chair, her legs bent like broken twigs. Fiona knelt at Agnes's feet, holding her limp hand and calling her name in a thin, plaintive voice. Across the room, Dwight spoke into the telephone, repeating Fiona's address. Estelle and Elmo clustered nearby like nervous sheep. Only the portly Natasha Velour stood near Fiona, studying Agnes with what George considered ghoulish fascination.

Adam rushed to them. "What happened?"

"Someone poisoned poor Aggie." Fiona nodded toward a punch cup lying on the carpet, its contents spilled.

Natasha snapped open her compact and held the mirror under the nose of the unconscious Agnes. "She's still breathing." She flipped it closed like a seasoned cop would his badge and checked her watch which like everything else she wore, was dark, boxy, and serviceable. The only exception was her felt hat which, though black, sported a magenta ostrich plume. No wonder a local columnist had described her trademark attire as butch with a touch of buccaneer. "Phillips," she bellowed, "tell 'em to get the lead out!"

"They're on their way."

Natasha started to lift one of Agnes's eyelids.

George shrieked, "Don't touch her, you barbarian!" Six stares leveled on George. Undaunted, George pushed past the startled Natasha and dropped to her knees beside Fiona who immediately burst into tears.

"Go ahead and get her away from here. I'll take care of Agnes," Adam promised.

George led the sobbing Fiona into an adjacent parlor and shut the double doors behind them.

"It's all my fault," Fiona wailed.

"Don't be ridiculous! The only way you could be responsible is if you poisoned her, which I wouldn't believe even if it was etched in granite. Sit down." Fiona sunk into a brocade-covered settee. "That's better."

"I'm so selfish. You, nobody can understand why. I got everyone here hoping someone would slip or we'd learn something, anything to clear this murder up before the other candidate and the papers can find something in this terrible mess to hurt Marvin." She grabbed a faded needlepoint pillow and clutched it to her chest. "For months I've tried to be so careful not to do anything damaging. It's so important that he succeed. Now I've made poor Aggie suffer."

George paced over an Oriental rug, thinking that her father's oft-repeated saying was correct: The sobs of the hysterical did sound like the laughter of the damned. "You had absolutely no idea anything like this would happen.

How could you? It's just that these filthy old scandals crop up here again and again. That's not your fault. People make mistakes. Marvin is your son. It's natural, no, it's absolutely imperative that you protect him."

Fiona's complexion blanched to alabaster. "But no one knows," she gasped.

"Of course, they don't. So far there are only rumors." That rotten Troy, George thought, spreading rumors about Fiona's gardener. What if some fool actually believed him!

"Rumors?" Fiona squeaked, growing ashen. She dropped the pillow. It rolled off her lap and onto the floor.

George opened her mouth to speak but stopped abruptly, a realization dawning. She and Fiona had been talking about two different things.

Knowing she had already seen too much, George lowered her gaze to the carpet, not wanting to take advantage of the moment, unwilling to read all the revealed truths in Fiona's eyes, ones that George knew instinctively the older woman was not yet ready to discuss. George decided quickly on diversion. "Jack Smith will be completely exposed so everyone can see what a rotten swine he is—though I hate to compare that odious creature to a pig. After all, some pigs can be awfully sweet, especially guinea pigs."

Fiona jumped up and started to the window. Beneath the forest green wool of her dress, her shoulders began to relax.

"Please don't worry. I'll do everything I can, I promise, and I bet Adam will too. We'll both help clear this murder up before Smith can use it against Marvin in the election. We have three weeks to figure things out. We'll start with motive, just as every good detective does. Why would someone want to kill a sweet, insane person like Harry? And now Agnes, right under our very noses!"

"The ambulance," Fiona said, now composed, and straightening her dress and hair. "I'd better go see to the details. Aggie must be all right." Then almost to herself, she murmured, "She just has to be."

At George's quizzical expression, she added, "I don't think I could bear the thought of arranging another funeral, especially not one for Aggie. The only real gift life gave

Agnes Clodfelter was life itself, and by God, nobody has the right to take it away."

George trailed behind Fiona, her mind clicking through the information like an old-style adding machine. Fiona was protecting Marvin, but the stakes were higher than Jack Smith and the race for city supervisor.

No wonder many San Franciscans claimed that Scarlet Street and scandal were one and the same, George mused. Now this place had proved fatal.

Chapter
6

Poking her face between her bedroom curtains, Georgette Richards peered down at Hangtown Harry's deserted house, searching the early evening shadows.

"You have bags the size of Monaco under your eyes. Can't sleep, running to the window every five minutes—I think you're getting paranoid."

George allowed the curtains to fall closed and turned to Marfa diBello, clad in a purple body stocking and lounging like a Roman princess among the pillows on George's bed. Fresh from exercise class, her legs stretched like elegant violet stamens emerging from the three overlapping petals of her short black skirt.

"Paranoid. Paranoid!" George sputtered. "Night before last, and mind you, right next door, a sweet old man was stabbed to death. This afternoon poor Agnes Clodfelter was poisoned, not fatally, thank God, but poisoned by a glass of plain fruit punch. Well," she mused, "I guess you couldn't call it plain. But that's not the point!"

Marfa propped her feet on a rare footboard, part of a bedroom set enameled in vibrant floral patterns that George had flown to Brussels to buy. "I don't see how going to the window every other minute is doing any good. If you need protection, hire a bodyguard."

She concentrated on giving Marfa her absolute best shriveling stare. "One of those motor homes you date? Not on your royal little life. I'm not the one who could write *Europe on Five Bodyguards a Day.* For your information, I was looking out the window for a dog, and not just any dog, but a champion Akita named Mr. Moto. He belonged to Hangtown Harry Frye, the murdered man. I should have such a loyal friend!"

Marfa raised the most envied female face in San Francisco and puffed her full lips. "I sent you all those costumes."

"And humiliated me with Little Bo Peep!"

Marfa dismissed the remark with an imperial sweep of her hand. "I gave you that lovely teddy and robe you're wearing. Need I remind you that they are hand-sewn silk with French lace and an exclusive. No other woman in San Francisco owns a set like it."

"A dog, now that's a person's best friend." George paced to her dressing table. "Do you know that both nights since the murder, Mr. Moto has gone back at dusk to patrol the grounds? Last night I finally forced him in at midnight. That's a kind of friendship I'll never know. It would take a keg of beer and six lusty pallbearers to get you to keep a vigil for me."

"Some sage said that we get the friends we deserve." Feet still in place, Marfa scooted her bottom across the coverlet and reached for a half-empty glass of wine. She raised the goblet in toast. "You deserve me."

"You don't have to tell me who you heard that from—one of those heathens like Hank 'The Tank' Muldoon." She grabbed her hairbrush and waved it at Marfa. "I didn't want that monster in my house, but oh, no, you insisted. You, who refused to even invite him to your apartment because of what the neighbors might think. You, who had to have a bodyguard while you housesat, whining 'I'm scared to stay alone.' Well, I certainly didn't deserve to have my beautiful sofa thrown through my two-story picture window."

"Actually, I thought it was kind of romantic. Tank only did it so he could shout that he loved me to the world. It was an act of extreme passion—"

"I suppose it was just coincidence that this passionate urge overwhelmed him in my house. Then you disappeared on a trip home to Milan while I'm forced to move! I couldn't bear to look my neighbor in the face—he loved that poor MG. He even painted flowers on the curb. And nobody would believe what happened. Daddy had to send his personal attorney to explain how a car could be totaled by a sofa. The insurance company was so confused they subpoenaed Louis the Fifteenth!"

"That week of pure bliss is long past. Now there's only Woody."

"Woody the . . ." George made a circling motion with the brush. "I'm asking purely for insurance purposes, you understand."

"Just plain Woody."

"Does this one throw furniture or gnaw on it?"

"Don't be silly. There's a perfectly logical explanation. It's a nickname. During the off-season he needs exercise, so he pushes around station wagons. Actually," she purred, "with my intimate knowledge, I would have called him Bronco."

George tossed her hands heavenward. "Marfa, these men are only using you for one thing."

She snuggled down into the covers, her mouth curving into a thoroughly lascivious smile. "I know. Someday, I'll find some nice, steady man with a title and a castle and get married. He'll lavish me with jewels to prove he can afford me, and I'll lavish him with children to prove how virile his own little jewels are. Meanwhile, it's bombs away."

"One of these days you're going to wake up with wrinkles and find out that the only men in circulation are either ones that don't have any jewels left or fortune hunters. That's called bombing out."

"Georgette, you act so hopeless about everything. You could have most any man you want, right now, just for the asking."

"They'd brag about it. I've heard them at parties. I refuse to be just another Saturday night conquest."

"So that's why you act like a nun! Listen to me, they brag most when they don't get it. Besides, you have to learn to ignore gossip. You're beautiful and rich, and yet you never have any fun, always going out with those jerks your father sends. Why don't you have an affair? Enjoy yourself for a change. Pick someone really different, some man who sends your body into long, smoldering fits."

"I don't know . . ." George tapped her brush against the tip of her chin. "But what if . . ." Adam Lawrence did fill out a pair of jeans and a T-shirt with a body straight out of her naughtiest fantasy. This afternoon when the police were questioning them at Fiona's house, she could hardly force herself to pay attention to the officer. Adam did his share of looking at her too, and it was exciting knowing that the attraction was mutual and a relief to know it was simply sexual. Going to bed with him would certainly be wicked and wonderful—as long as he kept quiet and didn't distract her with his infuriating logic.

Screeching with delight, Marfa bounded off the bed.

"Holy heaven!" George jumped, lost her balance and landed on the fluffy pink rug.

Marfa fell to the floor laughing and pointing, the strategically placed highlights shimmering in her dark hair. "You know him already. I can see it in your eyes. You've found him! Who is he? What kind of man is he?"

"No, he's really like all the rest. . . ."

"He can't be or you wouldn't want him. He can't be like one of those mummies you usually go out with."

George crossed her legs and clutched the hairbrush to her chest. "That's the funny thing, Marfa. In one way he is like the rest, sort of a stuffed shirt. You know, the ones who always speak in exactly complete sentences and never say 'uh.' Only when Adam says something, I usually don't notice because it's interesting."

And, she thought, that smooth, deep voice could drive an Eve to scour trees for an apple. "But, every time I really think about it, I mean it's hopeless. He probably winds his watch the same time every day."

"The better to be on time for a tryst."

"And knows how much money to the absolute penny he carries in his pocket."

"So he can buy you a drink after he makes you pant with passion."

"Ooooh, you don't understand!" George scrambled to her feet and planted her hands on her hips. "That gorgeous tan is a disguise! He's only pretending to be a gardener. Even the smudges on his jeans look orderly. So tell me, Miss Authority-on-Affairs, just how I forget everything and have a torrid affair with a fake gardener who most certainly balances his checkbook?"

Marfa rolled to a sitting position and sank her chin to her knees, an air of seriousness settling over her like an ill-fitting slipcover. "George, I don't know. It all sounds too complicated, way too complicated. My father always wrote that an affair must be simple, like fine wine. You drink, you enjoy, you remember. Then tomorrow comes another bottle. But this," she shook her head, her expression solemn. "Your feelings for him are already complicated, and that's all wrong."

"What do you mean, all wrong? It can't be; he'll be here for dinner in half an hour."

Marfa bolted from the floor. "Mother of God! I'll stay with you."

"Don't be ridiculous."

Marfa dashed to the closet, pressed the light switch, and started thumbing through the rows of clothing. Muttering in Italian, she emerged with a lapis blue skirt and matching sweater. "Here, wear this. Blue is very cold, and silver, you'll use silver accessories." She opened the top dresser drawer and started sorting through the jewelry.

Sighing, George removed her robe, and slipped the skirt over her teddy. She aligned the soft suede along her hips and zipped the skirt, then tugged on the matching wool sweater with suede appliqué. Marfa was definitely overreacting. She supposed it had something to do with her being an Italian clothing designer. As George adjusted the wide, fitted waistband of her sweater over her trim waist, she studied Marfa. Somehow, her derriere twitched seductively even when she was standing still. Her body language was obscene; she drove men wild. If Marfa was having dinner with Adam, Marfa would have something to worry about.

Marfa descended on her with a large silver choker and matching earrings. "Where did you get these? I don't recognize them."

"They were a gift from a client who liked the way Shannon and I remodeled her house. Shannon's set is a little different, but we both have the fire opal in the choker. It's the same shade I used as an accent color for the living room." George snapped on the earrings and necklace.

"How is Shannon?" Marfa asked, fussing over the way George's sweater lay against her shoulders and waist.

"My cousin is married, pregnant, and happy. I hardly see her anymore except at the office." Suddenly George recalled all the times she and Shannon had tried on clothes before dates, exchanging scarves and jewelry, running back and forth between their bedrooms, George up, Shannon down, both joking, always laughing. After eleven months of dismal loneliness in the house on Russian Hill, Tank Muldoon—bless his fateful lust—had given her an excuse to sell the perfectly wonderful but memory-ridden Victorian and move to Scarlet Street.

"There!" Marfa took a step back. Out of habit, George held the pose so Marfa could survey her handiwork. "You're lovely. I've achieved a bit of icy, but don't you dare take any chances. Send him home after dinner." She leaned down and pecked both of George's cheeks. "And don't despair. I'll find the right man for you, a fine, full-bodied wine."

George plastered on a false smile. "Forget it."

After Marfa left, she slipped into matching lapis-colored heels that, she calculated, lifted her to five-foot-three inches. Defiantly, she sprayed perfume behind her ears and knees. Resisting a man's advance was one thing; having no pass to resist was quite another.

Downstairs, she checked on the pot roast in the Crockpot.

All the goodies bubbled happily along. Bread warmed in the oven. Champagne cooled in the refrigerator. A celebration was in order. Everyone in the neighborhood had survived the day—at least so far.

She rechecked the dining room and paused a moment to enjoy the lone oasis of order amid scattered packing boxes. Over the dining table, the Venetian crystal chandelier and Marfa's peace offering over the Muldoon affair shimmered, two magnificent tiers of candlestick holders adorned with frosted clusters of grapes, serrated leaves, and clear prisms. In the tall china cabinet, soft light glowed behind the keepsakes she loved, Irish porcelain, Italian crystal, Belgian laces, mementos of her mother and her extended European tour, one that her middle-aged father had sent his twenty-year-old bride on alone. His decision seemed incredible, no more understandable to her now than at any point in all the years since an obnoxious gossip columnist had cornered her at a party and related every gruesome detail.

Her father must have been as unbending, dictatorial, and obsessed with business then as he was today. The only photographs on display in his house featured airplanes.

With her left hand holding her right wrist to steady it, George reached inside the cabinet for a china figurine—a miniature girl with auburn curls and an apron. As always, George imagined her mother whisking into a tiny European shop where she discovered the tiny beauty, and cradled her like a precious jewel in her soft hands. George struggled to feel the touch of the hand that had once warmed the porcelain so long ago, struggled to feel that glow of appreciation and acceptance enfold her own body.

Had her mother seen in the delicate features of the miniature a vision of her daughter, the one she would bear but never hold herself, the daughter that Marfa's parents would send from Milan to Harlan Richards along with the crystal, porcelain, and lace as just another memento of a lonely, long-ago journey?

She clutched the tiny figure to her chest, but as always no answer came. "You're being silly," she said aloud. "There is no answer." Quickly, she replaced the little girl, closed the cabinet and turned the key. She straightened the mixed bouquet of flowers on the table, then marched into the living room.

"Completely awful," she muttered, surveying the furniture. She pushed the sofa, angling it more toward the marble hearth. "Perfectly horrid," she said, guiding a chair alongside the sofa.

At the chime, she paused, puffing. The house smelled of paint. Boxes lined the walls. Adam Lawrence would have to settle for unsettled. What on earth did he expect anyway, inviting himself for dinner when she'd only been here for less than a week?

She opened the door. "Come in. But I'm warning you not to complain. Any polite person who invites themselves to dinner under these circumstances promises not to notice that the flowers on the table are arranged in a champagne cooler or that all the serving pieces don't match."

Adam smiled. "You certainly look lovely this evening."

So much for Marfa and her cool blue, she thought, triumphant. And this was no perfume-induced euphoria either; he wasn't even close enough to smell it. She beckoned him into the foyer. "Thank you. You look wonderful, too, except for the jeans, of course."

"Too informal?" he asked, glancing down at the crisp denim. "I did wear a sport coat."

"I like the coat. I've always been partial to wool tweed. No, it's the jeans. They're just wrong somehow . . ." she trailed off, trying to get a glimpse of what he had hidden behind his back. "What's that?"

"I brought you a small gift. I hope you like it." He extended a covered bird cage and smiled gently, his gray eyes sincere.

"That's . . . oh . . ." *Oh, God, he's gorgeous.* Her eyes clung to his even as she accepted the cage. She lifted the cloth canopy. A large bird with spindly legs bobbed over a perch. Plump and gray, it tilted its head and pointed a bright eye at her. "Is it a wild dove?"

Adam nodded.

"Where on earth did you get it?"

"Out of the mouth of a neighborhood cat. Unfortunately, doves aren't very fast. Fortunately, the cat wasn't either, and he ensured his flight to safety by dropping the bird. It's taken her a couple of weeks to recover, but she's fine now. She took a few practice flights in my room and she could be released at any time."

"But . . . I don't understand. If she can be released, why give her to me?"

He answered with an approving expression that told her that she had met his expectation.

"Letting her go is my gift, isn't it?"

"I had hoped you would see it that way."

"You were the one who took care of her all this time. It's not fair to you. You should be the one to watch her fly free again."

"I was hoping that you'd invite me to watch."

"Oh, yes! We can do it tomorrow morning. It's going to be beautiful. I mean, it already is beautiful; the most beautiful gift anyone's ever given me." George wanted to kiss him badly and did, a quick touch of her lips to his cheek. When she drew back, she realized that he was actually blushing.

George drifted around the room, waving her free hand high, then low, checking for drafts. "She needs to get a good night's sleep before her debut tomorrow morning. There," she said, setting the cage on a teakwood end table inlaid with rare ebony.

Adam retrieved a copy of *Architectural Digest* from a basket on the hearth and slipped it under the cage. "I think this precaution is necessary. I don't want to be responsible for any further damage to your home. It's getting expensive."

"It's all right about the rug. Mr. Moto is using it now that he's staying with me, at least when he isn't using my bed. I'll be sure to let you know when it's time to send the rug to the cleaners." With a wink, she ducked into the kitchen, hopefully tempting him to follow.

Once there, she busied herself by collecting a box each of wheat and rye crackers and starting to align them in a circle around grapes and sliced Havarti cheese. The second he stepped into the kitchen, she asked, "Will you open the champagne? You'll find it in the refrigerator. The glasses are in there too."

Adam retrieved the bottle and began untwisting the wire over the cork. "What are we celebrating?"

"Agnes not dying, I suppose. I can't really think of anything else to celebrate. It certainly isn't great news that the only fingerprints the police are going to find on that pitcher of nonalcoholic punch with the poison in it are yours and Fiona's since it's only reasonable that the murderer wouldn't leave fingerprints there. On the other hand when they find both sets of fingerprints there that will prove that you and Fiona are innocent. That's another thing we can celebrate."

"I agree with that conclusion even though I'm not the least bit certain how you arrived at it."

"People often have trouble following what I say. My cousin Shannon says it's because I'm already ahead of myself when I talk, so I leave things out. It makes a lot of sense, don't you think?"

"It certainly does."

She cringed, waiting for the pop of the cork. But he was an expert, releasing the pressure with little more than a sigh. After wrapping the bottle in a towel, he poured, tilting the flute and trickling the liquid down the side to conserve the bubbles. "I can't make any sense out of you. You're terribly confusing."

"I am," he said, seeming to brighten to the idea. He handed her the glass of champagne, and filled another. "Let's toast confusion."

"Really? Well, if you insist." She clinked her glass to his and drank deeply. Light and effervescent, the champagne slid down her throat as a wave of pure pleasure. Cupping the slender flute with both hands, she touched her tongue to the tip of the rim, looked over the dancing bubbles at Adam, and said softly, "Most definitely confusing."

"Explain that, please." Adam leaned back, his elbows

propped against the counter, his hands crossed loosely over his flat stomach.

Her gaze drifted down the firm length of him. "You have a body that belongs in *Playgirl.*"

A slow grin edged up the corners of his lips. "I do try to keep in shape."

She took another long sip of champagne. "But then the absolute second you open your mouth you sound like *Scientific American.*"

His smile evaporated instantly.

"Well, not exactly scientific, and actually not even quite American, and definitely not *The New Yorker.* Maybe more like *Forbes* or *Business Week.*" Muscle by muscle his body stiffened. "Why don't you have more champagne," she said, ending with a small yawn. "It will make you feel so relaxed."

He straightened as if to reach for his glass and hesitated. "If you are about to insult me, I can assure you that alcohol will not deaden the impact."

"It's not an insult, really. Oh, don't you see? No, I don't guess that you do, do you. To thine own self be true. I did it my way and all that . . ." she trailed off, her long sigh extending into an expansive yawn. "Ohhhhh, no, wait," she said. "I've got it now. It's perfect. Actually you're *Gentleman's Quarterly* masquerading behind a cover from *Field and Stream.*"

"You make me sound like Publisher's Clearinghouse personified. I think I will have more champagne." He drained his glass then refilled both.

She sensed his covert scrutiny and wondered what evaluation he was undoubtedly formulating behind those gray eyes. What titles might he use to describe her? *Glamour?* She glanced down at her chest and shuddered. *Boy's Life?* "Honestly, Adam. I didn't mean to offend you."

He scowled, an irregular crease appearing between his brows. She giggled. He was cute when he was angry. She felt like pleading for a truce and curling up on his chest like a kitten. She blinked away the fuzziness, and studied his face. The odds for a truce did not appear promising. "I'm really sorry."

"Apology accepted," he said, prying the champagne glass from her reluctant fingers.

"Why are you doing that?"

"Your eyes are glazed over. You had better lie down."

She released a long, sleepy sigh. "Can I curl up on your chest?"

Adam grabbed her arm and pulled her toward the living room. "I refuse to take advantage of a tipsy woman."

"I am not tipsy, only sleepy."

"When did you last eat?"

"I can't remember. It's this neighborhood, I can hardly do anything the way I'm supposed to. Wait . . . wait a darn minute. You're responsible for this too, you know, falling on my doorstep and keeping me awake two nights ago. Or was it last . . . Ohhhhh," she yawned. "I'm so sleepy. It hardly matters anyway. But the insomnia started when you fell on my doorstep so it's all your fault."

"Somehow I knew you would say that."

"Great minds think alike, don't they?" she mumbled. She could never remember the sofa looking more inviting, the soft cushions, the fluffy pillows, all ready to conform to every tired muscle and sore joint. George collapsed into its spongy depths with a sigh of sheer pleasure. "Oh, Adam?"

"Yes," he answered. He'd located the quilt, a rare indigo blue with red cardinals that after three hours of haggling at a street fair had still cost her an absolute fortune. It was nice that Adam liked birds.

"Adam, I'm being such an awful hostess. I even forgot the cheese and crackers."

"Don't worry about it." His face hovered near hers. Narrow lines creased his tanned skin, and she wished that she had the power to read them like tea leaves, to know if the small dimple in his left cheek came from laughter or if it was the companion of the worrisome crease between his brows, to understand what loves and hurts and passions had designed the finished man.

She shook her head from side to side, unwishing that wish. Suddenly she didn't want to explore from the outside in, to resort to some quick, easy, or superficial examination.

If Adam wanted to keep secrets he had passed out on the wrong doorstep. She was going to uncover every single one. She touched her fingertip to his nearly invisible dimple. She heard his soft laugh, and her hand and her eyelids slid downward. "Please," she murmured, "promise me that when I wake up . . . you'll tell me . . . all about . . . your wrinkles."

Chapter
7

Adam straightened in the wing chair, trying to ease a dull ache in his back from too much gardening in the past four days compounded by too little movement in the past four hours. Georgette had not yet stirred, but somehow Adam knew that she would soon. During her waking moments, she was driven by a restless energy that mandated constant physical and mental activity. Her sleep appeared to be equally all-consuming, manifest by her extreme stillness. Now, small, almost imperceptible changes in her expression—a quirk of her brow, a twitch of her nose—seemed to signal the resurgence of that irresistible force and personality that was Georgette Richards. He welcomed her back with great pleasure.

Abruptly, all signs of sleep vanished from her. She sat up, wide-awake, eyes bright and alert as though a magical cloak had been lifted. "My dinner is ruined," she moaned.

"No, actually it was excellent. I saved you some."

She jumped up and in four deft arm movements had the quilt folded. "Good, I'm starved. Is Mr. Moto back yet?"

"No. Why would you expect him to be?"

"Don't you remember that he's staying with me?" With stiff fingers, she combed her hair upward from her ears to her forehead then shook her head. Amazingly, her fluffy dark hair settled into the exact style he remembered from earlier in the evening. "We can't let Mr. Moto patrol all night. We have to get him to come in."

He followed her into the kitchen. "Only if you insist."

"I had a terrible time getting him away from Harry's house last night." Georgette fetched the leftovers from the refrigerator and began fixing herself a plate. "Wait a minute. If we reheat him a plate of pot roast, maybe we can lure him." She retrieved the large butcher knife he remembered from his tenure in bondage and started slicing the meat.

"It sounds like a bribe to me."

"I don't care what it sounds like as long as it works. Besides, I'd rather bribe him than get frostbite chasing him around the neighborhood. Wouldn't you?"

"Don't drag me into this."

Hands on hips, knife in hand, she sized him up with vivid turquoise eyes. "Well, that's gratitude for you. Poor Mr. Moto's an orphan now. Agnes Clodfelter is lying in the hospital after being poisoned at Fiona's house while that poor woman is desperately trying to protect her son from heaven only knows what horrible fate! You're already involved—from your button-down collar right down to your wing tips! You're her gardener!"

"And as such, I'm responsible for her yard. That's the entire extent of my responsibilities or liabilities."

"How can you stand there and say you're not involved! Not involved! You're a prime suspect!"

"Oh, really? Tell me why."

Her eyelids flew wide at his simple statement. She took a shaky step backward and stammered, "I don't believe it, of course."

"Of course, you don't," he said, amused. She'd really stuck her foot in it this time, bringing up Troy Hasselbush's speculation from earlier in the day. "Then explain how *you* can consider me a suspect."

She severed eye contact by turning to face the counter.

"It's not me. But they—I mean the police—they might because of the punch. You touched the handle of the pitcher with the poison in it, remember?"

"As you pointed out earlier, a murderer would be foolish to leave his fingerprints on a pitcher containing poison. You even suggested previously that the presence of my fingerprints proved my innocence."

Georgette sawed furiously on the roast. "You know, I seem to remember saying something like that."

"Furthermore, until the contents of the pitcher are analyzed, no one knows for certain whether or not it contained poison. No one actually saw Agnes drink from that pitcher, except you and Fiona, and Fiona poured that particular glass from the pitcher long before I ever touched it. You can appreciate that chronology since you witnessed both events."

"You know, you're absolutely right," she said slowly. "It's all coming back to me now."

In his driest of tones, he added, "I thought it might." He leaned against the counter and studied her. "The police will certainly consider the possibility that the poison was introduced only to Agnes's punch cup or to one of the hors d'oeuvres. Also, some poisons are slow-acting; she may have ingested the poison sometime before the party. It's merely conjecture that her collapse was the result of being poisoned anyway. People collapse every day from natural causes. Tell me now, how can I be a prime suspect?"

"Oh, I don't know," she answered in a small, high voice. "I just get carried away sometimes. My father says I jump to conclusions constantly. He says I've always been that way." She pushed a plate piled high with meat into the microwave oven then added her plate which contained mostly vegetables. She punched the digital pad and the microwave purred to life. "All those observations you just made are really interesting. Were you a detective?"

" 'Perry Mason,' weeknights, I'm addicted." But it didn't take a Perry Mason to figure out that she'd let the policeman's suspicions slip. He smiled inwardly, remembering her outrage in the hallway that afternoon. He'd overheard her defending him despite the fact that she knew nothing about his past, nothing aside from what she had cleverly deduced. Indeed, clothes did not make the man. She had easily and accurately pegged him which pointed up the exact reason he needed her help.

The timer *pinged*, and she removed her vegetables. "Like some?"

He shook his head.

She forked a piece of potato, popped it into her mouth, chewed thoughtfully, and swallowed. "I would have liked the Perry Mason show a whole lot better if Perry and Della had fallen in love and gotten married like other famous detectives, you know, like Nick and Nora Charles, Lord Peter Wimsey and uh . . ."

"Or Sherlock Holmes and Dr. Watson," he suggested.

"You're completely missing the point. What's wrong with romance, too? It adds something. Old bachelors with cigar ashes on their collars, and tough guys with lipstick on theirs, get boring after a while. When people are getting murdered right and left, there ought to be something going on that's lively." She attacked a piece of carrot. "And no matter what you say, some of those detectives are boring. But I always enjoy Perry Mason, even though he is stodgy."

"And you enjoy being with me, even though in your eyes I'm stodgy."

She stopped in midchew and nodded vigorously. Her cheeks seemed to pinken slightly. After swallowing she said, "Mr. Moto. We have to go get him before he catches his death."

"That animal has at least two inches of fur. He could sleep comfortably in a snowdrift."

"So tell me," she said, trading her virtually untouched plate for the one containing the slices of pot roast, "just where is he going to find a comfortable snowdrift in San Francisco?"

As he followed her through the wet bushes toward Hangtown Harry's house, Adam decided that if he only had one word to describe Georgette Richards that word would be *relentless*. His Omega read 1:30 A.M. and judging from the goose bumps on his body, the thermometer read forty-five degrees. Mr. Moto was undoubtedly warm wherever he was, but no one could reason with the lovely woman picking her way through the shrubbery ahead of him.

"You could shine the flashlight ahead of me instead of on my behind," she complained in a raspy whisper.

"I *am* following you."

"Give me that," she snapped, relieving him of the flashlight.

"Do you want the umbrella too?"

"I only have two hands, and I'll have you know this plate of roast is burning one of them."

He pulled out his handkerchief and exchanged it for the flashlight. Once she had the folded cloth positioned like a hot pad, she held out her free hand for the flashlight. He said, "Has it ever been mentioned that you're a bit grabby?"

"Never," she answered, pointing the beam toward Harry's deserted house.

Georgette crept noiselessly along the perimeter of the spiked iron fence, sweeping the beam of the light back and forth across the lawn. She held the plate of roast high, stopping every minute or so to blow across the meat to disperse the aroma. Although the whole scene contained the potential for humor, he decided that it definitely fell short. The atmosphere surrounding the murder house was downright sinister.

Heavy mist laden the still air. Droplets of water beaded every surface, the black iron fence, the leaves dying in the oak trees, the dark slopes and angles of the house. Unseen, the water collected, slid, and fell in a constant unnerving chorus of *drip, drip, drip*. No other sound penetrated the grounds, no hint of humanity or civilization, no hint of life. The atmosphere would have had Edgar Allan Poe inking his quill.

Bathed in and glazed by the mist, the house glimmered. The night was moonless, and he searched for the source of the light that the house reflected. Finding only a weakly glowing street lamp, he scrutinized the house again, puzzled. And then, despite his complete belief in pragmatism and logic, he came to a baffling conclusion. From chimney to foundation, the house seemed to radiate a vague sense of smugness.

"Mr. Moto," Georgette whispered.

She was a good twenty feet ahead of him, still picking her way slowly toward the rear of the house. Adam caught up and fell in step behind her. Obviously, her imaginative outlook on the world was already rubbing off on him. A smug house, he thought, enjoying the incongruity of his previous observation. Maybe this entire experiment would pan out after all.

He caught a glimpse of movement accompanied by a flash of light, the instant of gleaming brilliance near the rear of Georgette's house. He opened his mouth to alert her, but the vision had already disappeared. Tense, he studied the shadows, panning the gloom for additional signs of motion. Nothing.

Georgette stumbled, drawing his attention. She regained her balance. "Mr. Moto, Mr. Moto," she caroled with additional volume. She grumbled, "Of all the stubborn, obstinate . . . It's no coincidence that he's a mister."

He continued to scan the darkness, uneasy. "I take it that you hold the male sex in low regard."

"Years of experience. Wait, look over there. I think I see him." She trained the light on a large bush inside the fence. Two luminescent animal eyes stared back. She adjusted the beam to shine directly on the stocky dog, his distinctive upright ears pricked to attention with the sharpness of a military salute. "I don't know how on earth you got inside there, but come out this minute."

His large, white teeth gleamed against the black fur of his muzzle. His low growl exploded into an angry burst of deafening barks. "Stop that barking this instant. You didn't do this before—"

Suddenly, she broke off. Eyes wide, she opened and closed

her mouth, but no sound escaped, at least nothing that could successfully compete with the vociferous Mr. Moto.

"Is something wrong?" Adam shouted over the din.

"No!" she shrieked, tossing aside the plate and flashlight and throwing her arms around his waist. "Oh, Adam! Thank heavens you're not a murderer!"

the house, but no one came to check on it, which means the
owner with their remote or their switch came and went as
they pleased. A few people passed by and
took the time, no doubt, to note the light and trudge
on through the snow. When I think of it, how foolish of them
not to know, or even to try to know.

Chapter
8

George hugged Adam, her face buried in the folds of his
sport coat, her cheek pressed against his hard chest, not
giving a flying how-do-you-do that Mr. Moto's barking
might wake the entire neighborhood. So what if he woke the
entire city! Adam Lawrence was innocent!

His soft laughter stirred her from her euphoria. "While I
confess I'm growing somewhat used to your unusual pro-
nouncements, announcing loudly that I am not a murderer
is still a bit bizarre. It sounds like something of a back-
handed compliment."

"Oh, no!" she said. "Don't you see, Adam? Don't you
see? Mr. Moto barked, not last night but tonight, because
last night I was alone. Mr. Moto barked at *you.*"

She threw her head back. In the dim light, she saw that his
dark brows were drawn together in apparent puzzlement.
"All evening on the night Harry was killed, I was in my
bedroom. Mr. Moto was quiet the entire evening or I would
have heard him bark. That means that the murderer was
someone Mr. Moto recognized which completely rules you

out because he barks at you. See? You couldn't have done it. You haven't lived here long enough!"

"Hum," he murmured with a slight smile.

"The murderer has to be one of the neighbors. Harry made a point to introduce Mr. Moto to me, and now you know why. That dog is positively earsplitting. You be quiet!" she screeched. "There, that's better."

"Yet surely Harry had friends, visitors to his home who lived elsewhere that the dog also recognizes."

"His other friends weren't at the party when Agnes was poisoned. Oh, my, poor Fiona didn't realize she inadvertently arranged a gathering of the suspects."

"If we assume that Agnes was poisoned during the party, it does implicate the neighbors. Why would Harry's murderer try to kill Agnes?"

"She must know something, probably something she doesn't even know that she knows."

"You mean a clue."

"We'll have to question her the minute she's better."

"You're warm."

She cocked her head and said impatiently, "Of course I am. I'll have this murder solved in no time."

His hands slid over her waist and held her firmly captive. "I meant that your body feels warm."

Holy heaven, he had that right. His nearness, his words warmed her like sunlight on a fall afternoon. He appeared delectable and inviting in every way, clean-cut with a slight touch of rogue, his hair neat but still intriguingly uncontrolled, his lower jaw clean shaven but heavily shadowed, his face hardened by life in a way that only enhanced his angular features. Every movement of his agile body promised that his lovemaking would be an absolute feast of sensation.

"I'm going to kiss you again," she warned him.

"This time let me help." He lifted her to him, and she wrapped her arms eagerly around his neck. Emboldened by his receptiveness, she found the edge of his mouth and lingered at the junction of beard-roughened skin with smooth flesh. With small, teasing kisses, she meandered along the growing fullness then stopped at the firm, mobile center of his mouth and continued sampling him with the tiny, discerning sips of a connoisseur.

"Sumptuous," she murmured against his growing response, and smoothly, he seized control. His lips divided hers, and he began his own leisurely exploration, his tongue tracing her inner softness. On a shivery sigh, she surrendered to his gentle yet deliberate invasion, one that hinted at ultimate joining. Then his tactic changed, erupting into a masterful, urgent, potent seduction.

Inside her a longing welled from a secret place, a wicked, tingling, maddening, exhilarating longing, one to savor, one to consummate. "I want you to make love to me."

"Excellent idea."

The slight tremor in his arms telegraphed a clear message of strength barely restrained. His gray eyes had darkened to the color of thunderheads and lightning seemed to dance around their edges. He clasped her closer until she could feel that every part of him was ready and startlingly able to fulfill her request. She dragged in a shaky breath and panicked.

"How about tomorrow night?" she suggested in a high, strained voice that even to her own ears sounded unrecognizable.

"Tomorrow night!" He planted her firmly on the ground.

"I just can't go through with it, at least not yet. But by tomorrow—"

He interrupted her with a sigh through clenched teeth, the sound ending on a growling note.

"I see that you don't understand. Well, you're so different from any business-and-finance type I've ever known before. I've never encountered one quite as . . . uh . . . well, virile. I mean I expected you to be an absolutely marvelous lover, but a hurricane—well, that's kind of scary."

He pinched his eyelids shut. "Georgette, as usual I don't know whether to thank you or to strangle you. But if I ever kiss you again—"

"Oh, you will."

"If I *ever* kiss you again, please, just don't say a word."

"I promise. But to be on the safe side, you'd better remind me right beforehand or I'm liable to forget. Oh, Mr. Moto," she said, noticing that he had managed to circumvent the fence and was now munching contentedly on the scattered slices of roast. She managed to snatch a piece from his greedy chops and held it away from her body, ready to start back for her house. She paused, biting her lip, wondering if this time Adam was too irritated to follow. She picked up the flashlight and began playing with the switch. "Will you come back to my house for a glass of wine or some coffee? I'd like you to, very much."

"I only drink decaffeinated coffee at night."

"I can make it Irish too."

"It would need whipped cream."

"Is Cool Whip all right?" She stooped down to retrieve the plate.

He scooped up the umbrella and his handkerchief from the lawn. "Lead the way."

Near the house, she caught herself fairly dancing across the dewy grass, and the thought crossed her mind that she might be falling in love. She giggled. Her father would literally erupt if she told him about her affection for a gardener when he was so intent on her marrying a businessman as ruthless as he was. But Adam Lawrence—whoever he was—was more interesting than all her father's choices combined.

Adam opened the kitchen door for her, and Mr. Moto bounded inside, then spun, and affected a statuelike pose that signaled serious begging. She held the meat like a fish for a seal and dropped it into his eager mouth. With a contented sigh, he collapsed on the Oriental rug.

"Oh, my, it's nearly two. Shall we tune into Estelle's broadcast? Though I'm afraid of what she might say. I think that woman would hurt Fiona and Marvin without batting a false eyelash. What do you think?"

"She impressed me as the thoughtless type."

She dropped a filter in the coffee maker, loaded it with several scoops of coffee, added filtered water to the reservoir, and flipped the switch. "Not thoughtless, just one thought and one thought only, and that's about herself."

He watched, his head tilted at an angle that indicated curiosity. She waited for him to speak, but he remained silent. Finally, George said, "Will you turn on the radio and find the station while I finish up in here?"

"Certainly."

"It's in my soon-to-be office which is across the living room and on the other side of the foyer."

When she joined him a few minutes later, he had arranged several packing boxes into a cozy grouping around the alcove containing the sound equipment. He lay on an area rug, his broad shoulders propped against an oversize pillow, his long legs outstretched, his expression welcoming. She handed him his Irish coffee and sank down into the pillow he had placed next to him. Obviously he intended for her to sit close, and she did, happily, snuggling against his arm, her Irish coffee cradled between her hands.

Estelle's show opened with the lonely bleating of a foghorn followed by organ music eerie enough to send a chill up the spine of a stone statue. The haunting notes flowed then trailed off, replaced by Estelle's lilting voice.

"Tonight, evil walks among us, silent in the fog, moving closer, closer, ever closer. From the depths of the murky shadows a cry rings out. Wide-eyed with terror, a woman struggles alone against a strength too strong, a force too evil then vanishes without a trace, another baffling puzzle without a clue, another 'Mysterious Occurrence.' I am your host, Estelle Capricorn. For the next hour we will explore the latest of the unexplained horrors that happen every day in this city. But do they always happen to someone else? Not necessarily. Tonight, we have a very special show, a very special murder. One of my own neighbors and dearest friends, Hangtown Harry Frye was brutally stabbed to death in his Scarlet Street home. Joining me tonight in grief and with the hope that we will somehow help reveal Harry's murderer is my neighbor and best-selling novelist Natasha Velour whose scorching novel of love, betrayal, and dentistry, *Open Wide, My Darling,* has just reached area bookstores. Thank you for coming, Natasha."

"Glad to be here."

"I know that you have been taking exhaustive notes regarding this unfortunate murder—"

"For my next novel, Stell. *A Bloody Rancid Business,* out next year and a damn fine novel. Be glad to come back then and discuss it."

"Ugh, yes. Now, tell me about your careful observations regarding Hangtown Harry's murder."

"He was as crazy as a loon, panned gold in his front yard pond, ran off God knows where for weekends to prospect. Folks, we're talking about tramping off every other weekend for years here. Had yellow fever and crazy—"

"Yes, Natasha, we got that. Anything more to add before we take a few calls?"

"Keep your love beads on, Stell. Don't rush me. Like I said, crazy, and he was like that right up until somebody stuffed a knife into his back. Understand this, folks—killed him dead as a doorstop. Then yesterday, Miss Old Society herself, Fiona Breathwaite, invited all the neighbors over to her place for a wake. Two hours later, Agnes Clodfelter—another one of our neighbors, folks—keeled over, poisoned. Let me tell you, they're dropping faster than togas at a Roman orgy."

"Interesting analogy, Natasha."

"Two murders and a poisoning, right on Scarlet Street. And ain't it a hoot, Fiona's son is running for city council as a law and order candidate."

George sprang upright, sending hot coffee sloshing on her legs. "I should have known better than to trust a novelist!"

Adam silenced her with a look. He pulled out his handkerchief and began dabbing at the coffee stains as Estelle continued.

"I'm sure everyone agrees that Marvin Breathwaite running as a law and order candidate is an ironic coincidence, Natasha. Or is it? I want *you* out there to judge for yourself. Scarlet Street is known for scandals, but few realize that over the years, violent deaths have been almost as common. In 1949 well-known businessman Marshall Hoagsworth was murdered in a still-unsolved case that made headlines for months. Only one year later, Fiona Singer Breathwaite's mother committed suicide. Hello, caller, you're on the air. . . . Caller, are you there?"

"Estelle Capricorn?"

"Yes, caller, go ahead."

"She-devil, mistress of Satan! Evil—"

"Well, Stell, the bars do close about the same time your show starts. Hey, you look awful rattled. I've heard worse before on this show."

"We pride ourselves, Natasha, in presenting an open forum. However, we do maintain certain standards that are consistent with the interests of our listeners. Please, everyone, keep that in mind. Hello, you're on the air with Estelle Capricorn."

"Hey, Estelle. Love your show. I'm calling about the murder. My great-granddad said that before the quake and fire, there were houses on Scarlet Street for rich degenerates, ones who thought they were too high-class to have their fun on the Barbary Coast. They'd go there for fornication with women, you know, all sorts of depravity. Granddad said that he heard that if one of those women was to die, they'd just wait until dark and bury 'em out back. The street of a thousand miseries, Granddad called it, and it jinxed everyone who ever lived there. Didn't make any difference that they put the evidence of their evil deeds underground or that the flames of the 1906 fire cleansed everything. He said that those poor souls were just waiting to get their revenge no matter how long it takes."

"You've made a very intriguing point, caller. It was expressly because of my interest in contacting lost souls that I decided to move there. Coincidentally, Hangtown Harry Frye was also extremely responsive to lost souls, particularly to those from the Gold Rush Era. Harry and I often discussed our mutual desire to ease their suffering and were about to begin a series of joint séances to achieve that goal. There is no question that the psychic energy is extraordinarily high in our neighborhood, don't you agree, Natasha?"

"Plenty of good vibes to go around. Sometimes, you can read those dead folks as clearly as a piece in *Truly Bloody Crime*. By the way, next month—that's the December issue, folks—I'll have an article out in that same magazine, a true crime inspired by a vision that appeared to me right in my own kitchen and straight out of Scarlet Street lore."

"Yes, Natasha, and over the next two weeks, *I* will be conducting a series of séances culminating in a Halloween gathering right in my Scarlet Street home. These evening séances will enable everyone to tap directly into the fascinating energy of our unique neighborhood. My numerous clients think of me as a stone, strong and solid, embedded in the wall between this world and the other, a perpend, touching both realities, and easily able to help them or anyone to transcend that barrier and to awe in the mysteries beyond. Mastercard and Visa are accepted. In just a moment, I'll give you my telephone number that is your key to experience the thrill of this or any other lifetime. Hello, caller, you're on the air."

"Neither one of you gives a damn about Hangtown Harry! You're only exploiting his death to sell books and séances and to get publicity for a show that nobody even listens to in the first place. You're both the lowest kind of vultures!"

* * *

George slammed down the receiver and buried her face in her hands.

"Do you feel better now?" Adam asked, gently.

She wagged her head from side to side, ashamed of herself for being such a silly fool.

"It made me feel better."

She parted her fingers enough to glimpse Adam rising from the floor and extending his hands toward her. She went to him, and he enfolded her with a warmth and tenderness that made her sob all the harder. Knowing that he was trying to understand her, cared that she was hurting, perhaps even cared for her, tightened her throat until she could hardly breathe. She tugged in air, gasping. The oxygen snagged in her throat. She choked.

Panic gripped her and her diaphragm locked. Her chest went completely still; thoughts refused to make it move. She had forgotten how to breathe!

"Georgette?"

No air remained in her lungs to push out sound. Fear danced through her mind like a circle of wild gypsy women, their brightly colored skirts swirling before her eyes. Bitter liquid burned her throat. She managed a strangled cry.

A sharp blow hit her squarely in the back. The force pushed her into Adam, and she collapsed against him. A strange rattling sound erupted from deep in her chest, and air she had been certain wasn't there before rushed out in a long, jerky flow.

"Relax. Relax. Relax. Let your body go completely limp, every muscle, one by one. Better, now?" Adam asked, and she realized now that he had been repeating those words in a slow, sonorous voice for some time.

She wheezed, "I'm embarrassed."

"Don't be. You choked." With one hand, he cupped her head and pressed her into the hollow beneath his shoulder while the other moved in a long, deliberate stroking motion that miraculously erased every bit of the soreness from the blow and replaced it with the warm numbness that reminded her of that last, liquid instant she always experienced right before falling asleep on the beach in the summer sun. Her labored breathing eased to sighs.

"Feeling you can't breathe is a nightmare."

She tried to swallow, but her tight, sore throat resisted. She bore down and won the battle with a giant gulp. "How do you know that?"

"When I was a child, I had asthma. The sensation is different than choking though the panic is somewhat the same. The cure is totally different. No back-slapping for asthma."

"Were you living in England when you had asthma?" she asked, pulling slightly away from his body so she could study his face when he answered.

He grinned. "Perhaps you will solve Harry's murder after all. Yes, I lived in the United Kingdom until I was seven, father British, mother American. My asthma compelled them to send me to Colorado to live near a famous clinic. When I had recovered enough to leave, I elected to stay."

Unable to suppress her disbelief, she said, "Your parents sent you here alone?"

"Not entirely. They sent along my tutor and companion, Nigel, and we both lived with my maiden great-aunt. Harriet and he married about a year after our arrival. Nigel is a brilliant scholar, and Harriet is warm and kind. They were almost like my parents."

George pondered that aloud. "You said almost."

With an expression that suggested total honesty, he said, "No one can replace your parents. I don't believe that anyone can truly replace another human being emotion for emotion, role for role." He tilted his head and his gray-blue eyes captured hers. "Something puzzles me. I noticed it in the kitchen and again later during the broadcast."

"What?"

"While I commend you for your concern about Fiona and Marvin and their current dilemma, I don't quite understand your motivation."

"I want to help them."

"I know, but when you talk about them or people who

might effect them, your voice and expression change radically, almost as though a zealous determination had set in. You weren't aware of that though, I take it."

"I only think it's horrible how people feed on one another. There are Estelles and Natashas everywhere, just waiting to prey on someone's troubles and blow them all out of proportion. All they think about is what they can bleed out of the situation. Nothing else matters except their own selfish gains, and they don't care how much it hurts other people." She swiped her hair away from her face. "What's truly infuriating is that they always pretend to be helping someone!"

"You misunderstood. I agree with your viewpoint. But your desire to help Fiona and Marvin is so extreme."

"Extreme? Extreme!"

"Tying me to your sofa, for example, only because you suspected that I was working for the Jack Smith campaign. That was undoubtedly the real reason. If you had truly believed that I was a burglar, you would have called the police immediately."

She freed herself from his arms and planted her hands resolutely on her hips. "I only wish someone cared about me that much!"

He raised a stilling hand. "Back up. You mean care the way Fiona cares about Marvin?"

"Of course."

"I think I'm beginning to get the hang of this."

He smiled with obvious satisfaction, and she immediately felt the urge to kiss him again. He was irresistible. But she had promised to keep silent during their next kiss, and she still had things to say. "Fiona wants Marvin to succeed so badly she even promised to stay like a virtual prisoner in her house during the entire campaign. She says catastrophes tend to crop up in the oddest ways and felt it best not to tempt fate, especially with Jack Smith involved. Now this whole mess with Hangtown Harry and Agnes and the vultures has positively blown up in her face, and it's all so totally unfair."

"That entire speech proved my point. You've paced back

and forth at least a dozen times. Women doing aerobic exercises don't move that fast. Your voice was pitched so high, you were virtually screaming."

"Screaming? *Screaming!*"

"It's all well and good to support them, help them, but you've adopted it as your own personal fight. I'd like to understand why."

George began running her fingers over the cool metal and smooth stone of her chunky silver necklace. My fight, she thought, passing the idea through the reasoning center of her mind and coming up with mother, child, unconditional love, complete and total support. Suddenly she understood her feelings and saw the reason for her actions very clearly. "You were right, Adam. Nobody can replace somebody role for role. I suppose that when I realized how much Fiona was willing to sacrifice for her child, I saw firsthand something that I had missed." She closed her hand tightly over the necklace. "After that, I had to choose how to feel about it."

"I don't understand."

"Whether or not to feel happy that Marvin has such a supportive mother or sad for myself. I certainly didn't want to envy Marvin or be sad, so I decided to feel happy. On the other hand, my mother was dead before I ever got a chance to know her and the support that Marvin has will never be mine. What can I do about that? Absolutely nothing. But I can help make it happen for someone else. Of course, I only figured it out because you asked. It was something I did without thinking, like riding a bike."

The worry crease reappeared between his brows. He stared beyond her, sadness seeming to lengthen his face and glaze his eyes.

"I'm so sorry," she said, trying to ease her blunder. How could what she'd said hurt him? It had nothing to do with Adam. He practically had two mothers. She approached him cautiously. "Are you angry with me?"

That question snapped him quickly back. A smile flickered over his lips and disappeared. "Never," he said quietly.

Hoping to coax his smile back, she reached to touch his lips with the tip of her finger and brush them into a curve.

She sensed that they might need to talk a bit more before she kissed him again, but before she could make any contact with the firm line, the telephone rang.

Adam groped behind him, located the receiver, and put it against his ear. "The Richards residence."

Even she could hear the speaker on the other end. Whoever it was sounded like a squawking cartoon character.

Adam held out the receiver and covered the mouthpiece. "Do you want to speak to someone who's cursing in Italian?"

"Marfa!" She grabbed the receiver. "Marfa, for heaven's sake, calm down! Nothing happened." She glanced up toward Adam and found him waving good-bye. "Marfa, wait! No, I mean Adam . . ." She trailed off; he was already gone. She guessed he was tired. The night was mostly gone. She half-listened to Marfa's tirade, wondering instead how such a special man had ended up a stuffed shirt.

She found Adam's note at eight the next morning. He'd anchored it beneath one foot of the coffee maker. *Georgette: Fiona wants you to accompany her to Harry's funeral tomorrow at eleven o'clock. I'll bring the car around at ten. If this is inconvenient, please let Fiona know in the morning.*

She found his handwriting shockingly messy which, of course, was in total contrast with his appearance. The note itself was also disturbing; he had completely forgotten about the dove.

After setting up the coffee maker, she moved the bird cage into the kitchen and put it on the table. Meager light filtered through the heavy mantle of clouds enough, at least, to save the room from total gloom. She raised the cover gently and the dove bobbed her head, as if in greeting. After checking her seed and replacing her water, George let Mr. Moto out. "I want you back in here in five minutes!" she shouted as he bounded next door toward Harry's house. Boy, how she wished she had a fence.

When he failed to return after fifteen minutes, she pulled her serviceable London Fog raincoat over her nightgown and bathrobe and went out after him, raising the hood over her matted hair. She was absolutely certain she looked like a pup tent with legs.

The morning was cold, rainy, and quiet. She spotted Mr. Moto standing near the rear of Harry's house in the same place he'd been the night before. In the daylight she could see evidence that he had been digging. A small amount of dirt lay strewn over the green lawn. "Get out of there!" The dog appeared stunned at being caught, muddy paws and all.

Mr. Moto bounded across the lawn, disappeared into a knot of bushes, and reappeared outside the fence. "Shame on you for digging." She ducked under a low-hanging tree and padded back toward her house. Near the back door, Mr. Moto spit some dirt-crusted object out of his mouth with a mighty woof.

Covering her ears against his spate of barks, George turned toward the street in time to see a slender man dressed in jeans and a bomber jacket behind a camera with a mammoth telephoto lens. His cocked finger pulsed relentlessly on the camera.

Damn!

She resisted the impulse to march down there and tell him off, remembering that in the past her confrontations had never worked with reporters. They loved it. Instead she bent to the ground, snatched up Mr. Moto's brown object, and sprinted for her house. "Mr. Moto, come!" she screamed. Amazingly enough he trailed her and barreled inside the kitchen, whining and crying. "What's wrong?"

He tried to nuzzle her right hand that gripped his hard, grimy object.

"Let me wash it first." George dropped it into the sink and turned on the water. "Reporters in the bushes! What next?" she grumbled.

She washed her hands over Mr. Moto's strange treasure, letting the water dissolve its dirt disguise. She reached for a towel then stopped, gaping in stunned disbelief at a set of grinning human teeth.

Chapter
9

After bathing and dressing for the funeral in less than half an hour, George dashed toward Fiona's house intent on telling Adam about the teeth. Before she cleared the wall of her own house, an unfamiliar purr of talking and laughing caused her to hesitate. She halted behind the bushy limbs of a Hollywood juniper. Lowering one of the branches, she surveyed Scarlet Street, aghast.

Strangers wandered everywhere, along the narrow lane, over the lawns, some right up to the windows of the houses, many of them snapping pictures. In the center of Agnes's portico, a man in his early twenties posed, head cocked, tongue out, hand clutching his throat mimicking poisoning. A woman in a nylon raincoat glanced over her shoulder, then quickly tucked a brick from the border of Agnes's herb garden into her pocket.

George let the branch snap back into place. Estelle Capricorn and Natasha Velour deserved to be hanged for this! They deserved to have their invitations to her pre-Halloween party rescinded.

Holding her black Chanel handbag beside her face, she

bolted from behind the juniper and ran for Fiona's kitchen door. Just as she ripped open the kitchen door, she heard the unmistakable whirr and click of a rapidly firing professional camera. She darted inside and slammed the door in the face of a photographer and a reporter she recognized from a tabloid with his outstretched microphone. She threw the bolt with undue fervor.

"Vultures," she fumed, stamping around the kitchen and tugging at the sleeves of her tailored white overcoat. She peeled it off and straightened her plain, black, self-belted dress. Thank heavens she'd grabbed a scarf, she thought, surveying herself. Only the jewel-toned Chanel square draped across one shoulder saved the outfit from utter drabness. It was another gloomy day, and maybe that touch would please Adam.

Fiona appeared from the hallway, dressed in navy blue Ultrasuede, her normally composed features haggard. "Oh, George," she gasped. "I'm so happy you've come."

George flipped her head toward the door. "It isn't bad enough that those horrible reporters have no manners. I actually let them make me do something rude that I have never ever done before in my entire life." She slapped her coat and purse down on the table. "I walked into a house without knocking."

"Oh, dear, that's nothing. Nothing. People have been calling for hours. They keep asking me about Harry and Agnes and Estelle's radio broadcast. How could a two o'clock show cause all this furor? Did you hear it? What do they mean about lost souls? They kept talking about the dead bodies in our yards." Her hands shook; her lips trembled. "And someone asked if Marvin was here yesterday."

"Don't worry, Fiona. The two reporters who just followed me have nothing to do with Marvin. They've been harassing me because my father is under investigation for cheating on government contracts, and I'm the decadent heiress who's supposedly reaping all the rewards."

George stretched her arm toward Fiona's shoulders. Coming up several inches shy, she looped an arm around her waist then guided her toward a table surrounded by several Louis XVI lyre-backed chairs. "As far as any local publicity, there's only one thing that will quiet it down now, and that's finding out who stabbed Harry and poisoned Agnes. Once there's a suspect, the reporters will pounce on that person instead of us, and Marvin can go on with the campaign and beat that awful Jack Smith."

"I suppose you're right," Fiona mumbled, sinking into one of the chairs. She smoothed back her red hair and repositioned one of the pins that secured her severe French roll. Her arms dropped wearily to her lap. "I imagine the funeral is going to be a horrible spectacle now that all this publicity is involved. Lord knows, I tried to do my best for Harry, but he didn't leave any instructions." She clasped her hands together tightly. "I never want my children to have to go through making such decisions, blindly and wondering. It's always so hard to know what to do."

George bit lightly on her index finger, recalling a snippet of last night's broadcast. *In 1950 Fiona Singer Breathwaite's mother committed suicide.* Yesterday in this same room, Fiona had told her many things about her mother. But not that. True, some people still considered a suicide in the family to be a mark of shame. Could that be what she was trying to protect Marvin from? Somehow, that failed to jibe. A forty-year-old suicide hardly matched a present-day murder in impact. Still, there was something in all this. . . .

As the telephone rang, George decided to blame the whole thing on paranoia, at least temporarily. Maybe Marfa was right; maybe Harry's murder was making her jumpy. Still she refused to feel guilty about being suspicious of every little thing. How many people had endured what she had in the past seventy-two hours? How many people had a set of strange teeth in their sink?

George lifted the receiver and said impatiently, "Hello. Who is this?"

A male voice droned over the wire. "Mr. Brill at Chapel of Perpetual Peace and Tranquility. May I speak with Mrs. Breathwaite, please?"

George covered the mouthpiece. "Mr. Brill," she whispered. Fiona responded with a dejected shrug and accepted the receiver.

"We're planning to leave any moment—" Fiona's head tilted; she appeared puzzled. "No, I don't know of anyone by that name." She paused. As she listened, her face paled until her rouge appeared like circles of red color applied by a clown. "Yes, of course, in thirty minutes." She handed George the receiver. "Please dial Adam. It's the first button on the bottom row on that in-house telephone on the wall by the pantry. That's right, the black one. Tell him we need to leave immediately. A strange woman is at the funeral home demanding that all the arrangements be changed. Why, of all the nerve," Fiona chanted, as though suddenly gathering a new resolve. "She even wants to recall the order for Harry's headstone!"

Watching out a narrow window by the front door, George waited while Fiona paced the hall, tugging at her gloves. "We're going to be late."

That, George decided, was a minor problem. Outside, people continued to wander through the area. The tabloid reporter Don Dick Watson whom she had dubbed "Mr. Microphone" and his companion with the camera who'd chased her to Fiona's house were lurking near a lamppost trying to look important. She sensed they were waiting to cause trouble.

The moment Adam eased Fiona's white Cadillac sedan to halt at the curb, George said, "Let's go!" Fiona charged out the door. She followed Fiona in a mad dash down the short path to the street. The reporters converged on them as they reached the car. Mr. Microphone began working his mouth earnestly, scattering questions like confetti and using his lanky body to block the rear door.

The bystanders rushed closer to witness the event, gawking at the two real, live Scarlet Street degenerates they probably imagined her and Fiona to be. Wedged between Fiona and the reporter, George shrank against the side of the car. The microphone nudged her nose, and she had the awful sensation she might gag on it. She twisted away, shielding her face from the reporter and his inane questions. "Do you realize that you have purchased a house in a virtual graveyard? Aren't you afraid of being jinxed? How does your publicity-shy father feel about all this, especially in view of the government investigation?"

George bit her lip and tasted the faintly metallic taste of blood.

"Do you have a comment on Natasha's broadcast?"

Did she! It took every shred of self-control she had to avoid screaming it into his smug little face!

The car rocked against her as though Adam were getting out to help them. "Leave them alone!" he shouted.

She felt gripped by the sudden urge to scream at the total unfairness of it all. One bit of notoriety gave people a license to trample and upset your life, to invade your privacy, even take away a right as basic as getting into a car.

Damn!

With a force inspired by absolute frustration, she lifted her foot and drove the heel of her shoe into the reporter's instep. He flinched in pain, and George seized her chance. Putting her shoulder down, she bulled him aside and grabbed the door handle.

Next to her, Fiona threw an elbow that broke them free from the cameraman, and they both scooted into the rear seat of the car. Fiona tugged the door closed and locked it. Adam jumped into the driver's seat and shoved the car into gear. He hit the gas, and the Cadillac jerked from the curb.

Furiously, George tried to straighten her coat so the neck wasn't strangling her, and failing, flung her purse aside and began working her gloved hand against the top button. It came off in her hand. "Aughh!" she said, shoving the button into her pocket. "We've got to do something! I just know that it's only going to get worse. Fiona?" She turned to the panting woman. "Is it true that Scarlet Street used to be the rich man's Barbary Coast?"

Fiona gulped. "Before the earthquake and fire in 1906, yes. Why is that important?"

"Only because Natasha and Estelle emphasized that last night on the air, talking about how in the past they used to bury dead people at night and that there are these lost souls hanging around just waiting to get revenge."

"Lost souls?" Fiona murmured, hugging herself and sinking her chin against a huge fur collar. She shivered.

"Fiona?" George touched her hand, and the older woman turned her haggard face. "Do you believe that Adam and I are your friends and that we want to help you and Marvin?"

She nodded.

"I think that Agnes's poisoning and Harry's murder must be linked. It seems too much of a coincidence otherwise. Other than Troy, the only people at your house yesterday were the neighbors. To start with, we need to know everything you know about Scarlet Street and the people who live there."

Fiona looked past her and out the rain-spattered window, her eyes shiny with tears. She remained that way for so long, George thought she might have gone into some form of trance or lapsed into shock. Through it all, Adam simply drove, competently and patiently.

Suddenly, Fiona patted her eyes with a handkerchief. "I'll try," she said in a weak voice.

George retrieved the notebook she normally used for design notes on houses and flipped to a page she titled "Neighbors."

"Let's work our way around the block starting with Natasha on the southeast corner. How long has she lived there?"

"What you must understand is that every home with the exception of yours is owned by a descendent of the original builder. They have always stayed in the families, at least until your purchase. It sounds a trifle odd, I know, but then the street is somewhat unusual." She dried her eyes and crossed her arms. "After the fire, the Hoagsworth family came to own all the land the street and homes now occupy. Marshall Hoagsworth, Jr.'s grandfather built a house at the apex of the cul-de-sac. As years passed, they sold parcels to various people."

"Not all at once?"

"No, from what I understand it was a gradual process that

spanned the teens and twenties. That's probably one reason why we have such a blending of architectural styles. Natasha's father built in a Moorish style. The family name was Trimmer, every last one of them plump. Natasha's been that way all her life. All three of her brothers were killed in World War II, so she inherited the house. Natasha Velour was originally a pseudonym, but now she uses it exclusively, much to the relief of her living relatives, I hear. Her significant other is a cartographer, presently in Tierra del Fuego. *She* makes an annual pilgrimage."

"What about Agnes?"

"Agnes's parents were kind, decent people, always opening their home to vacationing missionaries or any men and women in service to God or country. They were great philanthropists, dedicated a great deal to the promotion of the fine arts and various charities. Unfortunately, they gave themselves wholly to the community and paid little attention to their only daughter. Agnes was pathetically shy." Fiona's voice cracked. She dabbed her eyes. "We used to go into the turret room at the top of my house where my grandmother kept her old clothes. She still had trunks full of clothing from her trousseau, Paris fashions that she wore before they settled in San Francisco. Agnes and I would put on the showy party dresses with swishy skirts and lace ruching and pretend that we were princesses high in our tower, waiting for our Prince Charmings to take us away and make us happy." She held the handkerchief briefly to her nose and sniffed. "The doctor says she's better today, thank God."

"I know. I called too." They were within a dozen blocks of the funeral home which gave George anywhere from five to ten minutes to get the information she needed, depending on traffic. Fiona might not be as talkative after Harry's funeral. "Dwight Phillips?"

"The eldest of six boys, all brilliantly successful in business. Dwight was a world-class hurdler."

"He never married?"

"Everyone said he always ran too fast for any woman to

catch him, and, believe me, they've been trying for years. He's had a slew of girlfriends."

"Could that be a cover for . . ." George gestured in a loose circle, "you know?"

"Certainly not. One of my friends was his Miss 1952." Fiona raised a brow and murmured under her breath, "The stories that woman tells. She's been married three times since then, and she's still smitten with him. She stops by my house all the time just hoping to catch a glimpse of the man. Oh, wait," she said slowly, "he did marry, once while I was living in the East, during the fifties. I remember because my grandmother said she was redheaded like me. Apparently, it didn't last long—no children, I think. But his house is spectacular inside, full of antiques, not the fussy kind, but the large, stately type—and marble statuary. He has a sculpture of Venus that's breathtaking."

Fiona continued to babble as they crawled down the hill toward the mortuary, obviously stalling to avoid talking about the largest and oldest home on the street, the Hoagsworth mansion. Who was Fiona so desperate to avoid discussing: the Hoagsworths themselves, the strange middle-aged man and his reclusive mother, their elderly servant Elmo Burroughs, or Estelle Capricorn?

Adam guided the Cadillac around a corner and onto Vallejo Street.

Fiona craned her neck to read the sign. "Adam, you've passed the street. The funeral home is on Green, not Vallejo Street."

"My mistake," he said casually. "I'll turn around and circle back."

"Just turn left at Larkin. It's only one block over to Green."

George smiled into her hand. Adam's turn was probably intentional. Maybe the crafty, resourceful man was trying to buy her extra time. Maybe Adam Lawrence wasn't so stodgy after all.

She pressed on. "What about the Hoagsworths?"

"You know nearly as much as I do about them." Fiona

scooted forward to the edge of the leather seat, her hand gripping the headrest. "Turn here, Adam."

"Which Hoagsworth actually built the mansion?"

"Zeb Hoagsworth. It's his grandson Marshall, Jr. that lives there now. And Marshall's mother too. Both are virtual recluses. This is Green, Adam. Turn right."

"But doesn't Estelle Capricorn live with them?"

"Oh, no, she's a tenant," Fiona replied impatiently, her eyes fixed ahead on the traffic crawling toward North Beach. "I heard they partitioned the house into three units, one for Marshall, one for his mother, and one to rent. I suppose they needed the money. Over the years, they gradually let all their servants go except that good-for-nothing Elmo Burroughs who's lived in that detached cottage out back since I was a girl."

"How long has Estelle lived on Scarlet Street?"

"She certainly didn't grow up there, if that's what you mean. Estelle was renting when I returned from the East a year ago. I've no idea how long she was there before that."

Immediately after he turned onto Green Street, Adam stopped behind a parked delivery truck. Leisurely, he glanced from mirror to mirror, waiting for an opportunity to merge into the through traffic.

"And Harry?" George asked quickly.

Fiona managed a wan smile. "Hangtown Harry inherited his house quite some time ago from one of his wives. She was a Reed, and very unusual. She became Harry's fourth or fifth wife about twenty or more years ago. He had at least seven maybe even eight. Grandmother lost count as she got older. He possessed an almost childlike quality that women apparently found endearing. But you met him, that's right. Humm, I wonder if it's one of the former wives who's making all those demands of Mr. Brill. . . ." She trailed off, looking perplexed.

"And Dr. Emerson?"

"That's your house now. Your home is the newest on the street and the most beautiful, I think. Dr. Emerson commissioned a very well known architect to draw up the plans during the midtwenties, someone with three names that I can't ever recall. Anyway, Emerson went ahead and had it completed despite the stock market crash."

She seemed about ready to say something, paused, then shrugged. "I suppose some professions are truly depression-proof. Dr. Emerson's specialty was obstetrics and gynecology, and apparently he accumulated a great deal of money. He was always endowing something or establishing another foundation mainly for endangered species. I suppose he was a good man, and his death was certainly tragic, but I can't in all honesty say that I ever liked him. With all Father's trophies, you can imagine how he felt about me. After I returned from the East I hardly exchanged ten words with the man even though we lived side by side for nearly nine months."

George glimpsed the white and gold funeral home sign. Her fingers tensed on her ink pen. She felt like a contestant on "Beat the Clock." "You said that your house was originally owned by your maternal grandparents."

"My father turned it into the monstrosity it is today. After Grandfather died, my father convinced Grandmother to let him redecorate the house. We were living with her, and I'm sure he worked on her until she finally gave into his plans. As soon as I finish selling my property in the East, I'm going to gut the entire house, get rid of that depressing array of artifacts, and update everything."

Fiona waved her hand toward George's notepad, her expression disdainful. "I don't see how any of that is going to help. On the other hand if I was a perceptive woman, I would have known better than to move back into my awful house in the first place. Maybe what they say is true. Maybe the entire street and every person who lives there is jinxed."

"I disagree," Adam said. He drew the Cadillac to a smooth halt beneath an elaborate porte cochere where a uniformed attendant waited to sweep the car door open. When he did, Fiona jumped out, obviously relieved to make her escape.

As George slid across the seat, Adam reached back and

closed his hand over her arm. His gray eyes seemed to capture her inside a bright ray that bathed her in lovely, shining light. He made her feel beautiful.

In a low voice he said, "I want to see you again."

"After the funeral," she whispered softly, "will you come to my house?"

He nodded. "We need to talk."

"We also have a dove who's waiting to be freed."

He squeezed her arm. "I never would have thought seeing someone as wealthy as you are could be so economical."

"Economical only in money," she breathed. "There are other methods of exchange."

His gaze flickered over her, paused on her scarf, then met her eyes. His approval flowed over her, spreading warmth throughout her body. Suddenly, she wished it was last night again with his strength surrounding her, his beautiful words in her ears, his firm hands adoring her body. Tonight her mouth would utter only yes, freeing her to discover every magical part of him.

Once again his hand tightened on her arm, then he let her go. "People are staring."

She glanced up to see the attendant crouching and watching them both with embarrassingly clear understanding. Judging from the expression on his face, their intentions had been as recognizable as the outline of Coit Tower on a clear day.

With careful dignity, George extended her hand to the man in uniform and alighted from the car, knowing her cheeks were warm. She asked herself if that was because the attendant had seen what had passed between her and Adam and realized that was not the reason. Her face was flushed with happiness, which was improper for a lady arriving to attend a funeral.

The moment she entered the Chapel of Perpetual Peace and Tranquility she decided that whoever decorated the funeral home believed in one thing, mahogany, mahogany, and more mahogany. The walls, the pews, even some of the floors were a uniform and lustrous reddish brown. George hurried down a long, claustrophobic hallway struggling to remind herself that she was still firmly and happily above ground, even though it didn't seem that way.

After running for what seemed like forever, she finally located her first sign of human life and, thank heavens, a window. Fiona snagged her arm and dragged her into the large room with a desk and several stuffed chairs with embroidered backs and cushions. The air seemed heavy and smelled faintly of dead roses. "This is Georgette Richards."

George disengaged her arm from Fiona's grasp and shook the hand of the gaunt man. "It's a pleasure," she said, lying. He sported a coal black toupee, a tight suit, and a spectacular tan for the middle of October.

"Mr. Brill," he said, stonily. He released a loud, rumbling cough into a handkerchief. His wretched rattle sounded as if he smoked four packs a day or had a horrible cold. She took two steps backward.

"As I was saying, Mrs. Breathwaite, I have made every effort to follow your instructions to the letter. That has always been my policy. Always. But I fear that circumstances have escalated beyond even my control." He blew loudly into his handkerchief, then carefully wiped his nose. "Remembrances have been pouring in. Normally we see the standard arrangements, mostly tasteful, sometimes not, but always holding to a reasonable standard of decorum. In this case, however, the flowers are . . ." He lifted his hands, palm upward toward the heavens, "shall we say, extraordinary."

Fiona bristled. "Harry was a very well liked man. He was also quite flamboyant. I'm not surprised that the remembrances, as you put it, are lavish, possibly even extravagant."

"You misunderstood me, as you will soon see. They're garish."

"But Harry enjoyed unusual things."

"Remembrances aside," Brill said sharply, "certainly our most pressing problem lies, rather sits, in the next room. A Miss Joan LaRose wishes to provide her own, as she put it, entertainment, for the funeral. Her costume does not bode well for its tone. A burlesque number, I fear."

"What's wrong with having an upbeat song?" George

99

broke in, confused. "Not everybody insists on dirges these days."

"Miss Richards, that is only the tip of a very nasty iceberg. Miss LaRose has also contacted my associate and insisted that the order be changed so that she and the departed may share a common headstone. The difficulty with that being, if you remember, that Mr. Frye is to be buried in a plot next to his departed wife Jane Reed Frye where *they* will share a common headstone."

"Maybe there's a vacancy nearby," George suggested, "something sort of overlooking Harry's plot."

Brill turned to Fiona, plainly ignoring George's idea for compromise. "When I explained that everything had been prearranged and prepaid by Mr. Frye himself, Miss LaRose jumped to her feet and threatened to block the burial. Even if space was available for Miss LaRose," he said, casting a glance of extreme distaste at George, "which fortunately there isn't, I could hardly condone a ménage à trois."

Fiona released a long, loud sigh ending with "Merciful heavens."

"Mr. Brill," George asked, "did you ever ask this woman who she is?"

"I assume that she was the deceased man's paramour."

"Then she's obviously overwrought. Put yourself in her place."

Mr. Brill responded by blowing into his handkerchief indelicately which only solidified her determination to defend the woman. She pulled herself up to her full height and began to gesture. "Harry didn't have any living family so when he was murdered one of his friends graciously took charge of the funeral arrangements." George stretched to put a hand on Fiona's shoulder. "But in this Joan LaRose's mind, she was simply left out, totally alone with her grief. Several days pass, the morning of the funeral dawns, then finally overcome by her anguish, she arrives on your door-step, desperate for some shred of consideration, some way to pay tribute to the man she loved." Warming to the role, she clinched her hand and cast her gaze heavenward, striking the pose of the heroine Azucena in the famous opera *Il Trovatore.* She could almost hear the score building in the background complete with anvil strikes and singing gypsies.

"And what did you do? What did you do to this poor woman's soul as it lay prostrate at the toes of your patent-leather loafers?" She swept her eyes over Mr. Brill who appeared a trifle dumbounded. "You talked about prepaid funeral plans, adjoining plots, and marble headstones. What could be colder? You stood there and callously denied her one last chance to bid a final farewell to her own true love. You left her no alternative. What action was left to her other than threatening to block the funeral?"

Fiona sniffed, "Oh, George, what can we do for the poor woman?"

"There's only one thing left to do." George stuck a pointed index finger in the air. "Negotiate."

Mr. Brill looked as though he'd bitten into a lemon. "I will not talk with that woman."

George appealed to Fiona, "What's really important here?"

"We need to get Harry buried," Fiona answered without hesitation.

"Then why not allow her to perform her song? In exchange, we'll insist that she back down about the headstone so that Harry can be buried."

Fiona nodded. "That sounds reasonable to me."

"I'll not be held responsible when this turns into a dog and pony show." Mr. Brill's lips pulled away from his too-perfect teeth as he sneered, "She doesn't perform solo, you know!"

Chapter
10

George selected a pew in the rear of the chapel, and Adam took the seat next to her. Dwight Phillips ambled up the center aisle, leading Fiona toward the front.

Much as George hated to admit it, the funeral director, Mr. Brill, was right about Harry's remembrances. Over the years, her father had forced her to attend several funerals, and she'd never noticed anything like the rose-encrusted horseshoe draped with a ribbon that read Good Luck, Harry or the replica of the Seal of the Great State of California executed in carnations.

She'd always read that San Francisco was famous for encouraging eccentricities in its inhabitants, but she really hadn't seen much evidence of that until the remembrances banking Hangtown Harry's coffin and the music provided by a guitar, fiddle, and accordion now playing "The Gold Diggers Waltz" as the mourners took their seats.

Fiona and Dwight slipped into the front row, joining Natasha Velour and Estelle Capricorn who both sported dark hats. George glanced over her shoulder just as Elmo Burroughs slouched into the chapel accompanied by a gray-haired woman and a tall, rail-backed man. She guessed Elmo's companions must be Ina Hoagsworth and her son. A brief glimpse of Marshall, Jr.'s face confirmed Fiona's description of him. He was handsome in a broken sort of way. His mother appeared stooped and gaunt. George scoured her mind for some tactful way to introduce herself to the two recluses as they passed, and failing, hoped for an opportunity after the service.

The mourners who filed into the chapel were a mixture of attractive men and women mostly well past middle-age. Unusual black bands circled the left arms of the men, unusual because they suspiciously resembled garters. The other unusual thing about the so-called mourners was that they were all smiling.

She wondered if Harry's murderer was here, hiding behind a placid expression. Her eyes wandered over the crowd, searching for some telltale clue. They all appeared so calm. How did murderers betray themselves anyway?

Her gaze swept over the backs of Harry's neighbors, cataloguing a range of nervous gestures. Dwight and Fiona fidgeted, Estelle tapped her cheek with her finger, and Elmo tugged on his ear. Natasha craned, then bent over her lap, probably to jot down another note. Only the Hoagsworths remained unnaturally still. But they weren't at the party when Agnes . . . Lord, George thought, seized by inspiration, Marshall or Ina Hoagsworth could have sneaked into Fiona's kitchen from the backyard and poisoned the punch! They knew all about the party, and none of these other people did!

An elderly, bearded man stepped to the podium with a small stack of index cards. Surrounded by a riot of red and gold flowers, he tugged his vest over his paunch, then smoothed the lapels of his coat and straightened his bow tie. "My friends, we are gathered to bid a final farewell to our friend of many years, Hangtown Harry Frye.

"In this life we all knew Harry as a man set apart from others because of his great kindness, his great humor, and, yes, because of his great oddness."

Easy laughter emanated from the seated guests.

"He charmed every woman he met, enriched the life of every man, and drank deeply from the cup of life—as well as any other cup that happened to be passed his way."

Again, laughter rippled throughout the room.

"Harry would be pleased to hear your gentle laughter today, laughter that is tribute to the great joy that Harry brought to all of us during his short lifetime."

George whispered to Adam. "I thought Harry was sixty-nine."

"Time is relative, I suppose."

"Helping us to remember him today is Joan LaRose."

George gawked as Joan glided from behind a curtain in a magnificent full-length rose silk dress with an ivory lace décolletage. Stopping in front of the remembrances, she dropped in a slight curtsey and flipped her fan demurely. George reasoned that she must be over fifty even though her face and figure said forty maximum. Her magnificent gown was complemented by an elaborate coiffure, her blond hair a cascade of loose curls.

"Accompanying Joan today is Ricardo Pena on the guitar. As Harry once said, 'When I go to my great reward, I want Joan's voice in my ears singing me on my way with a song of life.'"

Joan bit on her lip, her wide eyes watery, and for a moment, George thought she might burst into tears. Then Ricardo the guitarist picked soft, opening notes that suggested a haunting Spanish ballad. After swallowing hard, Joan mouthed the first words in a barely audible whisper. According to the lyrics, a man looked into the brown eyes of his lover, asking her to say a prayer for his life. Joan raised her voice. But the young outlaw knew all hope had vanished. The gunmen would never take him back to Texas alive. Joan choked as she repeated the woman's pleading reassurance that God would save them and keep them free.

Sadness closed around George's heart. The lyric echoed a young girl's optimism, a tragic, desperate hope too fragile to withstand the reality of living. Their beautiful love was doomed.

Joan's voice lowered for the chorus, her tone becoming brandy hued. Seven Spanish angels were praying for the lovers that fate would tear apart forever.

Joan dropped her hand to one edge of the closed casket, gazing along the length of polished wood. Her voice breaking, she sang of the girl praying over the dead body of her lover and asking God to forgive her for taking her own life.

Seven Spanish angels, Joan repeated, in a melodic lilt, unshed tears glimmering in her brown eyes. Her hand caressed the casket bidding her own lover a final farewell. The music ended. Joan paused a moment then withdrew her hand, pressing it immediately against her breast over her heart.

A tear slid over George's cheek. Why must life hold such bitter sadness?

"Thank you, Joan, Ricardo. That was very moving." The bearded man once again followed his elaborate procedure with his vest, lapels, and tie, straightening each in turn. His hands gripped the edges of the podium, and he tilted his head. "In the long days since Harry's tragic death, we have all, each in our own way, mourned this loss of our friend. Our loss has been great, but overall our gain has been greater. Over the many years, Harry gifted us with his companionship, gifted us with so many joyous memories.

"Then what shall we mourn about Hangtown Harry Frye? Shall we mourn the ending of his life on earth?"

His eyes swept the room. He lowered his voice meaningfully. "But how can we? Harry believed in life everlasting."

He boomed, "Then shall we mourn the fact that he has gone from us forever?"

Once again, his eyes swept the room. "But how can we? Harry believed in life everlasting.

"Shall we mourn that his life was cut short?

"But how can we? *How can we?*" He shook his head slowly. "Certainly, we, of all people, cannot, we who believe that Harry will be back to dance on this earth once again.

"Alexander Pope once said, 'For he lives twice who can at once employ the present well, and ev'n the past enjoy.'

Perhaps no one understood Pope's words better than Harry. Harry lived twice! Harry employed the present and enjoyed the past, in fact, reveled in it. He lived twice within one lifetime—a life again more than most men."

A pervasive silence followed his proclamation, a silence so complete it seemed to envelop the room. George was barely breathing. The bearded man's tiny eyes roamed over the assembled people. When he met George's eyes, she was mesmerized by his challenge, his intensity, his incredible intelligence.

The speaker raised a clenched fist. "What then is left for us to mourn?" he roared.

He sent the challenge straight to her soul. *I have given you the answers. What is left for you to mourn?*

Suddenly, tears brimmed in her eyes. Her fingers dug into her purse as if it were a lifesaving island in a dark, wild sea. Something inside her strained to tearing point, like a sail in hurricane wind. The force was as terrifying and mysterious as a gale in the night, coming out of nowhere, unstoppable, unfightable, frightening. Then the wind died, the light returned, and it was over.

She glanced from side to side, to see if anyone, especially Adam, had noticed her lapse of reason, but, thankfully, everything appeared normal. The elderly man had descended from the podium and, along with others, was distributing tiny crystal aperitif glasses filled with brown liquor. As he handed her one of the stemmed glasses, the elderly man's eyes were kind and smiling, nothing more.

She sniffed the contents of the glass, guessed that it was whiskey, and felt grateful that it was straight. She could use it.

The elderly man returned to the podium. "Hangtown Harry was very partial to quoting Arthur Macy's long-ago address to The Papyrus Club. Today, as we say one last good-bye to our friend, I think it's appropriate to repeat a few of those wise words." Extending his glass toward the people in the pews, he exclaimed:

Sit closer, friends, around the board!
Death grants us yet a little time.
Now let the cheering cup be poured,
And welcome song and jest and rhyme;
Enjoy the gifts that fortune sends,
Sit closer, friends.

He thrust his glass toward the closed casket containing Harry's body. "Godspeed!"

"Godspeed!" chanted the crowd, and everyone drained their glasses.

Still feeling somewhat numb from the funeral, George watched Fiona dash through the light rain toward her house. When she disappeared inside, George shifted her attention to Adam. He snapped the padlock in place on Fiona's garage doors. He pulled on the lock several times to check it, then caught her arm and began guiding her toward her house. He seemed to be a man with a mission. The dove, she supposed. But today seemed too gloomy to be a first day of freedom for the lovely bird.

Somehow the concept of freedom made her think of Harry and the matter-of-fact attitude he must have had toward life and death. His praiseworthy philosophy had won him such remarkable friends, and, she supposed, great freedom throughout his life. She instructed herself to remember Harry's wisdom of acceptance during those rare times in the future that she railed at situations that were impossible to change. "It was a beautiful service."

"It was," Adam replied, still forging forward. "You've seemed sad ever since."

"I have? You mean sad as if I were grieving?"

"Yes, I suppose so."

"That's strange. My father told me that grief is a totally useless ritual, and he always forbade those sorts of things." Her heels beat a rapid tattoo on the stone walk. Actually, they walked together quite smoothly since his stride equaled precisely two of hers. His hold on her arm was firm and possessive, a grip that could withstand the force of a hurricane. . . .

She instantly attributed that strange thought to her experience at the funeral. Some alien feeling inside her had become almost as real as a heart or a lung or a spleen, and then it had nearly exploded. The sensation had been terrifying, more frightening than being unable to breathe, the consequences seemingly worse than suffocating. She shivered.

What could be worse than suffocating?

"Cold?" he asked.

"No, not really." She looked up at the sky. Overhead the clouds parted, revealing patches of blue. The drama unfolded rapidly, as quickly as an ocean breaker crashes against the shore.

Sunlight drenched the sky, spreading like gleaming wave tips over wet sand. The burgeoning sun forced even the stubborn clouds to relinquish their somber grayness, painted their borders with brilliance, and transformed them into innocuous, plump bits of white fluff. Now totally disarmed, they seemed to float like whimsically shaped buoys over a calm, azure sea. "Oh, look, Adam. It's a rainbow!"

Adam halted and stared in the direction she pointed, his head thrown back. His grip on her arm tightened as though strong emotion had surged through his body. George's eyes were no longer on the sky, but riveted on Adam. An extraordinary change was coming over him, a change as dramatic as the antics of the heavens.

The worry crease between his eyes faded. The determination, the seriousness that usually formed his every expression ebbed from his face.

Sunlight washed over his features, softening the hardness and bathing them in an amber glow. Against his temples, even the silvery threads in his hair edged his dark curls in light.

When it came, his smile was glorious. It deepened the dimple in his cheek and answered the question she had so often wanted to ask but had failed time and again to conceive of the right words to use. How could you ask someone if they possessed the capacity to know joy—to experience love?

Adam Lawrence did! She knew it now. A rainbow had written the answer over his countenance.

"Oh, Adam. Please kiss me!"

Before her heart could beat again, she was off the ground and in his arms, her tiptoes brushing the ground. As his mouth descended to hers, the golden beauty she'd seen before still lightened his face. He looked upon her with the same joy as he had the rainbow! Happiness flowed through her like liquid wonder.

His mouth slanted against hers, and she knew bliss. She used her arms to circle his neck, her hands to twine through his hair to draw him closer. His lips caressed her with a skill that coaxed every part of her to tingling life. A flood of sensations assailed her senses, the heat of his skin, the softness of his lips, the tickling wisp of his breath, the male scent of his body. He smelled as intoxicating as the woods in fall and as clean as winter wind.

When his nibbling kisses demanded that she open her mouth to him, she gave herself willingly. She had already purged the word *no* from her vocabulary. For him, there was only yes.

At first, his tongue teased her, sliding in and out, swirling gently over her sensitive flesh, sending her provocative signals that were nearly too astonishing to contemplate. What secret pleasures would he teach her when they were alone together, naked, and making love?

She opened herself to him wantonly, and he thrust his tongue deep within her softness. A tremor rocked her body; he gripped her harder. "Oh damn, Georgette," he groaned against her lips.

"What's wrong?"

Instead of answering, he lowered her to the ground, his hand pressing her face into his chest with such force that her nose was crimped against his silk tie.

"I can hardly breathe," she said, her words echoing inside his suit coat.

"I know. Keep your face hidden against me. Someone is concealed behind a shrub near Fiona's house. I glimpsed a flash like sunlight glinting off glass, but now I've spotted him. His telephoto lens is sticking out of one of Fiona's camellia bushes."

"I don't care what those vultures do anymore. Let them take our picture. Let them print it in their awful magazine!" George tried to push at his hard chest, but one of his arms was locked around her waist, the other clamped against her head. She was pinned like a bug on a board. Frustration bubbled up inside her. She wasn't even sure he'd heard what she'd said. To get his attention, she bent her knee and drove it into his shin. "I don't care what they print about me anymore!"

Adam lifted her and began running. "Well, I care," he ground out. "Try to keep in mind that I'm doing this for your own good. And stop kicking. You're only going to hurt yourself."

It took moments of appalling helplessness like this to remind her how small she actually was. She thought his grip might loosen as he jogged, but it didn't. How infuriating to be hauled around like a Raggedy Ann doll!

His shoes tapped against the wooden stairs. She found herself swung around and set on her feet in one smooth motion, her nose only inches away from her own back door. Adam's body framed her back, his arms circled her waist protectively, and his chest rose and fell evenly. His power and strength was tantalizing. He was hardly winded.

She retrieved the key from her purse and fit it into the lock. "I suppose I should be grateful that you didn't drag me by the hair."

His deep laughter caused his chest to pulse against her. His breath stirred the curls on the top of her head, and a fresh set of tingles rippled down her spine. "Believe me, that position was as much for my protection as it was yours."

"Oh? Oh!" she blurted out with sudden understanding. "I mean of course, I noticed. I could feel that . . . well, you know." She stepped inside the kitchen, silencing Mr. Moto with a sharp "no."

Adam followed without releasing his grip. He kicked the door closed behind them and began slowly turning her around to face him.

Her eyes drifted up over his thin gold belt buckle, his fitted shirt, his silk tie to his dark suit that announced Italian from every thread. The rich material was tailored to conform closely to every sharp ridge and masculine curve. Seeing the way his muscles bulged against the tight cut across his shoulders gave her an alarmingly clear image of how the pants must fit now. Her cheeks flushed at that intriguing image.

Adam freed the first button on her coat, then the second and the third. She fought the urge to panic as his long fingers spread across her shoulders and slipped the coat off her shoulders. He tossed both her coat and purse across one of the chairs. Her scarf drifted to the floor.

Her stomach convulsed in a maddening series of flip-flops. She buried her burning face in his chest, hiding herself beneath one flap of his suit coat. Her mouth went utterly dry as he glided the zipper of her dress down her back. His hand slid in languid circles over her silk slip moving ever lower until he caressed the globes of her hips.

His free hand sought out her chin and lifted it until she was forced to stare into the gray thunderclouds of his eyes. She drew in a shaky breath. The lightning was back, the brilliant desire for her.

"You were hiding. Are you frightened of me?"

She shook her head no, then changed it to a tentative nod.

"Do you want me to go on?"

Her eyes flew wide. "Oh, yes!"

His mouth descended on hers, sealing her submission on her lips. His kiss demanded, and she opened herself willingly. She stretched on tiptoes, wanting him to draw her to him, and he did. Her dress fell away from her. He reached beneath her slip and tap pants and brushed his hands over her bare bottom. As he pressed her to him, the lace clinging to her breasts teased her nipples to points.

Cupping the softness of her derriere, he raised her, trailing her up the hard length of him until the heat of her collided with his arousal. Instinctively, she wrapped her legs around him, cradling his hardness and snuggling against it. He felt so wonderful, she thought she might just die from pleasure. She arched her back and undulated against him.

"Good lord!" he shouted. Her breath caught in her throat as his gaze traveled over outthrust breasts, her parted legs. "Where's the nearest bed?"

"Upstairs," she murmured, hugging his chest. "Adam, do hurry."

She needn't have made that request. He swept her upstairs and into a bedroom almost instantly even though it was the guest room, she noticed as he rushed through the archway. He laid her on the old four-poster bed, and she settled into the soft depths of the real feather mattress, aching and needing, but resigned for the moment to waiting while he stripped off his clothes. He shrugged out of his coat and ripped off his tie. His fingers traveled down the buttons of his shirt, releasing them magically.

He flung his shirt toward the chair, then bent to remove his shoes. His shoulders were magnificent, his chest broad and lightly sprinkled with hair that narrowed to a tight line and disappeared beneath his belt. As she traced the provocative trail with her eyes, she absently raised her leg and began to unfasten one of her black stockings.

He dropped his shoe and pounced on the bed. His hand closed over hers, stilling her movement. "I want to do that," he murmured, his lips nuzzling her neck. "I want to do so much to you."

Her free hand found his belt, and she burrowed her finger beneath it. "Then show me."

With a growl, he snatched her hand away and pinned her wrists over her head. His long body framed the side of her body, and he began exploring her with his fingers. His hand meandered over her breasts, his palm circling the aching points. His mouth followed, sucking up a nipple and rolling the lace over the erect flesh. While his mouth continued to minister wildly to her breasts, his hand unfastened her stockings but only to brush away her skimpy tap pants. He eased her slip up over her hips until the dark lace barely edged her soft triangle of curls. He propped himself on one arm. His gaze swept over her nakedness as gently as the fronds on a feather fan. "You're beautiful."

Words refused to form in her mind. Every thought was held in thrall by the exquisite sensation of his touch, the erotic promise in his eyes. His gray gaze held her captive as his fingers found her. He parted her gently and began a tiny flicking movement.

She arched her pelvis against him, but his fingertip maintained a steady, stunning, maddening pulsing. His mouth found her breasts, nibbling the sensitive crests. The tide of pleasure grew inside her until it threatened to peak. "Too soon," she moaned, lowering her hands to his shoulders. She rolled herself to couple her desire with his. She felt his gasp as her eager fingers found the belt buckle. As she tugged on his zipper, he pitched her onto her back.

Suddenly, she was beneath him, her legs parted, her stockinged legs wrapped around his naked hips. He penetrated her swiftly, filling her completely. He rocked against her, nestling deep inside her. She tensed against his hardness, trying to hold him. But he pulled back with excruciating slowness, almost to the brink of withdrawing before descending with equal slowness into her again. Sliding in and out, he continued his erotic massage until she whimpered her pleasure.

Her fingers dug into his shoulders, trying to coax him to take her faster, but he maintained his leisurely pace. Her hands slipped against his skin, now slick with sweat. She bit her lip as the very tip of his pulsing need paused at her opening, and she screamed with the need for him to enter her instantly. "Oh, Adam!" She thrust her pelvis upward.

With a low moan, he plunged into her. Her body exploded into a fireball that melted into liquid gold.

She opened her eyes in time to see the strain in his face disintegrate into pure release. He pulsed deep within her and a new heat filled her. As he sank with a sigh against her, she locked her ankles over his back and vowed to never let him go.

Chapter
11

Adam took several long, deep breaths. He planted his elbows on either side of Georgette and raised himself in bed slightly to ease the pressure of his weight on her. Her dark hair lay in disarray over the flowered quilt. She held her eyelids tightly closed, and the way she was smiling was enough to make any man feel outrageously smug if not downright arrogant.

Her legs still gripped him, holding him inside her warmth. Earlier in her plain black dress she had been a beguiling temptress. But, damn, in bed she was a pagan goddess.

Hell, he was thirty-nine years old and she was already making him hard again.

Her erect nipples beckoned him, the lazy twitching of her hips, an irresistible seduction. He tested her willingness with a tender thrust. She closed hotly around him. His breath snagged on something deep within his chest; his mouth descended on her neck.

At his touch a shiver seemed to dart through her, vibrating through the core of her until a provocative wiggle played over his hard, embedded shaft. "My God," he groaned, "you feel good."

"Mummm," she murmured.

"You're so responsive."

"Mummm?" She lifted her eyelids to reveal two startlingly blue eyes, now hazy with desire.

"A siren," he said, sampling her skin which was as soft and addictive as ice cream. His lips drifted down her throat. "In other words, intoxicating, irresistible, tantalizing . . ."

"It takes two to dance. . . ." She released a long, shaky breath. "It can only be as good as whoever leads."

He began to chuckle, his chest shaking, rubbing against her slender body. "I forgot to mention how delightful you are." He buried himself deep within her, and her legs tightened around his hips, demanding more. "I want you again, and I know you're ready for me. Tell me you want more."

She rewarded him with a lazy, dreamy smile. She extended her arms in complete compliance as he stripped off her lacy slip. He flung it aside.

He bent to suckle her breast, laving the tender crest with his tongue. Her fingers urgently pulled him against her. When he ran his teeth over the nubby pink flesh, she moaned softly, her hips undulating around him in primitive rhythm.

"Hold on," he rasped. Gripping her tightly, he rolled on his back, carrying her with him. He pushed gently against her shoulders, and she straightened atop him. His eyes drank in the sight of her as she rode him, her head thrown back, her rose-tipped breasts swaying. Suddenly, her brow knit, and she increased her wild pace, her moist pressure. A cry escaped her parted lips, and she shuddered.

Then he lost control. His hands cupped her bottom, clasping her tight to him as he spilled his seed inside her in a series of mighty thrusts. With shaky arms, he gathered her to his chest, reveling in her softness as the after-tremors subsided.

Lucidity returned to him slowly. He shook his head, hoping to resettle the power of reason firmly in his mind.

He gripped Georgette harder as reality descended on him with a vengeance. Why had he wished it back? Why face the fact that he'd just had the best sex of his life with a woman he could never have permanently? A socially prominent heiress was completely incompatible with his present lifestyle and all of his plans for the future.

His hand twined in her bountiful hair, pressing her face against him. And yet, Georgette was exactly what he'd been searching for, the rarest flower in the forest, the magical bloom that possessed the power to give him everything he wanted. She was the key to the eventual success of all his plans.

Her breath tickled his ear when she whispered, "I always knew that you would be a wonderful lover. I think it's because of the way you move, almost as smoothly as a current in a river. Ever since we first met . . ."

Georgette bolted up, her dark hair flying. "Dear heavens, I still don't know a thing about you! You haven't told me anything! For all I know you could be anyone, even one of those loathsome reporters!"

He extended his arms to pull her to him but embraced only empty air. Somehow, she had nimbly bounded from atop him.

"I'm not a reporter," he said, hoping to coax her back. Reluctantly, he rose on his elbows, wishing she would rejoin him in bed, yet knowing now that that hope was likely futile. "I've not deceived you in any way, I promise."

She tossed her hands heavenward. "How do I know that? How do I know anything!"

He marveled at her beauty, naked except for the black stockings slipping down her legs. Her creamy skin glowed in the fading afternoon light that streamed through the window. More than anything, he wanted to hold her for hours, listening to her melodious voice utter inventive riddles and unexpected truths as he stroked the exquisite silkiness of her skin and hair. But the indignant expression on her face told him that she was disinclined to comply with his vision of the perfect afternoon.

He sighed, then decided to revert to a tactic that had

worked once before. He pushed himself to his feet and applied a veneer of sternness. "Come back here," he commanded.

"I will not!" She lunged past him, reaching for her slip, but he caught her easily at the waist and dragged her to him. She fought him furiously, shoving and pushing flattened hands against his chest, but, of course, he won. He sank to the bed with his prize, pulling her onto his lap and clamping down on her flying limbs. "Georgette, please stop struggling. We're going to pull back this quilt and get in bed like two civilized human beings, and then I'll answer every question you put to me. Fair enough?"

She ceased her struggle immediately. "Promise?" she puffed out through a veil of disheveled hair.

He chuckled at her audacity. Physically, she had no choice in the matter. Though surprisingly strong for her small size, she was completely outmatched. At last accounting, he could bench press over two hundred pounds. Yet in actuality, she knew him better than she realized; he would let her go if she only asked. "I promise," he said, carefully maintaining a straight face.

With an exasperated-sounding sigh, she blew her hair from her face. When he released her, she announced in an overly loud voice, "That's better." She straightened herself with dignity, rose from his lap, and tugged the quilt away from the pillows, revealing navy blue satin sheets.

The incongruity of the dark sheets caused him to finally take notice of his surroundings. He glanced around the room at the walnut furniture, probably antiques, all decorated with carvings of the masks of lions. The massive posts of the tester bed ended with feet, more specifically furry-looking lion paws. The extraordinary furniture appeared masculine, but was devoid of personal possessions; even the matching tablelike nightstands were barren of both telephone and alarm clock. "This must be the guest bedroom."

"Of course. This Italian Renaissance bed is much too small for me."

He surveyed the bed, perplexed. Though short, the four-poster appeared nearly as wide as a double bed. Another riddle, he thought, watching her scramble over the spongy mattress and under the covers. She tugged the down-filled quilt over her breasts, then clamped her arms straight down the sides of her body sealing herself inside a fluffy cocoon. Her lips were set in a determined pout.

He was having none of this. He angled himself next to her, reached for her hand, and squeezed it. She kept it stiff and inflexible.

He brought his lips to her ear and feathered the tiny lobe. "Georgette, we've just made love twice with what I would describe as incredible sincerity. I'm planning to repeat the experience very soon." She recoiled and glared at him with sparkling turquoise eyes. "You gave yourself honestly and completely and without reservation so I have to believe that deep down you must trust me. I have a lot to tell you. Please move your arm and lie against me."

The quilt slipped from her body as she rolled into his welcoming embrace. Her arms encircled his neck. "I really do trust you, Adam. But I need to know who you are now, truly, and why you're masquerading as a gardener."

"This is no masquerade. I made a change in my life, and I intend to stick with my decision."

"You are a business-and-finance type."

"Was. I worked at Pacific West Bank and Trust. And to answer your question of yesterday, I was successful, very much so."

"Why didn't I ever meet you? My father has fixed me up with every eligible man-on-the-rise bachelor in the building. Were you married?"

Adam skimmed his finger along the ridge of her cheekbone, clearing her pale skin of errant raven strands. His hand dipped into the fullness of her hair. "I suppose I was, in a way."

At her confused look he continued, "After I had been with the bank a few years, a young woman joined my staff. Claudia was bright, determined, and attractive. We both shared ambitious career goals, and we also discovered our common tastes in art, food, vacations, everything that makes for a smooth, easy-to-maintain relationship."

"But boring," she added with mischievous pleasure.

He grinned back at her. "So you've already heard this story."

"Go on. I'm all ears."

His eyes swept deliberately over her nakedness. "Thank heavens that's a barefaced lie."

She giggled. "Keep your mind on business."

He slid his hands to her waist, then lower. "You're too much of a distraction."

She snatched back his wandering hands and planted them firmly on her waist. "Just repeat the word *debenture* over and over like you do in your sleep. Maybe that will help."

He eased his hands down the curve of her hips. "I don't want help; I want cooperation."

"That's it. You're impossible." She jerked the pillow from under her head and plopped it between them. "That stays until you finish. No story, no cooperation. Daddy says to get what you want from a worthy adversary you always need a tactic and to get the best results you must deal from a position of strength. Since I don't seem to have enough strength to deal with you, I'll use whatever tactic works for me, and this is it." She anchored the pillow with a slender knee and an elbow then dropped her chin to her palm. "Now, let's go back to the smooth, easy-to-maintain, boring relationship."

"*Boring* was your word, not mine."

"Then it was exciting?" she countered with a lifted brow.

"Uh, well . . ." he struggled for the right word. How did one describe a relationship that was satisfactory in every way except emotionally. "The relationship was functional."

"In other words, it was boring."

"Right," he replied, admitting defeat.

"Did you live together?"

"Same building, same floor, different condominium."

"Close enough to put you off my father's list." Georgette wagged her head, obviously expressing dismay. "How long did this go on?"

"A long time."

"How many years?"

119

"A long time."

"You promised, remember? How many?"

"Seven years."

"Holy heavens!" Georgette gathered the pillow to her body and sat up cross-legged in bed. "Surely you must have loved her?"

"Wait," he said, throwing up a stilling hand. "Let me go back to the beginning." He rubbed his face. She was effectively diverting him from the whole point of his foray into the past. Carrying on a conversation with Georgette Richards always proved a challenge. Her mind and her mouth worked as quickly as a pretzel-tying machine and with similar results for him—all knots.

"As I was saying, we worked long hours, which earned promotions but didn't allow much time for a social life. It was easy for us to drift into a convenient relationship, and when you're comfortable enough and busy enough, you can get out of the habit of asking important questions like 'Do I actually love this woman?' Two years ago Claudia met a man who worked on the ski patrol at Boreal Ridge. She became totally infatuated with him, and the change in her was incredible. Nothing mattered to her except him. She resigned from the bank, sacrificed a very high and lucrative position that she'd struggled for years to attain, moved to Donner Lake to be near the slopes, and took a near entry level job in a tiny branch of a savings and loan."

"Where she and Mr. Ski Patrol lived happily ever after," Georgette added, sounding hopeful.

"He made her miserable."

"Then she tried to come back to you."

"That's not the point of—"

Frustration seemed to virtually leap from her eyes. "Did she try—"

"Yes," he interrupted. "Actually it had been over between us for a long time only I'd been too busy to notice. Her leaving made me realize that. Her returning couldn't change it." He paused, sadness nudging his insides as he recalled Claudia's tears, her pleas when all he could ultimately return to her was her job. He'd had nothing else to give.

Even in the best days of their relationship, she'd never completely possessed his heart. Ironically, Claudia herself had enlightened him to that sad truth.

He crossed his arms over his chest. Georgette studied him with an intensity that left him vaguely uneasy, his discomfort stemming from an inkling that she was deducing the direction of his thoughts and silently demanding that he pursue it. He cleared his throat. "When Claudia first left, I felt pretty awful, lonely, depressed. One night I did what every American male is supposed to do when a woman leaves him."

"I know! You got drunk!"

"So you're aware of that masochistic tradition."

"I *have* heard country music," she replied indignantly.

He couldn't argue with that logic. "Sometime before I passed out, I finally asked myself why I felt so damned bad. Was it because I really loved Claudia, or was it only a battered male ego, or maybe some combination of the two? Of course, my pride was a bit wounded, but I also knew from previous experience that the primal instinct to maintain possession of a mate couldn't account for such a deep depression. Then it hit me. If Claudia had asked me to sacrifice my lifestyle, my job, and move to the mountains to be with her, I would have said no. I'd never cared for her enough. I had *never* been in love like that."

"Shannon and Mark," Georgette murmured. "My cousin and her husband love each other the way you're talking about. Sometimes it's hard not to be jealous."

He'd been right; she had anticipated him. Her uncanny insights left him astounded again. "I remember thinking that Claudia need never have to wonder what might have been, need never deal with a ceaseless litany of 'what if?'"

Georgette dropped her chin to the pillow and stared at her feet. "Falling in love is such an awful risk. So often trouble comes because of it. And great hurt."

"True." He released a long sigh. "It devastated Claudia."

Georgette cast off her pensive mood and brightened visibly. "Okay, tell me what you did after the hangover wore off."

"That's when I started to examine my own life and found that the meaning I had hoped would magically appear somewhere along the line was missing."

"That's what you get for going into banking," she said solemnly.

"It had nothing to do with *what* I was doing." He scooted up in bed and hunched forward, frustration tensing his shoulders. "What I did was important; it impacted people's lives, their children's lives for years to come. It had everything to do with how I *felt* about it. My job had become a meaningless ritual, and hell, I did it sixty, sometimes eighty hours a week, whatever it took. My whole life had evolved into a series of trivial details and nonsensical motions. My idealism had disappeared. My personal growth was nonexistent. I was too busy running on a treadmill of appointment calendars, fighting to avoid being swallowed up by meetings, lunches, and plane flights. My God, I'd never even been in love. It didn't fit into my schedule. And I thought if Claudia could quit her job for a bum, then by damned I could quit my job to save my own sanity."

"So you just quit?" she asked meekly, and he realized that he must have been shouting at her. Her eyes had widened to ovals, and something glowed in their brilliant depths, perhaps total understanding.

"Better than that. I burned my bridges. Two weeks ago on my last day at the bank, I skateboarded down the hall, onto the elevator, then right through the lobby and out the front door." He swept a hand across his flattened palm. "I pitched my briefcase into the trash as I rolled down California Street."

She rocked back and forth, clutching the pillow. "Oh, Adam, that's wonderful. Do you realize what that means! You simply can't be the stuffed shirt you seem to be!"

God help him, he wanted to cheer. Instead he punched the air with his fist and shouted, "Damned right!"

She giggled, her nose crinkling. "Then you became a gardener." A hint of a frown crept over her face. "Do you really think you ought to stay in landscaping? You're not very good at it, you know."

"I have to work. I'll do my best for Fiona until I discover what it is that I'm meant to do. Then I'll move on."

"Hum . . ." she said, her brows knit. Her demeanor grew contemplative.

He reached his fingers to trace the delicate arch of her foot. Every part of her seemed fragile and at the same time pulsing with life. He explored her ankle then higher to the swell of her leg, over her knee, along the milky flesh of her inner thigh.

"Oh, no!" she caroled, obviously gleaning his destination. With a giggle, she tossed the pillow at him and scampered down the bed. He pounced, snatched back his squirming booty, and rolled across the softness of the quilt, shaking with laughter. His arms tightened around her tiny frame, capturing joy and wonderment and Georgette Richards.

Chapter
12

George slipped a loose fuchsia top edged with a touch of tangerine on over matching silk pants. In her closet, she upended a large box of shoes and sorted through the pile until she located a pair of flats. Hurriedly, she shoved her feet between the soft leather, eager to return to Adam and extend the magic of their perfect afternoon into the long, cool evening. She fluffed her hair, flipped off the light in her bedroom, then dashed into the upstairs hallway to find him.

Adam emerged from the guest bedroom, his suit coat slung over his shoulder. The collar of his shirt hung open, the tails of his tie draped over the crisp, white fabric that covered his broad chest. He ran a hand through his dark hair still tousled from their afternoon of lovemaking. As ever, he looked positively gorgeous.

She said, "I'm glad that you didn't comb the character away. It's such a nice reminder." She felt color rising in her cheeks, but Adam would know her blush had nothing to do with embarrassment. She had already informed him of her decision to banish any self-consciousness about her body where he was concerned. He had seemed a bit puzzled, but pleased, and she understood. Whenever she discovered she'd surprised him, she often felt a bit puzzled, but pleased.

He extended an arm, and she scooted underneath it. Wearing his embrace like a mantle of distinction, she matched his steps two for one as they marched toward the staircase. "I'm starving!" she exclaimed. "Shall I reheat the pot roast or send out for Chinese food? Wait," she said, remembering his tight budget and his determined pride, "all that food in the refrigerator will go bad if it doesn't get eaten soon, and after all that work I did, too. That does it. I'm reheating the pot roast. Will you stay for dinner?"

"I'd like that," he answered, his voice so soft she could hardly hear him.

His response seemed almost reflexive. Worried by his sudden meditative mood, she stopped. His arm slid from her shoulders, as he descended the final step into the foyer alone. Swinging his suit coat over the banister, he turned to face her.

She remained a step above him on the staircase, her eyes level with his mouth. But the soft lips that had explored her that afternoon had become passive and unsmiling. "Adam, what's wrong?"

"Nothing."

His expression darkened, and she understood why. Deception and Adam Lawrence were incompatible.

"There's something you're not telling me, I can tell. Early this afternoon you said that we made love twice with what you called incredible sincerity. Now we've done that three times, and I think you ought to tell me the rest of what you're thinking." She tilted her head and tried to penetrate the grayness in his eyes, but they appeared shrouded in a dense, concealing fog. "It's only fair that I should know what you want from me."

He started, obviously stunned. His features became tight with emotion, maybe confusion. "How do you know that I want something from you?"

"Everyone wants things from other people. It's normal. Men are usually after my money, but I believe you aren't. I know you like my body, and we do fit perfectly together, but

125

I also believe you want more than that from me, at least I hope so. I mean I'd prefer to think that you're interested in more than sex . . ." She broke off when his hands closed over her shoulders.

His expression relaxed a fraction. "You mean you went to bed with me thinking that sex might be all I was after?"

"No, I told you that I believed you wanted more. I mean I wanted to believe—"

"I understand," he interrupted.

"But even if I had thought that sex was all you wanted, I might have . . ." She trailed off, pinching her lower lip with her teeth. "I might have anyway, but probably not—unless there was some tiny hope."

"I understand," he repeated. "Georgette, how old are you?"

"Thirty-three."

"You are?"

"Thank you for looking so shocked, though everybody does."

"I'm not surprised they do. My point in asking your age was this. A few weeks ago, when I turned thirty-nine, I made a promise to myself that I would break free and experience life before mine was over and gone. I finally confessed to myself that I was a bit of a stuffed shirt. When you met me that was nearly the first thing you pointed out, and it hurt because I knew it was true."

"I'm sorry. That was awful of me, and I'll never call you that again."

"Whether or not you do is not nearly as important to me as removing the reasons the term fits. I want to change but the simple truth is that I don't know how."

"I don't think it's supposed to take practice, only determination."

"That's what I thought at first too. I planned my escape, took all the basic, conventional steps, chucked the job, the briefcase, the lifestyle, and suddenly everything went wrong. According to you, I can't even pull off wearing a dammed pair of jeans."

"Adam, that's hardly a drawback. Try to picture Cary Grant in jeans. It doesn't work."

"What am I supposed to do? Wear an Armani suit to spread fertilizer?" he roared, jerking his head toward the coat. "A normal, everyday midlife crisis—that's all I want."

"That's your problem, Adam. You're too normal to have a crisis." At his bewildered expression, she continued, "You don't plan to do unexpected things. If you'd just relax and stop planning everything, you'd give them a chance to happen."

"Like getting myself tied to your sofa. I see your point."

"That's *not* a good example. There was nothing crazy about that. Remember, I explained—"

"I know, Jack Smith, Marvin, Fiona. I know." The worry crease appeared between his eyes. "Georgette," he began, squeezing her shoulders, "you're the only good thing that's happened to me since I left my old life behind. You possess a sense of joy in simply living, and *joie de vivre* is exactly what I set out to find in myself. I don't have the vaguest notion of how to go about changing myself." He paused then said softly, "But I'm convinced that you can help me. Would you?"

She lowered her eyes and began studying a pearly button on his shirt. Helping Adam meant taking a terrible risk. After only three days, she was falling in love with him. What would happen if she spent three more days with him—or heaven help her—a whole week? Transforming a business-and-finance type would certainly take that long. It could take a year!

Twenty-four hours ago, her feelings for Adam were already too complicated; now they were as baffling as local politics. Marfa, the silly fool, had been right for once. What if she said no to Adam now? Would she regret it forever? What if he was the perfect man for her to fall in love with? What if she missed out on her chance to be loved? *What if?*

She'd have none of that regret business now or ever, she suddenly decided. "I know it's going to be a challenge, but I'll try."

The button on Adam's shirt began to move. He had been holding his breath.

Holy heaven, she thought. *I am taking the biggest risk of my life.*

George's hands flew to protect her ears from Mr. Moto's latest eruption of shrill barks. Palms still clasped to her head, she rushed past Adam in search of the dog and found him in her soon-to-be-office, his paws planted against a windowpane.

"Quiet!" she shrieked. In the moonlight she saw him glance over his broad shoulder at her, his curled tail wagging tensely over his back. "Good boy," she crooned, lowering her hands.

Mr. Moto angled his head toward the window, a low growl humming deep within his chest. Following along one wall, George crept nearer the window-lined alcove. At the junction of milk-washed paneling with the window frame, she eased her face so one eye could peer through the curtainless window. The narrow lawn between her house and Fiona's appeared deserted. She scratched Mr. Moto's fuzzy head. "Good boy."

"I'm going out to take a look," Adam said from behind her.

"It's probably one of those odious reporters."

"Maybe, but I'll be back before the leftovers are heated."

Minutes later, as he set down the flashlight on the kitchen table, Adam said, "Someone was out there all right. There were footprints in the flower bed."

"Reporters," George snorted.

"I counted four different shoe types. It looks like they held a square dance out there."

George helped Adam out of his coat and hung it over the back of a chair. "We must get this murder solved. It's ruining the neighborhood."

"According to Estelle's radio show, this neighborhood was ruined long before Hangtown Harry's murder."

"First, we need to interview the suspects. I have plenty of free time away from the office. What with Shannon's pregnancy and all, we've hardly taken on any new projects, and there's not a thing on the calendar for at least another week. Fiona said you could postpone the gardening. She gave us great background on the way to the funeral. I'll take more notes. Then we can gather all the clues——"

"I'm relieved that you didn't say suspects."

"Then we'll know who did it. Oh, Mr. Moto," she said, dropping to her knees and taking his black furry head in her hands. He released a small groan of contentment as she massaged his ears. "You know who did it, don't you? If only you could talk . . . Wait! Somebody wrote a book on why dogs do what they do and how they think. We'll go to the bookstore, or to the library! We'll psychoanalyze Mr. Moto!"

"Good God!"

George spun around. Adam bent over the sink, gaping downward in frank horror.

The teeth!

She jumped from the floor and rushed to Adam's side. "In all the confusion I forgot all about them. I meant to tell you. This morning Mr. Moto dug them up in Harry's yard, and I looked the same way you do now when I first saw them. But isn't it wonderful! We have our first real clue!"

Adam arched a brow.

"After the funeral, when they opened the casket for the last time, I kept trying to work up enough courage to touch Harry's cheek to see if he had his teeth, but I just couldn't do it. It seemed so barbaric."

"The man *was* murdered," Adam pointed out, "and these are pieces of evidence."

"I kept trying to visualize Harry's smile to see if they matched, but I don't ever remember him pulling his lips back far enough."

"I'll take these to the police."

"You might as well wait until morning, don't you think?"

"Where did you say they came from?"

"Harry's yard. I think it was the exact same spot where we saw Mr. Moto digging last night. I don't see what you think the police are going to do if Troy Hasselbush is any example of their talents."

"Unquestionably, Hasselbush is only an example of the lower strata." Adam turned his back on the teeth. "I could certainly use a drink," he muttered.

"I haven't unpacked the liquor yet, but it's in the wooden box in the living room marked 'gargoyle.'"

A smile teased up the corners of his mouth. "Let me guess, you concealed your liquor because you didn't want the movers to be tempted to raid your cache, get drunk, and drop your antique furniture."

"No, but that's really good advice. I'll have to remember that the next time I move."

After they downed the leftovers, Adam retired to the sofa with a brandy. George snuggled against his chest, enjoying its slow rise and fall and the steady drumming of his heart. "It's too bad we don't have a nice fire to look at instead of all these packing boxes. And it looks like it's not going to get any better soon. I was going to use the free time I told you about to get settled." She sighed. "A murder can certainly throw a wrench in the works."

Adam slid his hand beneath the hem of her top and fanned his fingers over her midriff. The tip of his thumb traced the undersides of her breasts. Every nerve in her body tingled in anticipation.

"It's too bad the dove has had to wait a whole other day to be free, though I can't see the point in releasing her in the dark. Where would she go? Should we let her go tomorrow morning?" she asked, not particularly caring about the answer.

Deep in his chest she heard a rumbling sound that she realized meant yes. His thumb journeyed higher and began flipping idly across a sensitive crest. When it stiffened, he moved to the other, teasing until it too roused against the rough pad of his finger. She closed her eyes, shutting out the distraction of sight, wanting only to revel in his ministrations. Soon he would bear her, his willing captive, away to an unearthly cloud beyond thought or reason where nothing existed except she and Adam, sensation and pleasure.

"Oh, dear heaven," she grumbled at the door chime, but

her expletive was mild compared to Adam's. Mr. Moto bellowed in deafening unison with the second chime.

"Quiet," she screeched. "Good boy," she said, dragging herself to her feet and heading to the closet for a coat. Her clinging silk blouse told a story the world needn't know. What confronted her when she opened the oak door made her grateful that she'd taken the precaution of covering herself.

Her father's chauffeur touched his hat. "Good evening, Miss Richards. I have a message from Harlan Richards. A reply is requested."

Grumbling, she snatched the note from his gloved hand. She ripped open the envelope. The chauffeur obliged her with a penlight, pointing the small beam on the crisp, white stationery.

Georgette:
Once again your escapades have become public knowledge. Your irresponsible actions have jeopardized my current endeavors. I expect you at the Oakland house at 11:00 A.M. tomorrow. No excuses.

H.R.

George crushed the note in her hand. "Where is he?"

"I believe he is en route from Tel Aviv, Miss. Will ten o'clock be all right?"

She straightened to her full height and glared at the insolent man. He knew what the note said and what her answer must be. "No. Leaving at ten-fifteen will allow plenty of time."

"I'll be here at ten, Miss."

"Then look forward to waiting."

"Very well, Miss Richards."

Absently, George shut the door. Head bent, she considered her options. Naturally because her father was involved, there weren't any. He planned to force her to see him then forbid her to have anything to do with the murder or any other scandal. Damn!

"Who was at the door?" Adam asked from his spot on the sofa.

She ambled slowly toward him. "One of my father's minions, at least that's what he always calls them. He never uses the word *servant* because that's how he made a living when he first started building airplanes, and I think he wants to forget that he ever took orders from anyone. Anyway, he sent me one of his famous directives. I'll be called for at ten tomorrow morning for an eleven o'clock audience. He's going to be furious."

"Why?"

"He's always in a bad mood whenever his company is under federal investigation. You'd think by now he'd be used to it. If he'd only stop trying to cheat on the government contracts, he could avoid all these problems." She paced in front of the fireplace. "I don't feel a bit sorry for him."

Adam studied her with a quizzical expression. "You suspect your own father of dishonesty?"

"It's a proven fact. Sometimes I think he's really not a very nice person." Would she ever get the furniture right in this room, she wondered, scanning its contents. French looked too stiff somehow, but art deco might just work.

"Does your father often summon you like this?"

"Only when he's upset. He was always against me moving to Scarlet Street. But he really got angry when he saw a picture in a tabloid of this house with the caption 'Defense Spending?' They promised a feature on me in the upcoming issue. That reporter Don Dick Watson seems to think that I live off his ill-gotten gains. He's the one who cornered Fiona and me at the car."

"How did your father find out in advance about the story?"

"Somebody probably wired him about the radio show. Everyone on his personal staff is a professional busybody. How he hates publicity! Unless it's about the company, then it's promotion." She tugged a chair around, grouping it with an end table, decided it looked horrible, then pushed the chair back to its original position. Art deco, she mused. Definitely.

"He can't force you to move." Adam lifted his snifter of brandy and drained the glass.

"I know exactly what he's going to say tomorrow." She lowered her voice, scowled, and said huskily, "George, don't get involved in this murder business. I have several important contracts in the works. Gossip is bad for business. You're a Richards. Act like one." She groaned. "He can be such a nuisance."

She opened her hand and glared down at the wad of paper. What an infuriating message! She sucked in a deep breath and scrutinized the *chaise à l'officier*. When she put it up for sale next week the antique dealer in her building was going to flutter with ecstasy. He'd practically burst into tears when she'd outbid him for it two years ago, though just why he became so emotional about a nineteenth century chair that accommodated a man wearing a sabre was beyond her.

She tossed her father's note in the direction of the fireplace and sank into the sofa next to Adam. "I have to see him tomorrow. That doesn't give me much time. First thing in the morning, I'll start with Dwight Phillips. He jogs so he must be an early riser. Joggers always are. As soon as visiting hours start, I'll go see Agnes in the hospital. But it's so hard to know where to start, except the murderer must be someone who was at Fiona's party. Unless the poison was slow-acting. I wonder how we could find that out?" George shook her head. "After seeing all Harry's friends and what he meant to them, I mean I'm more confused than ever. I just don't understand why anyone would want to kill Hangtown Harry."

Adam gathered her into his arms. "Often appearances can be deceiving."

Chapter
13

George scanned the entry on Dwight Phillips in her notebook; the key points of Fiona's information boiled down to
short phrases.

> brilliantly successful in business
> world-class hurdler
> married once to redhead, no children
> actively pursued by women
> real pistol in 1952

She slapped the book closed and tucked it into her purse,
reminding herself to be observant and remember everything
he said. Or did.

She struggled into her coat asking herself if she should call
ahead before dropping in. After all, it seemed rude to show
up on his doorstep at eight in the morning. But this was
murder. Standard conventions hardly applied.

She trotted up the front walk to the Phillips mansion,
blinking and wishing she'd thought to put on sunglasses.

The textured stucco of the Spanish-style house reflected the morning sun in blinding whiteness.

She depressed the buzzer on a gate executed in ornate black grillwork that guarded a tiled courtyard. Giant palm fronds drooped over a centered, circular fountain that gurgled pleasantly.

"Miss Richards," Phillips intoned. He crossed the courtyard in surprisingly few strides and released the lock on the gate.

"I suppose I should have called. I know it's rude to arrive on your doorstep at such an early hour." Taking in his attire, she concluded that he might not be the early riser she'd assumed. The towel hanging from his neck combined with his terry-cloth bathrobe and wet hair suggested that he'd just hopped out of the shower.

"A beautiful woman is never an intrusion," he said, gesturing her into the courtyard. "Contrary to what you might think, your timing is perfect. I always eat breakfast after my morning swim. If you're willing to tolerate my casual dress, I hope you'll join me."

"I'd like that very much," she said with sincerity. Dwight Phillips was one of the most attractive men in his sixties she'd ever met, tanned, brown-haired, lanky, and very, very tall. He moved with the fluidity and confidence of an athlete. His trim body dwarfed her.

With a light touch on her shoulder, he guided her into a magnificent morning room, glass-walled on one side and filled with the largest specimens of exotic houseplants she'd seen outside the Hall of Flowers in Golden Gate Park. Interspersed among the hodgepodge of foliage, rattan furniture invited with plump white cushions. Freshly cut bird-of-paradise blooms, at least twenty of them, adorned a glass-topped table set for one. Copies of several newspapers and a telephone completed the arrangement.

He took her coat, draped it carefully over the couch, then pulled out a chair in front of the single place setting. "Please," he said. As she settled into the seat obviously meant for him, he lifted the receiver, punched a button, and instructed whoever was on the other end that a guest would be joining him for breakfast.

"Oh, my heavens," George breathed, staring open-mouthed at the enclosed atrium directly across from her. "She's absolutely lovely."

Sunlight bathed a white marble statue of Venus, the voluptuous goddess of love and beauty. In the almost unearthly brilliance, her creamy skin glowed translucently; her calm expression radiated serenity, modesty, and vulnerability. A robe draped from her shoulder, flowing alongside her full bosom, narrow waist, and flared hips. Orchids and pumeria bloomed at her feet. George felt her soul soaring with joy from simply looking at her. She fully expected the lifelike Venus to move at any moment. "Absolutely lovely," she repeated.

Dwight swiveled slowly toward the statue. A change came over his face. His eyes appeared to mist, his lips tighten.

The sadness she glimpsed in him was heartbreaking, heartbreaking because the atrium housing the statue clearly opened to three rooms and a garden. He'd designed a house of beauty and centered it with a glorious creation that only made him sad. Had it always been that way?

Dwight turned his back on the statue and sank stiffly into a chair. He lounged back, each hand gripping an end of the towel hanging around his neck. "Everyone has the same reaction to her."

Along with sadness, sincerity shone in his blue eyes. "Do you mind if I ask why the statue makes you so sad?"

"You are a perceptive young lady." He shook his head repeatedly from side to side as though trying to convince himself of something. "Buying her was a mistake. Now that I have her, I can't give her up."

"Why?" she blurted, shocked by his honesty but hoping for more.

"She reminds me of a woman I saw once a long time ago. For years I couldn't forget the lady. Now the statue of Venus won't let me forget."

George murmured, "Venus steals even the wits of the wise."

"True. If you've read mythology, you must know she had two sides, beauty and a mocking, treacherous nature."

"Who was the woman, the one you saw years ago?"

"That's the hell of it. I don't know. Nobody does. I watched her dance for five minutes forty-one years ago and she's haunted me ever since." He pulled the towel from his neck and slapped it over the back of a chair. "I see that you're surprised that I'd tell you this. Actually, it's only another part of one of those scarlet scandals everyone gossips about. Somebody even wrote a magazine article about my mystery woman and the murder a while back." He gestured behind him. "And the statue is hardly hidden either."

"Murder?"

"Marshall Hoagsworth, Sr. He was shot to death forty-one years ago. Surely you've heard about that."

"Estelle mentioned it briefly on the radio, but I didn't know whether or not to believe her." She sniffed her disgust. "I think she'd say or do anything to boost her ratings. Everybody always talks about these things like I should already know what happened, but I don't. How can I when I've only lived here less than two weeks?" Pushing back the sleeves of her red wool sweater, she scooted forward. She tried to look irresistible and beseeching. "Please tell me about the murder."

The entrance of a white-coated man bearing coffee, steaming home-baked rolls, and fruit cups interrupted Dwight before he could answer. The scowling servant added a setting for Dwight, then arranged a footed crystal globe containing assorted fruit and berries at each place. After pouring the coffee, he padded away.

"He doesn't approve," Dwight said when the servant disappeared. "He thinks you're too young for me which you are. Nowadays, in deference to his sensibilities, I always wait until a woman enters her thirties before I ask her here for a meal."

George spread her napkin on her lap, happily accepting his mistake about her age as a compliment. The gleam in his eyes told her she had succeeded in being irresistible. She picked up her fork and stabbed a strawberry. "Now, can we go back to the murder?" she inquired hopefully.

Dwight set aside his china coffee cup and folded his arms over his broad chest. "Do you know anything about Marshall, Sr.?"

"Only that Fiona once said he was handsome."

"Marshall was that and wild. He made a career of spending money and seducing women, and he became a master at both. He was fifteen years older than I, and when I was a teenager, I thought I wanted to be just like him.

"It was his father, Zeb, who made all the money and built that mausoleum next door for his young wife. He was well into his fifties—hard, rigid, and very religious by the time his son came along. Marshall was too smart to rebel while Zeb was alive. The old man would've cut him off. So he waited. When his father died, he got it all."

"What about the mother? Didn't she get anything?"

"Zeb had divorced her by then. One afternoon he'd caught her in the conservatory with Elmo who, as Marshall used to say, was picking himself a flower. After Zeb died, Marshall invited Elmo back. He said he liked to have a constant reminder that at least one man had screwed his father, if only by proxy."

"Marshall sounds awful. How could he joke about someone having an affair with his mother?"

Dwight sipped his coffee. "He was bright, witty, and manipulative—a Svengali in the truest sense. He joked about everything, maybe to hide his true feelings. It's hard to say."

"What's his wife like?"

"Ina used to be beautiful. She sang, danced. She gave up her career for him, and he destroyed her with one affair after another. Both she and her son, Marshall, Jr., suffer from some type of mental illness. I have no idea what."

George glared at Venus. "So much for the idols of our youth."

"Marshall ended up making my own father look like a saint."

She squirmed in her chair thinking it would take the second coming of Al Capone to do that in her father's case. At least he hadn't murdered anyone, that is, anyone she knew of, or driven anyone crazy—except maybe her. "How did Marshall get murdered?"

"The men at his club threw him a big fortieth birthday bash, almost like a bachelor party. God knows he lived like one, and everyone knew it. He kept an apartment for his assignations, even offered it to me."

With a wink, she asked mischievously, "**Did** you ever take him up on his offer?"

"A time or two," he said. "Remember, I was in my early twenties then. It was the first time I'd returned home in seven years. I was no longer used to the restrictions of the family home."

Dwight glanced down at his hands, looking sheepish. No wonder women chased him; he still had a beguiling boyish charm.

"Seven years?"

"I had a disagreement with my father. He demanded that I attend Stanford, get a degree in business, and enter the field of finance just as he had. I disagreed, and he threw me out. I returned seven years later with a degree in classical literature and an assortment of ribbons and medals for hurdling, both of questionable merit as far as earning a living." He laughed. "After Marshall's murder, I went to Stanford. My father was right; business and I were and are a good fit."

She didn't believe him about fitting into business. Everything else he'd said rang with such sincerity, it was easy to pick out that statement as sounding automatic and too firm. He probably only told himself that so he'd feel better.

He rubbed his hands on his legs. "For Marshall's birthday party the club members had hired live comedians, strippers, you name it. A real bawdy-night show on a ramshackle stage. Mostly the club men milled around, smoking, drinking, telling stories, hardly paying attention to the show."

"You were there?"

"With a couple of my younger brothers. The highlight of the evening, according to this porn-house-type barker, was to be the appearance on stage of Marie Antoinette risen from the grave with all her wicked, wanton wiles, her breasts so beautiful they were models for champagne goblets. About ten o'clock the lights dimmed, and the men stopped circulating in anticipation of the finale. The curtain parted, and she glided on stage. The room became so quiet that I could hear her dress rustle softly as she moved. She was costumed in a white wig stacked with curls and a scarlet dress similar to the ones they wore around the time of the French Revolution only gaudier, you know, low cut, corset waist, puffy skirt, ornate, with lace. A scarlet mask hid the upper part of her face, but anyone could see that she was beautiful, very young, obviously very scared.

"I realized that she was there to take her clothes off. My throat went dry. I started to elbow my way to the stage, all the while straining to penetrate the smoky haze to get a better look at her. Her freshness astonished me. She looked completely untouched, virginal. And she was terrified, so terrified her breasts quivered with each breath.

"The music of a harpsichord tinkled offstage, and she began a halting little dance. I managed to gain a position close to the platform. Her movements mesmerized me. They were as tentative as a first kiss between lovers, just as promising, just as sensual.

"Her skin was like snow, her lips like a bud about to open. She possessed the moist softness of a flower. She was poised on the verge of womanhood, and I suddenly wanted more than anything to be the man she'd willingly trade her innocence to love. I kept thinking: she can't do this here, not now, I must stop her. When her fingers touched the laces on her gown, I leaped to the platform.

"She froze, her lips trembling. Yet, somehow, I sensed a certain relief in her. She fixed me with her magnificent green eyes, and, foolishly, I hesitated.

"Behind me, I heard a roar like a freight train. Someone thrust me aside. It was Marshall. He grabbed the girl by the arm. She released a sharp cry of pain, but Marshall only raged at her. 'You little idiot,' he shouted. He swept her up and disappeared between the flaps of the curtain, the terrified girl sobbing.

"I jumped from the stage feeling like a complete fool. A quartet began to play, and the party resumed in full deafening swing as though nothing out of the ordinary had happened. The president of the club slapped me on the back and asked if I'd welcome his sponsorship to become a member. He complimented me on my audacity. I remember getting very drunk.

"About an hour later, a series of yells sounded from behind the stage. A man screamed, 'He's dead! He's dead!' We rushed backstage and found Marshall sprawled on the floor of the young woman's dressing room, shot dead with his own gun, his hand still clutching the discarded scarlet dress."

"And the young woman?" George asked.

"She had vanished."

"Holy heaven," she breathed, sinking back into her chair, drained. Even listening to the story was an ordeal. She reached for her coffee which, she quickly discovered, was stone cold. She pretended it was iced and drained the cup. "No one heard the shot?"

"It was a noisy party and the dressing rooms were quite a distance away from the main room. Everyone including the performers was questioned. I know it's uncanny, but no one saw or heard a thing.

"The ensuing investigation paraded all of Marshall's sordid affairs through the tabloids. The headlines followed the vein of 'Sin and Depravity on Scarlet Street.' The papers ran blow-by-blow accounts of the search of Marshall's so-called love nest, tales of his womanizing; they didn't miss a trick. Whatever was left of Ina's mind slipped. Marshall, Jr. was a teenager at the time. He's hidden himself behind the shutters in that old house ever since. I don't even think he finished high school. Elmo says he carves medieval warriors, armies of them, and reenacts the Crusades."

Dwight tilted his head back, seeming to stare over her head at nothing. "Maybe if they had found the murderer things would have been easier for Ina and Marshall, Jr. It's hard to say. According to the police there were no clues, no leads. It's as though the woman in the scarlet mask only existed for those few short minutes as Marie Antoinette then stepped back into oblivion."

"Do you think she killed Marshall?"

His eyes dropped to her. His expression grew tortured. "No," he said softly. "But perhaps that's because I refuse to allow myself to believe that the memory of a murderess has haunted me all these years."

"Oh," George said, thinking what sense that made. Dwight was biased, all right, and Venus was certainly the perfect symbol of his obsession. He'd become infatuated with a mythical woman. "Didn't anyone who worked in the company know her?"

He appeared sad again. "The young woman had paid the real stripper to allow her to perform in her place. The stripper couldn't even give the police a description. I seem to remember that she was high on something."

George pushed the fruit cup away from her. She'd only had time to eat one strawberry before Dwight's story had caused a knot to grow in her stomach. He wanted a mysterious woman he could never have, which was probably the exact reason he wanted her so badly. It was a convenient and easy thing he could point to in order to explain his misery to himself, her cousin Shannon would say. After she married Mark, she had embroidered on a wall hanging Avoid Using Something or Somebody You Can't Change as an Excuse to Avoid Change in Yourself. Maybe she could convince Shannon to do one for Dwight.

"I didn't realize how isolated I've become."

George whisked on a smile. "Isolated?"

"I hardly allowed you to say good morning before I launched into my history. What did you come to see me about?"

"Ugh . . ." She bit her lower lip. "Well, actually I'm

142

taking a survey. I'm polling everyone on the street for a dear friend of mine. A dental student named Cecil," she babbled, using the name of her father's butler. "He's doing a project, for a paper for school, and he's desperate. If he fails this class, he'll have to go into another home . . . I mean another field . . . I mean back to the fields, and be a migrant farm worker like all the other Rodriquezes."

Dwight squinted at her. "Cecil Rodriquez?"

Realizing her mistake she corrected, "His real name is Ernesto. Cecil is only his nickname."

"Still, Cecil seems like a strange nickname, especially for a man of Hispanic origin."

"He's always pumped gas on the side. That's how he got it. You know, Cecil. Diesel. Anyway, Diesel, I mean Cecil, who's really Ernesto, wants to be an archaeological dentist, so it's easy to see why he chose the topic of lost dentures. . . ."

George crossed Dwight's courtyard, her shoes clicking against the tile. She really didn't understand why Dwight had laughed so hard when she asked him if he'd lost any dentures lately. And it was certainly embarrassing when he wrote out a five hundred dollar check to Ernesto Rodriquez so the poor dental student wouldn't have to pump gas while he worked on his project. The real Ernesto Rodriquez owned a Greek Revival mansion in Hillsborough valued at over four million. She knew; she'd just redecorated it.

Her watch read nine-fifty. She only had a few, precious hours left to solve this mystery. If this was an episode of "Perry Mason," it would be titled "The Case of the Disappearing Dentures." She noticed they were gone after Adam had left for home late last night.

She dashed across the street. When she reached the curb on the opposite side, she spied Fiona standing outside near the entrance to Adam's basement apartment wringing her hands and talking animatedly to a man in a business suit.

Dread raced as a shiver down George's spine. She rushed

toward Fiona, hoping, praying that nothing had happened to Adam. She grabbed Fiona's arm.

She started. "George!" she exclaimed, throwing her arms around her and hugging her hard.

George pushed her away. "What's wrong? What's wrong!"

"They've arrested Adam," she said in a high, thin voice. "They think he murdered Hangtown Harry."

Chapter
14

"Adam arrested?" George shrilled, searching Fiona's face for some sign that her remark had been a joke or a wrong guess or a mistake. But the wrinkles and lines on Fiona's face appeared to form brush strokes of anguish.

"Mother, Adam has been taken in for questioning. He hasn't been arrested—not yet, anyway. Miss Richards," he said, extending a hand. "I'm Marvin Breathwaite."

She accepted his hand and said hurriedly, "I recognize you now. I've seen your picture. Please call me George. It's nice to meet you. Now tell me what happened to Adam." Her voice shook just like the rest of her.

"The police obtained a search warrant for Adam's basement apartment, and they found some incriminating piece of evidence."

"Evidence? What evidence!"

Marvin glanced at his shoes, shuffled his feet, and shoved his hands into the pockets of his pants. "I don't know. I arrived just as they were putting him into the police car."

George's breath snagged in her throat. *The teeth!* They must be Harry's and a real clue, just as she'd thought. But now they were incriminating evidence. Why had she let Adam take them? This horrible misunderstanding was all her fault. She pushed out the trapped air in a rush. "I'll go after him. I'll explain everything. Where did they take him? Where's the station?"

"George, no." Fiona clamped a hand on George's arm and held fast.

"Mother's right. You might make matters worse. I have a friend who's one of the best criminal lawyers in town. I'll call him now. He's the one to handle this situation."

Marvin sounded as levelheaded and cunning as her father. Reason suddenly clicked back into place. She could easily cause Adam more harm than good. Hadn't she already done enough damage? "The best in the city, really?" she asked, swaying toward his point of view.

"Honestly," Marvin reassured. "He's the one who got Rafe 'The Blade' Boils acquitted last month."

"Adam is innocent. I know. Tell the lawyer that Mr. Moto barked at Adam, but he never barked the night of the murder. I would have heard him. I was right *there*. Don't you see? Mr. Moto knew the person who killed Harry, that's why he didn't bark that night. But Mr. Moto barked at Adam."

Marvin appeared confused. "You say that the dog knows who did it?"

"Of course. He saw or heard anyone who came to see Harry. He must have. He patrols the grounds every single night. But he didn't bark the night Harry died. Not once! He's earsplitting. I would have heard him. Then two nights later he barked at Adam. That proves Adam is innocent!"

Fiona released George's arm, her anguished expression replaced by relief. "Marvin, she's right. Harry trained the dog to ignore his friends and neighbors. He only barks at strangers. Adam is a newcomer to the neighborhood. He was only here two days before Harry's death, and he was working day and night between the yard work and getting himself settled."

George clasped her hands together, pleading. "Adam never met Mr. Moto until after Harry died! He's innocent!"

Marvin ran a hand over his thinning red hair. "Does this Mr. Moto bark at Adam now?"

"No . . . of course not," she said haltingly. "They've become friends."

"Were you the only one who witnessed Mr. Moto barking at Adam after the murder?"

George threw her hands in the air. "Yes, but—"

"Mother, could you hear this Moto when he barked?"

"Sometimes. But I was out the night Hangtown Harry died."

"Who lives on the other side of Hangtown Harry?"

Fiona sniffed. "That good-for-nothing Elmo Burroughs sleeps in that shack nearby, but he's dead drunk most of the time. As far as the Hoagsworth mansion, Ina occupies the part closest to Harry and I doubt if Ina Hoagsworth could hear it thunder. She's virtually deaf. What are you getting at?"

Marvin turned an intent gaze on George. "It sounds as if it's only your word that this Moto didn't bark the night of the murder then barked at Adam afterward. Correct?"

"I'm right! I'm telling the truth! The clue they found in Adam's apartment is a set of teeth. I think they're Harry's. Mr. Moto dug them up in Harry's yard yesterday, right before the funeral."

"Harry's teeth?" Fiona gasped, the color draining from her cheeks. "You do mean dentures, don't you?"

George nodded.

"It's ghoulish. . . ." Fiona continued. "Still, I have to wonder why that Mr. Brill at the funeral home didn't mention that they were missing."

"Adam was going to take them to the police last night but I talked him out of it. He was going to do it this morning. I'm the one that found them! He had nothing to do with this. He's innocent!"

"I don't doubt that," Marvin said slowly, raising a hand palm out as though trying to placate her. "I see honesty and concern in your eyes. I also see more. I don't want to embarrass you, but Mother says that you and Adam are seeing each other. The police are liable to question your motives for making statements."

Her hands balled into fists. "He's innocent! If Mr. Moto and I can't prove it to them today, we'll find a way to do it tomorrow. I swear it!"

"I don't doubt that either. Mother, show me the closest telephone so I can call the attorney. I want both of you to stay inside and uninvolved. George, perhaps Adam was trying to protect you by taking the teeth to the police himself. I think he wants you out of this, so please respect his wishes. It's a sticky mess, certainly a dangerous one."

"Why don't you stay with me, George?" Fiona brightened. "I'd feel so much better if we both weren't alone."

"Great idea, Mother."

"Thank you, but I have to go to Oakland to see my father."

"Maybe you should stay with him until this whole thing is resolved," Marvin offered.

George glanced up at Marvin. He radiated a sense of benevolence, but it was obvious that he was trying to get rid of her. "I'll think about it," she replied politely though she had absolutely no intention of staying with her father.

Her response obviously satisfied them. They delivered the parting pleasantries. With her son trailing behind her, Fiona headed toward her home, and the two of them disappeared inside.

Spying the open door to Adam's apartment, George hiked toward it. At the very least, the police could have locked up, she thought angrily. She descended the stairs and paused at the entrance to a large room. She scanned its interior.

Like Adam, the room was well ordered and scrupulously maintained. The contents reminded her of a luxurious hotel suite decorated in classic, rich hardwood furniture. At the foot of his bed, a low-slung bookcase cradled hardbound editions ranging from Shakespeare to Dick Francis.

His skateboard leaned against the wall beneath a window. As she stared at the sill, tears blurred her vision. Small clay pots with mismatched saucers marched across the narrow ledge, each filled with a single dandelion plant. The little weeds that had once grown in Fiona's lawn now flourished in Adam's window. He'd dug them up and repotted them.

A small sob escaped her lips. He couldn't even kill a dandelion.

"Hey, you're not supposed to be in here!" A man with a graying walrus mustache popped into the room. He watched her a moment then said in a kinder tone, "I'm afraid you'll have to leave now."

She wiped her eyes with the back of her hand. "I didn't mean any harm."

"It's all right," he said gently. He straightened his corduroy coat and hiked his belt up over his skinny hips. Tall and reedy, he probably drank coffee instead of eating. His sympathetic-looking smile revealed slightly stained teeth. "Who are you?"

She pried open her handbag and extracted a tissue. As she blew, she cast a covert glance at the man. He appeared intense, the sort who either works or sleeps with no speed in between. She squeaked out her name.

"Dan Hernandez," he said. He pumped her hand with the overblown enthusiasm her teenage boyfriends had always displayed when first meeting her father. But he was definitely fortyish, his quickly moving eyes shrewd and penetrating. "Are you a friend of Adam Lawrence?"

"A neighbor," she replied, her suspicions mounting. "Are you a policeman?"

"Detective," he replied matter-of-factly.

At least that beat another reporter, she thought, stuffing the tissue back into her purse. Still, she edged toward the door, worried that something would spill out of her mouth that might jeopardize Adam. She sensed that almost any word she said might prove somehow enlightening to this man. "I really have to go now."

"Which house do you live in?"

"Twelve Scarlet and I really, really have to go."

He hovered around her. "I need to talk with you. I have a few questions, nothing much."

She backed up to the first step. "If you're on this case, why haven't I seen you here before?"

"I received this assignment late yesterday. It'll be mine from here on out."

From the manner of his statement, she got the impression he meant that his department had called on their finest—meaning himself. "The questions will have to wait," she said in a trembling voice. "I have to go." She rushed up the stairs and across the lawn. The detective terrified her, and now she realized why. Dan Hernandez had gotten a search warrant because he believed Adam was guilty of Harry's murder.

Adam needed her help. Agnes Clodfelter was the next step which meant that she had to see her father and return to San Francisco before hospital visiting hours ended.

She dashed between the houses, grateful to find her father's chauffeur had arrived early as promised. He opened the door, and she scooted into the backseat of the Rolls-Royce knowing she was in for a full, roaring lecture. Her father only sent the Rolls when he was outraged. The elegant car was supposed to remind her of his accomplishments. Harlan Richards first polished the car for the original owner; seven years later he had owned it himself.

Facing her father was like Dorothy confronting the thundering Wizard of Oz. Only bravery gained his approval. She straightened stiffly, her jaw set.

"Hello, Daddy," she caroled in a forced singsong. She glided into his study and sat in a cold leather chair on the darker side of the mammoth room.

She chose not to glance in his direction. Her father's anger filled the room like scorching desert heat.

Carefully, she folded her hands in her lap. Her toes squirmed in her shoes, but his desk blocked his vision of the one release of tension she allowed herself. "As you can see, I'm right on time, just as you requested."

Slowly she raised her eyes to him, her breathing rapid.

He squeezed a pair of hand grips at an even tempo. Ever since his stroke, his body had evolved into two mismatched halves, his left side withered yet slightly functional, his right strong and muscular from two years of intensive physical therapy. He challenged himself daily and coped without complaint.

Now he glared at her, his eyes blue-black with rage. The mere force of his presence dwarfed the massive hardwood desk, his face rocklike.

George's heart hammered. Why didn't he get on with it? She had to help Adam! "Why did you want——"

"Do you realize what you've done?" he boomed, rattling the glass panels in his bookcases.

"What's that?"

He thrust a newspaper across his desk with such force, it sailed off the edge and landed on the floor at her feet. She strained toward the paper and plucked it up. Angry red lines circled a portion of a daily gossip column in a local newspaper. The subheading read "She's at it again."

Georgette Richards, well-known heiress to the Richards Inc. fortune and daughter of aviation mogul Harlan Richards, accosted reporter Don Dick Watson yesterday in front of her Scarlet Street home. Calling the former award-winning newsman a vulture, she drove her heel into Watson's instep. X-rays revealed a cracked bone, and Watson, who is described as resting uncomfortably at home, plans to sue. Known as George to her friends, the thirty-three-year-old interior designer is no stranger to litigation. A lawsuit filed against her last spring involved the bizarre destruction of a vintage automobile when an antique sofa sailed through the front window of her former residence on Russian Hill, no casual lob for the four-foot-ten, hundred-pound woman. No explanation was ever offered for the incident, and the case was recently settled out of court for an undisclosed sum.

No wonder Daddy was furious, she thought, scanning the column, using the pretense of slow reading to buy time. But what was the best way to deal with his anger quickly? She tossed the paper aside and straightened herself up babbling, "That's libel. Heaven and half the country knows I've never weighed as much as one hundred pounds in my entire life.

And imagine, four-foot-ten. I'll sue them. I'm five feet tall, and they've as much as accused me of being a dwarf."

"That's only the latest," her father snarled, slapping a stack of papers on his desk. "There's more to your chronicle of irresponsibility. Now you've gotten yourself involved in this bizarre murder investigation." He tapped the papers. She had no idea what they said and therefore had no idea of how best to defend herself.

She bluffed, "It wasn't my fault that the man next door got murdered. That's something you can hardly predict, and you can't expect a realtor to point out embarrassing neighborhood trends that might endanger the sale."

"Your idiotic whims and escapades jeopardize everything I've worked my whole life to achieve. I know that matters little if at all to you, but have you ever stopped long enough to think that when you harm me, you also harm my employees? You jeopardize the lives of innocent people, people with serious responsibilities to their families, people who unlike you understand the meaning of responsibility. You're lazy and spoiled, and you think of nobody but yourself."

His words sliced like the lash of a whip. *Daddy, why do you say such horrible things to me?* She searched her mind for a soft, quiet refuge. Adam's handsome face began to form, his expression crystallizing.

"I realize now that I shouldn't have fixed that Russian Hill incident. You only saw it as the license to go out and do something else to embarrass me."

"You didn't settle that. The attorney did, and I paid him."

"You flagrantly ignored my advice and moved to Scarlet Street. I swear sometimes I think you spend your life inventing ways to denigrate the Richards name."

Adam's image stayed with her, even though she was growing weary and frustrated. Nothing she said seemed to penetrate because her father refused to listen. Adam seemed to smile at her and say, "You can bear this, no matter what he says." She steeled herself for more, her hands clutching her knees, holding herself together tightly.

"I will not permit you to continue to live this way."

Her arms ached from holding her knees. God surely would make him stop soon. She had to help Adam.

Dread seeped into her soul at the relentless *thump, thump* of his cane. "Look at me," he commanded.

She hesitated, then in halting little stages, she raised her head and arched her neck. Either her prayers had gone unanswered or God had no influence over Harlan Richards. He stood over her slightly stooped, both hands resting on the ball of his cane.

"I've tried to find some man fit enough to take control of you and manage your finances. Selfishly, I also wanted a reasonable son-in-law, possibly someone with the intellect and capability to join the company and truly contribute. I've been at this task for over a decade without results. Invariably, my expectations have been futile where you're concerned.

"I also wanted heirs, and I will have some, albeit from my great-niece. Maybe one of them will be equal to taking on the challenge of managing what I've built.

"Of you at this point, I have distilled my expectations to one simple demand—marriage. All I ask of your choice is that he be presentable so when he comes to work for me he won't be an embarrassment. In return, I'll be very generous financially."

She gaped at him. "I . . . I . . . I won't—"

With deliberate softness, he said, "You will. You don't have a dime I can't find a way to control."

"But my business—"

"Doesn't make enough to maintain a house like the one on Scarlet Street, support you, and pay your overhead. You couldn't make it without the income from investments derived from my money." He rocked once, forward then back. "I want you to put that place up for sale anyway. Day after tomorrow you'll leave for Baja. I've arranged for you to stay a month at one of the private resorts down there. And find someone to marry. The next time you do something crazy, it will be his responsibility, not mine."

He limped back to his desk and sank into his chair. George watched him, too numb to even respond.

"I insist that you stay completely clear of any of this neighborhood murder business. I'm giving you forty-eight hours to get everything in order, the house up for sale, arrange for movers and so forth, then you go to Baja. I want your promise—"

"Oh, my. I'm running out of time!" George jumped up, wringing her hands.

"What do you think you're doing? Get back in that chair," he commanded.

"I can't stay any longer. I really can't. I have to go," she babbled.

He shouted. "I'm not finished!"

"I understand everything. Completely . . ." she trailed off then dashed for the door.

Chapter
15

By the time George alighted from her father's car in front of her house in San Francisco, she was good and mad. The chauffeur rounded the end of the car, but she defiantly slammed the door shut and stalked toward her house. Her impossible father had struck again. Sell her house! Go to some stuffy resort in Baja! Get married!

How dare he threaten her! She had a murder to solve.

In reality she had nobody to blame but herself. He had talked, she had babbled. But if she had argued with him, she would still be there, her resolve being worn down with the relentlessness of sand shaping rock. He never gave up. Ever.

Take away her trust funds? After all the entertaining she'd done, all the command performances at his endless parties, all those dates with those insufferable number crunchers. She'd earned every dollar! How dare he! The largest trust fund had originated from her mother's estate anyway!

She pounded up the front porch steps. Soon her business with Shannon would be very profitable—it was going to be stupendous. Who cared if Don Dick Watson sued her. Who cared what that tabloid printed!

Mr. Moto bounded toward her and rained wild licks around her knees. "Oh, Adam," she said in a breathy whisper, thinking of their afternoon together gloriously naked—or nearly so. She dropped to the floor and hugged Mr. Moto. He stood obediently still as she buried her face in his fuzzy ruff.

Only last night, she'd promised Adam to help find joy. Now, less than twelve hours later, she was at least partly responsible for him being hauled in for questioning and heaven only knew what else. "Mr. Moto," she murmured, "we just have to find a way to help him."

Agnes Clodfelter must know something that could help Adam. She had been the murderer's second target.

George checked her watch, relieved to find it was only two. As she hustled through the house to let the dog out, she decided to visit Agnes first, then the library. Mr. Moto panted happily as she unlatched the door. "After Agnes, you, you charming little rascal, are going to be grilled."

Staggering under the weight of a *Ficus benjamina* that stood taller than herself, George peeked through the foliage at a nurse. "Can you please give me the room number for Agnes Clodfelter?"

"Four-oh-four," the woman answered just as George was sure that her arms were ready to snap like dry twigs.

She waddled down the hallway, checking numbers. She found the correct door, thumped it with her knee, and received a shaky, "Come in."

"Is that you, George?" Agnes asked.

"How could you tell?" George puffed, lowering the pot to the floor near a virtual flower show of arrangements. "Mercy, that's heavy. And I specifically asked the florist for one that needed watering. I should have guessed he was a sadist where women were concerned. He *did* have a two-day beard." Approaching the bed, she asked again, "How did you know it was me?"

Agnes pressed a switch and the bed began to raise her upper body. She smiled warmly. "You're the only person I know who wears leather shoes in fruit motifs."

George giggled and clasped the hand of the older woman. Surrounded by white, Agnes appeared sallow and frail, but her eyes gleamed brightly. "How are you, Miss Clodfelter?"

"I'm much better, and thank you for all the calls and flowers. The hyacinths are still so fragrant." She twisted toward the lavender blooms and sighed. "Sweet but deadly—they are quite poisonous. Still, they're one of my favorites. I love herbs and flowers."

Odd, George thought, that Agnes had mentioned a poison in such a mild, off-handed way, especially considering the ordeal she'd just been through. "I meant to get here sooner, but . . ." George trailed off expectantly.

"I know, Harry's funeral and the like." She angled her head in George's direction. "Fiona told me all about it and that Joan LaRose. Who would have thought that a man Harry's age would have a paramour?"

"Men seem to be able to pull that off all the time without anyone batting a brow. But it's positively infuriating what people say about women who sleep with younger men."

"Somehow I always knew that man had a secret nature. An evil one. I always thought he married the Reed girl for her money."

"You mean the daughter of the family that built Harry's house?"

"Yes."

"I suppose that follows his pattern of younger women. But marrying a girl. How young was she?"

"Barely forty. She didn't live much longer than that either." Agnes straightened her fussy bed jacket and smoothed the lacy collar. "He had two other wives since then, but they didn't die, just divorced him."

Agnes's tone implied that she considered death preferable to divorce. George suppressed a smile. The accountant for her and Shannon's business might even agree. When Shannon had announced her engagement, the nervous little man had delivered an inspired lecture on nasty divorces and prenuptial agreements. It was enough to make George conclude that lawyers, accountants, and judges had conspired to make the consequences of love and marriage more frightening than an audit notice from the Internal Revenue Service. "How long did Harry live on Scarlet Street?"

"Twenty-five years. He wasn't a native, of course. I never heard him say where he came from." She lowered her voice confidentially, "I often thought that his poolside chats with Emperor Norton were shams. Even while he claimed to be conversing with the spirit, his eyes were always alert, too alert and watchful. No, I don't think he was crazy at all."

Neither did George—especially after seeing his youngish and attractive girlfriend Joan LaRose. Few men Harry's age could boast such a catch, especially one who would grieve so over his death. "Somebody said he used to go off all the time on gold panning expeditions."

"Ridiculous nonsense. You saw Harry. Can you honestly imagine him hiking through the Sierras leading a burro? I don't believe it, and now that we know he had a woman, wouldn't you guess he was with her in some love nest?"

"That certainly seems reasonable," George mused. "You obviously knew Harry well. Do you have any idea why anyone would want to kill him?"

Agnes scooted up, crossed her arms, and proclaimed indignantly, "I hardly knew Harry at all. We rarely spoke."

"I only asked—"

"I understand," she said with a limp wave of her hand. "You can't help but be curious. You couldn't help but think us curious. We are! Natasha Velour and her tawdry books. Her map-making 'friend' is bad enough but that Estelle woman . . . A few more face-lifts and she'd be telling fortunes through her navel.

"Dwight Phillips and I are the only normal people there, except you, of course, and Fiona, though I can't say I approve of her drinking. Ever since her grandparents were expelled from the temperance union, the liquor has flowed freely over there. And Dwight." Agnes rolled her eyes. "Well, I'd forgotten until just now about that statue. He *does* have a fixation. I guess that only leaves you and me."

"I suppose so . . ." George trailed off. "I haven't had the chance to meet Marshall Hoagsworth and his mother yet. I thought I might bake some cookies or something and take them over."

Agnes picked up George's hand and squeezed it. "You are a sweet thing. Don't bother, dear. They both gave up on life a long time ago." She stared beyond George, looking wistful. "I used to bring Ina Hoagsworth special herb teas and little things from my garden until she just stopped talking altogether. It was a gradual decline. Finally, she got to where she'd sit staring at her hands or picking at the seams on her clothes. If that wasn't distressing enough, every time I went near the house Marshall cornered me and babbled on about the Crusades or started raving sermons about fire and brimstone. He's a big man, and he can be frightening." She sank back into the pillows, her eyes misty. She clung to George's hand. "My parents raised me to be a Christian and do good for people, but they didn't gift me with their stamina. A stronger person would have kept going back, but I just couldn't. It was painful, seeing them, knowing exactly what they'd gone through—especially Ina, while I was trying so hard to bury my own bitter memories. I've never actually faced things head-on the way some can."

Alarm bells rang in George's head, and she struggled to suppress her excitement at Agnes's slip. "Miss Clodfelter," she said with what she prayed was appropriate calm, "you can only do the best you can."

"Agnes," she corrected. "You are a sweet thing. Did you know that I'm to be released in the morning?"

"Are you sure you're ready?"

"I'm looking forward to getting home to my garden. I don't like all these medicines they force on a person. Why I hadn't taken a laxative in my life until I came here."

"Feel free to come stay with me—" George stopped, stunned by Agnes's look of horror. Agnes pushed away George's hand and drew the covers up near her shoulders. Until that moment she'd been more relaxed than George ever remembered seeing her, so relaxed that she'd betrayed herself. Now, she began carefully folding the blanket into precise accordion pleats with her trembling hands.

"I really couldn't," she murmured, "but thank you, thank you for everything, for the flowers, everything. Thank you for coming."

"What's the matter, Agnes?"

"I'm just so tired all of a sudden."

Her words were intended to be a dismissal and George took the hint. She left with a wave and a smile. Outside her door, George jotted a few notes in her book, including Agnes's bizarre reaction to the invitation to stay in George's house and her remarks about the Hoagsworths. She paused, watching the nearly deserted nurses' station. Only a young woman manned the area, and her look of frustration coupled with her feverish search of the desk indicated that she was new and inexperienced.

A slow smile spread across George's face, but she replaced it with what she hoped was a look of intense concern. Adam's freedom might depend on her performance. She forced the consequences from her mind. "Nurse," she called as she approached the station. The poor girl spun around and accidentally overturned a tumbler full of ink pens. While the hapless girl gathered them up, George spied the charts and squinted to make out the names and room numbers.

The girl righted herself and swept her bangs out of her face. "How can I help you?" she asked haltingly as though unsure if she could.

"I was visiting a friend on this floor, and when I came out I passed this poor man wandering down the hallway with this glazed look on his face. I mean he didn't even see me! I'm certain he was delirious."

"Was he a patient?"

Gad, George thought, is this girl thick. "I'm certain he was. He had one of your gowns on, the ones that gape in back. I noticed that fact as he was walking away from me. Also, that he was barefooted. You can't possibly miss him. He looks just like Mel Gibson, and I mean even right down to the er . . . well." George stretched toward the stunned woman and raised her eyebrows. "Did you ever see *Lethal Weapon?*"

"Which way?" the girl stammered.

George pointed and the girl ran, a flash of white. The second she disappeared around a corner, George swept behind the desk, yanked Agnes's chart from a circular file, and stuffed it underneath her coat. Just as she rounded the desk hugging her prize, a cool voice on the intercom announced "Code Blue, room four-oh-eight." The words echoed in the empty hallway, but George knew enough from being a high school volunteer at the Catholic hospital to know that it wouldn't stay that way.

Her heart thundering in her chest, she hugged the chart and told herself to calmly walk toward the stairwell. The fifteen feet to freedom yawned ahead as formidable as a desert mile. Two nurses rushed toward her followed by an orderly. She forced herself to smile at them. They passed, ignoring her.

She halted in front of the door to the stairs, pressing the chart against her abdomen. Her palm slipped against the plastic folder as she tried to work the heavy doorknob. She needed two hands.

Wheels and shoes rumbled against linoleum, the sound coming closer.

Bracing the chart with the backs of her elbows, she put both hands on the knob, twisted and pulled. She wrestled the door ajar. The binder slipped free and landed upright on her feet in plain view, its markings unmistakable.

Before she could react, a cart propelled by running white-clad people rounded the corner, heading right toward her. She was trapped. For an instant, she hesitated, blood beating in her temples. Then she squatted, fanning the bottom of her coat, desperately trying to cover the bright chart like a hen does an egg.

The cart speeded by in a blur of flapping lab coats. No one even glanced her way.

Alone again in the hallway, she eased the chart up under her sweater, wincing as the cold plastic contacted her bare skin. She jumped up, pried the door open and ran down three flights to the ladies' room. In the last stall she read every letter of every entry that had M.D. signed at the bottom. She was able to understand that Agnes had been poisoned, experienced convulsions and unconsciousness. George copied the diagnosis. When she finished, she polished the plastic with a tissue, shoved the corner of the chart back into her waistband, and buttoned her coat. After she'd hiked the three flights upstairs, she rested in the stairwell until the burning in her chest subsided.

In the hallway, she peered around the corner at the nurses' station. Three new nurses milled behind the desk, their movements relaxed and efficient. George paused, biting her lip, considering her options. She needed to either replace the chart or leave it in a location where a nurse or doctor might have logically abandoned it. Otherwise, questions might be asked, suspicions raised. Some innocent person might even draw the blame.

After a moment, she crept the other way toward Agnes's room. She tiptoed in without knocking.

"Why did you come back?"

George started, dislodging the chart from her waistband and sending it slithering down her thighs. She doubled over, frantically grabbing for the chart, knowing she couldn't stop it in time.

The chart snagged on the hem of her skirt. She released a shuddering breath as her fingers closed around the illusive binder. "Ohhhhh," she moaned, trying to inch the slippery plastic up her pantyhose, hoping to work it up far enough for her to walk. "I have terrible cramps. Can I use your bathroom?"

"Why of course, dear. Do you want me to call a nurse for you?"

"No! No, thank you." Still bent, she edged her way toward the bathroom. "I'll only be a minute." She closed the door, waited, then flushed the toilet. She departed with a smile for Agnes, leaving the chart behind on the sink.

Chapter
16

"Stop here," George instructed the taxi driver. The man obediently glided the Chevrolet to a halt in front of Fiona's house without breaking his monologue about wanting to write a novel.

"Just do it then," she advised, counting out ten dollars. "Wondering what might have been is far worse than failing. The truth is that I don't know how to do half the things I set out to do so occasionally I make big mistakes," she said, thinking of Adam and Harry's teeth, "but that doesn't mean I'd ever consider giving up."

She collected the huge stack of library books, bounded from the taxi, and after a thumbs-up gesture scurried up Fiona's walkway.

Sadness overcame her immediately. Evening shadows bathed the stark trees and quiet houses of Scarlet Street. Even the birds had deserted the trees. A chilly silence hung like smoke in the stillness.

Halloween loomed two weeks away, but she could easily imagine restless spirits already hovering nearby, waiting for their chance to roam through the midnight darkness.

Shivering, George negotiated the irregular stepping-stones forming the trail to Adam's doorstep. Only the regular *chip, chip* of her heels against the slate stones broke the enveloping silence. Clutching the heavy books, she increased her pace, somehow certain that a pair of eyes followed her progress through the gloom.

Her gaze darted over concealing shrubbery, shadowy corners, and dark windows, each appearing empty, each potentially deceptive. Even her own house appeared different, suddenly forbidding. One mention of staying in it had terrified Agnes. Why?

Relief flooded her at the sight of the light escaping around the drawn curtains in Adam's window. She bumped her hip against his door, praying for the first good news of this horrible day, that Adam was home, and safe, and wanting to see her. God answered her prayer in triplicate.

Adam pulled her inside and hugged her, books and all. After a long, satisfying moment of closeness, he freed the books from her arms, put them aside, and snuggled her to him. Her body found the right-at-home places against him, her arms draped over his waist, her head beneath his chin, her cheek against his chest, her soft hips against his hardness, welcoming him.

Without a word, he took her to his bed and removed her clothes. He made love to her with the tenderness of a man who saved dandelions and doves and ultimately possessed her with the fierce determination of a man who relentlessly pursued life.

Lying on her side, her dew-covered body still joined with his, she raised her eyes to study his face. "Was I right to stay away from the police station today? I felt responsible because of the teeth, and I was so afraid that I would say something to make things worse. Marvin and Fiona stopped me. Marvin said he would send a fantastic attorney; did the man help you?"

His fingers framed her face. "Yes—on three counts. I'm glad you weren't there; the press was. The entire scene was a circus."

"You look so tired."

"I am." His hand glided down her arm. "But I am worried about you. How did your conversation go with your father?"

She traced the straight bone beneath his neck with the pad of her finger. "I'd rather not talk about that now." She hoped he would leave it at that, and he did, breathing evenly, sound asleep.

Adam was perfect, everything she wanted, everything her father wanted. Living with him, being with him all the time, seemed like a perfect idea. Maybe someday he might even fall in love with her.

Of course, if she somehow got Adam to marry her that would stop her father's harassment on that topic. But there were major problems with that. In the first place, they hardly knew each other and such haste would be unseemly. Also Adam had never even mentioned love, much less marriage, in any circumstance any time she could recall in the past few days. *That* she certainly would have remembered. Worse still, the last book she'd read on men warned that older bachelors "were tough nuts to crack" which seemed crude in literal practice but probably quite true in context.

Also, her father might not like the fact that Adam was a murder suspect. Actually it was Adam's determination to stay out of business and finance that posed the real dilemma where her father was concerned. He was not above psychologically torturing anyone who defied him, and she certainly hated the thought of seeing Adam miserable.

As far as she was concerned, Adam's stuffed-shirtedness was still a minor drawback, though the skateboard and his desire to change were good signs.

All she really wanted was to learn more about Adam because the more she learned, the more she seemed to fall in love with him, and so far the experience had been extraordinarily wonderful.

Still, she did possess an unfortunate tendency to rush into situations she knew virtually nothing about. This love was no exception; she'd only felt something like it years before.

Now, suddenly, she was plunging into a maelstrom of deep, confusing emotions with the bravado of a cliff diver.

Why she'd vowed for years never to fall in love! The stakes were simply too high, the potential for hurt too great.

Her mind raged but her heart, dormant for so long, quickly silenced all protests. She huddled against Adam, absorbing the sensations of him, the texture of his skin, the tickle of his breath, the male scent of his body. Her eyelids drooped, and her thoughts floated through a dreamlike valley, an idyllic, enchanted place free of ogres, money, and murder.

Refreshed from her nap, George nestled cross-legged in the center of Adam's bed, hugging a pillow. "That's when I snatched Agnes's chart from the nurses' station—but only for a few minutes."

"You what!" The rigid outline of Adam's muscles appeared in bronzed relief, flexing as he pulled his trim, naked body to a sitting position. He bent one knee. "You might have been caught."

"Huh?" she mumbled. She tore her attention away from his sleek torso, chiding herself to stick to business even if it wasn't nearly as exciting as the man whose bed she shared. "You see, when I interviewed her in the hospital, Agnes made a giant slip. Remember I told you what Dwight said, that forty-one years ago Marshall, Sr. was seducing women right and left and that caused his wife, Ina, to go over the edge? Agnes said she understood *exactly* what Ina had gone through. Not only that, Agnes used to visit the Hoagsworths but stopped. It was too painful because she was still trying to bury her *own* memories. What if Marshall, Sr. seduced Agnes then cheated on her just like he did on his own wife?"

"You're suggesting that Agnes had an affair with Marshall, Sr., who then cheated on her, his mistress. That caused her to disguise herself as Marie Antoinette and eventually kill Marshall because she was jealous."

"Hard to believe, isn't it? Especially the part about thoroughly bewitching Dwight in less than fifteen minutes as Marie Antoinette. I guess we have to keep in mind how all that happened over forty years ago and he was in his twenties and very . . ." she trailed off delicately.

"Salacious."

"If you say so. Anyway, it seems odd that Dwight wouldn't have recognized her later. They were living right next door to each other at the time . . . but who knows? She was wearing a mask. Even so, I certainly can't imagine Agnes as a siren and certainly not a murderer which makes perfect sense. Dwight was there, and he's always believed Marie was innocent, still does."

She tossed her hands in the air in frustration. "Even after all the stuff about understanding Ina's pain, I still can't imagine Agnes killing Marshall, Sr. I can't even imagine her dancing in public! Not only that, it seems like the police would have questioned Agnes at the time, and my experience with her proves that she has problems in the keeping secrets department. Even she admits to that weakness, and I think she would have collapsed under any sort of intense investigation, don't you?"

Adam draped an arm over his bent knee and flipped his hand. "It seems to me that while interesting, the events of forty-one years ago have no bearing on Harry's death. Harry didn't even live here at the time."

"That's true. Agnes said he moved to Scarlet Street twenty-five years ago. Still . . ."

"That makes sense," Adam interrupted cryptically. "Now go back to the chart. What prompted you to take it?"

"Two other things Agnes said really stood out. She mentioned all the medicines the hospital forced on her, how she'd never taken a laxative until then. Anyway, Agnes has a huge herb garden, and I got to wondering when she mentioned hyacinths being poisonous that maybe that was a clue. It seemed too offhanded a remark for someone who'd only just been poisoned so I got her chart and guess what?"

"It was a clue," he said, reaching for one of her hands.

She squeezed his hand then set it firmly back on his knee. "I'd really love to hold hands with you and explain this, but it's just like kissing. I can't do both well at the same time."

"Go on," he said, his understanding tone suspiciously verging on laughter.

"Anyway, I copied down the diagnosis which was convulsions and unconsciousness. It took them a while to figure out what caused it. They sent specimens all over the place to all these experts who did all sorts of tests. Anyway, they finally decided she was poisoned by tansy. Well, I called Dr. Pelton ship to shore, and he said that he was old enough to know what I was talking about."

"Dr. Pelton, the fake ichthyologist, who took out your tonsils when you were three years old." Adam rubbed his kneecap, his eyes narrowing. "Let me decipher this. You mean Pelton is old enough to know about tansy poisoning because it relates to the practice of medicine decades ago."

"Of course." Adam only grinned back, seeming to derive extreme pleasure from his deduction. At least he'd finally learned to keep up with the conversation. "He said that tansy is a plant and even though it's poisonous, people used it as an old folk remedy. That's when I went to the library."

George bounded off the bed and dashed to the stack of books. She grabbed the volume on poisoning and returned to his bed.

He watched her, his gray eyes glowing. The thunderheads were back in his eyes, complete with lightning. Other evidence of his arousal appeared as well. While she found his interest inordinately pleasing, she was determined to get through the clues. She plucked up a pillow and placed it gently between his legs hoping to reduce the temptation.

He didn't take her action lying down. He cast the pillow aside.

"Come here, Georgette."

She flipped to the correct page and began reading, "Oil of tansy . . ." and continued as he dragged her to his side and pulled her close. ". . . was used as a home remedy often in the form of tea to calm nerves . . ." Her breath caught as his fingers began a lazy exploration of her tummy. ". . . help feminine complaints, and induce abortion. Symptoms of overdose include spasms, convulsions, and unconsciousness." She slammed the book shut and began tapping it with her finger. "I think that Agnes poisoned herself."

"Why would she do that?"

"I don't know—not yet at least."

He traced the swell of her breast, circling inward to the nipple and teasing it to tingling life. "Let's talk about Agnes later," he said, his voice beguiling her with a huskiness that surely must be sinful.

She sighed, sliding down the sheets and opening her arms to him. "I'm beginning to wonder how Nick and Nora Charles ever solved a case."

When he whispered a throaty promise against her breast, she forgot to wonder about anything except how it was going to feel when he actually fulfilled it.

"Oil of tansy," he sighed, looking pained. "I believe you. Now, come back to bed."

George pulled on her red sweater and fluffed her hair with her fingers. "Adam, I'm only trying to clear you of murder. The least you could do is quit seducing me long enough to help."

With a growl, Adam hopped out of bed and pulled on his shorts. He dressed quickly, locked up, and escorted her home.

Mr. Moto welcomed them with licks and snorts and trailed them through the darkness, tail wagging, across the street to Agnes Clodfelter's herb garden.

Adam fanned the beam of the flashlight over the tightly packed plants while she plowed through the snarl of prickly leaves and thorny branches. She kneeled next to a likely-looking candidate.

"Do you realize what this means?" George asked, holding the herb book next to the plant for Adam to see. The deeply saw-toothed leaves matched the picture of tansy in the book—perfectly. "If Agnes poisoned herself, then someone *other* than the people at the party could have killed Harry. The murderer could be anyone Mr. Moto recognizes, including Ina and Marshall Hoagsworth or even a friend of

Harry's." She rose slowly, still clutching the book. "That doesn't make sense. Maybe Agnes poisoned herself because she killed Harry. Naturally, she'd try to divert suspicion from herself. Why else would she take such a risk?"

Adam clicked off the flashlight. "Let's take Mr. Moto for a walk. I think it's time you understood why the police suspect me of Hangtown Harry's murder."

Chapter
17

"I can see that you haven't read the evening edition of the newspaper," Adam began.

George's hand felt warm and snug nestled in his as they meandered down Scarlet Street, but her stomach churned in anticipation. She sensed from the weariness in Adam's tone that the news was bad. Then again, wasn't it usually if it came from the press?

She matched his strides two for one as they meandered down the deserted sidewalk toward the Hoagsworth mansion following the prancing Mr. Moto. "I was in the library this afternoon for what seemed like hours. But I don't take a paper anyway; they're too depressing."

"Today saw a new wrinkle added to the murder case. Apparently when they did the autopsy on Harry they fingerprinted him. I suppose that's routine in these sorts of situations. From the prints they discovered that Harry wasn't really Harry Frye, but Arthur Mossbeck, a con artist with an extensive record of arrests who dropped out of sight to avoid imprisonment twenty-five years ago."

"Really?" she gasped. "Oh, goodness, Agnes was right.

Harry was a fraud. Agnes might be right about everything, that Harry really did marry the Reed woman for her money and probably as a cover too. That was exactly the time he changed his identity." George squinted at the darkness, her mind clicking. "My father always says that people never really change. Mercy, he ought to know. Anyway that probably means that Harry was only masquerading as a sweet old insane person. But why?" Her steps lightened; she bounced on her toes. This news wasn't bad after all.

"I know!" She danced in front of Adam then backpaddled. "A vendetta, that's it! Harry was afraid that someone would recognize him as being Arthur and someone did. That person wanted revenge, to punish Harry for bilking somebody a long time ago, but Harry, still thinking like a con artist, tried to convince that person that he was crazy. Finally, the murderer saw through Harry's scheme and murdered him. How does that sound?"

Adam slowly shook his head.

She stopped in the middle of the sidewalk, arms akimbo. "I don't understand, Adam. Didn't the police question you after they knew Harry was really Arthur?"

"Oh, yes, they knew."

"Then how does that revelation about Harry's past make you a stronger suspect than you were already? It seems to me that it would only broaden the possibilities to all sorts of people. You don't even have a motive!"

Adam's face grew somber. He seemed to focus on something in the distance, perhaps the meager glow of the lone street lamp. "Unfortunately, the police don't see it that way. If you'll recall, I told you that I did meet Harry two years ago through my work at the bank. Harry came to me with an idea about setting up a memorial foundation for Emperor Norton. I succeeded in talking him out of it. We had a couple of meetings; end of story as far as I was concerned. The police, however, view the incident as the hatching of a conspiratorial partnership."

Adam caught her hand again and resumed walking. "You probably realize that Pacific West Bank and Trust is by far the largest, most prestigious bank in northern California and is preferred by many San Franciscans. But what's not common knowledge is that the bank is particularly popular among older depositors who tend to leave large savings accounts untouched for extended periods. Today when I was being questioned, the police implied that certain irregularities have been discovered at the bank.

"As soon as I was released, I called an old friend at the bank's computer center and learned from her that some accounts have been tampered with. At present Lois doesn't know who or how, but she'd heard gossip that those large, inactive accounts I mentioned were targeted—possibly drained of funds. She promised to get back to me soon, hopefully by tomorrow, and provide me with more detailed information. Lois is the best there is, honest and hardworking to a fault. It's gratifying to know she believes in my innocence."

Adam wore a weary expression, and it hurt her to see him so morose. "That's the whole point. Why would anyone automatically assume that you're the one involved? Harry must have met other people at the bank."

"According to the attorney, the bottom line is this. The police suspect that Harry and I somehow collaborated in a scheme to raid large bank accounts, that I then quit and managed adroitly to hide the proceeds from the embezzlement—at least for the time being. They further contend that Harry and I had some sort of disagreement, that I moved to Scarlet Street intent on blackmailing him, harassing him, or some such thing, and eventually killed him."

"Wow," George breathed. "So those coincidences may be what they used to get a search warrant. But they don't have one single shred of hard evidence, do they?"

"If they do, they aren't saying. The attorney guessed that they probably lack adequate evidence to charge me. But my abrupt resignation from the bank coupled with my move to Scarlet Street are viewed by the police as telling actions. Still, I can't honestly believe that they can make a case against me."

"That's because you're a logical person. It's natural that you'd forget that law and logic have virtually nothing in common. What about the teeth; how do they fit in?"

"You were correct. They were Harry's, and the police withheld that fact from the press to trip up any phony confessors to the crime. The attorney implied that device is standard practice. The detectives were not amused when I told them that the dog had buried them. They appeared unconvinced of my honesty, at least until the laboratory detected traces of leaf mold."

"I would have told them!" She stopped and tugged on his arm, coaxing him to turn and face her. He obliged her, adding a wan smile. He still looked tired. "I bet that you didn't mention my name, did you? Even when you knew that I would have confirmed your story and gotten you released sooner. I bet you said you found the teeth."

He canted his head. "I did find them. I just omitted where and when. There was no point in involving you."

What a special man he is, she thought, also an honest and strong one too. Perhaps he was truly growing to care for her. A warm glow settled around her heart. "Adam, chivalry went out with capes and tricorn hats. I happen to know that for a fact because I have a friend who runs a costume business on the side. Marfa can't rent Sir Walter Raleigh these days. Men even refuse to pretend to be that way."

"Then I guess that makes me old-fashioned in some ways," he said, leading her up the walkway toward her front porch.

She swiped at the pavement, scuffing the sole of her shoe. Why couldn't he be just a heartless fortune hunter like all the rest? She could find a way to overlook that in Adam yet still have the certainty and security of understanding him. Their relationship would be so simple, manageable, and straightforward that way. But, damn him, he was different and he was making her do something she'd promised herself since Michael to never do again. Adam was making her fall more and more in love with him.

"You're a stuffed shirt, and you're not my type—" She

stopped, her voice breaking. "I'm sorry. I know I promised not to say that but—"

She swallowed hard, hoping to somehow stem her fear. At the porch step, she whirled to confront him. "I'm going to save you. I promised to help you find *joie de vivre*," she murmured, then ducked her face, self-conscious over massacring the French expression. "I said I'd help the best way I know how, and I will, no matter what."

"In that case," he said mildly, "I release you from your obligation." He paused, then turned and strode away.

"Whaaaat?" She snapped her mouth shut and darted after him. When she caught up, she tugged on the sleeve of his tweed jacket, jogging alongside him to keep up. "What do you mean, release me?"

"Just that," he stated. "I release you. I'm confident that it is the right thing to do."

"I won't let you," she blared, suddenly perturbed at his cavalier attitude. "Here I am trying to help you and all you can do is say, 'I release you.'"

He halted. He gripped both her arms and leaned close to her face. "Georgette, your father doesn't want you involved in this any more than I do."

"How do you know?"

He cast a glance heavenward as though seeking divine guidance. "The man detests publicity; it's common knowledge."

"Yes, but—"

"But nothing." His hand still gripping her right arm, he began walking back toward the porch, dragging her along like a sack of flour. "What did your father tell you today? He ordered you to keep out of this. He told you to go away, move, get out of here."

"How?" she blurted, stunned by his perception.

"Those are the smart options, and your father is a smart man. This situation doesn't only reflect badly on your father, your involvement will reflect badly on your own business and most importantly on you. I know about the lawsuit Watson is planning to file against you. Jack Smith mentioned you in an interview today. The stakes are increasing. More and more people will gain or lose according to the outcome of this investigation. If that wasn't dangerous enough, just think what those gossipmongers— especially Watson—would print about you if they knew about our relationship. For God's sake, I'm a murder suspect! If Watson knew, he would crucify you in that rag he works for."

When they reached her porch, he guided her in front of him. Lines of strain marked his brow. "Today at the police station I realized how much these scandals are escalating."

The sadness she read in his eyes terrified her. In a low, strained tone, he said, "We have to stop seeing each other."

Pain, hurt, and confusion reeled through her mind and seemed to swirl through her like a brutal arctic wind. Adam leave? Now that she cared deeply for him? She would be alone again only hurting more than she'd ever hurt in her life. Suddenly she shook, freezing, her fingers icy, involuntary tremors rocking her body. Her teeth clattered so hard, she couldn't speak.

Adam wrapped her in his arms. She buried her face beneath his coat, willing herself not to cry at the sheer comfort of his embrace, the beauty of his scent, the hard textures of his body.

She searched her mind for a way, any way to stop the inevitable. He was right, that was the horror of it. As things stood, they could never be together.

But she refused to be sorry that she loved him.

I'll make him change his mind, she thought. I'll find Harry's murderer. Then Adam can go back to business to what he did so successfully. He doesn't have to be a gardener. Once he loves me too, he'll change his mind. He could work for my father for just a little while.

Dear heaven, she had less than forty-eight hours before her father would try to force her to go to Baja. Maybe if Adam knew about her father's threat, she could convince him to delay breaking off their relationship. Then she could use the two days and nights to make Adam fall in love with her. Risky and unlikely, but what alternative did she have?

"Adam," she said slowly, carefully choosing her words in advance. She knew he could hear her; she felt the answering movement of his chest. "My father insists that I leave day after tomorrow for a resort in Baja." She waited for a response and received one. His hold on her tightened. "What I do between now and then doesn't really matter. I can't make my father any angrier than he already is, and I don't care what they print about me. All the gossip only helps Shannon's and my business. Last time I was sued, our clients doubled." She took in a deep, steadying gulp of air. "Anyway, what I'm trying to say is, I may be able to figure out some way to deal with my father. Since you insist that we stop seeing each other anyway, couldn't we at least share the little bit of time left until I have to confront him?"

His hand found her chin and tipped it up. Though she was unsure that her question had made complete sense, Adam answered with a kiss.

When Adam's breathing became slow and even, George gently raised his arm and slipped out of her bed. She glanced at her bedside table to check the time. The digits read 11:35 P.M., leaving her barely enough time to carry out her plan.

She realized her scheme to smoke out the murderer was potentially dangerous. But she was desperate. She had to help Adam.

A few well-placed prods roused Mr. Moto. She lifted Adam's arm, and the furry beast crawled beneath it and collapsed with a sigh of sheer contentment. Tonight Adam had used his last moment of wakefulness to whisper that her warmth ensured his peaceful sleep. She lowered Adam's arm, hopeful Mr. Moto could pinch-hit for her for the next hour or so.

She crept into her closet and pulled on black slacks, a painted sweatshirt with rhinestones, and the tennis shoes that matched it. After one last look at Adam, she tiptoed past her sleeping lover and dashed downstairs.

Buttoning her coat, she mustered her determination. Outside, she dragged in a deep, steadying breath of chilly air then dashed toward the forbidding countenance of the Hoagsworth mansion.

Chapter
18

George hesitated, concealed behind a tree trunk in front of Hangtown Harry's house. She tugged the collar of her coat up over her throat to block out the midnight cold. A sudden queasiness gripped her stomach. Fear, she supposed, and dismissed it.

She stretched around the mammoth oak, straining to make out her destination. The Hoagsworth mansion presided stiffly over the head of the street, a monument of decayed elegance. Stains trailed from the corners of the pediments, streaking the gray stucco with tracks that resembled black tears. Every window appeared to have cried, while above, along the stringcourse, a row of grotesque, hysterically countenanced gargoyles laughed from their perches.

Dim light filtered through three of the curtained windows. She scoured her memory for the exact words Fiona had used to describe the partitioning inside the house. George worried her lower lip, trying to concentrate on their conversation on the way to the funeral. Nothing jumped out at her.

She scanned the facade of the house, searching for some

sign of remodeling. Spotting nothing, she came to the unsettling conclusion that the only way to locate Estelle's apartment was to explore the exterior of the grim house.

The damp coolness had worked its way into her shoes. Shivering, she wiggled her toes, reminding herself of all the reasons she must enter that house and talk to Estelle. Four came to mind, Adam, Fiona, Marvin, and Adam. As much as she liked Fiona and Marvin and disliked favoritism of any kind, she had to count Adam twice because she loved him.

Figuring that the lone front door was an unlikely candidate for Estelle's entrance, she dashed along the driveway that banked the side of the mansion, sticking close to the hedges. At the rear of the house, she caught her bearings using Elmo Burroughs's cottage. Voices hummed from the tiny house. The bluish-gray luminescence flickering in the window said the chatter came from a television, but she pushed herself to her tiptoes and raised her eyes over the sill to make sure.

Elmo, his arms splayed over the arms of a stained recliner, snored peacefully to a rap music video. Against her nose, the windowpane pulsed to the beat. Elmo was either deaf or dead drunk.

She sank her heels to the ground and darted up a staircase and across a tiled terrace that backed the entire mansion. The rear of the house appeared as unkempt as the front; dirt, leaves, and pine needles littered the dull tiles. Locating French doors, she pulled the flashlight from her pocket. Arching her hand, she used it as a shield hoping to block the beam from escaping to the upstairs windows. She clicked the switch and played the light over the door and moldings. Finding no markings, she turned it off.

A rustling noise sounded behind her. She whirled, her heart pounding. A gust of wind lifted the dry leaves and sent them swirling and crackling over the deserted terrace.

She rubbed her numb hands together and tried to convince herself that the noise she had heard before was only wind and dead leaves. She wanted to run away, hide in

Adam's arms, and ignore the danger to him until it simply blew away in the fall wind.

Instead, she forced herself to turn and face the Hoagsworth mansion.

Using the cold stucco wall as a guide, she groped her way through the darkness to the next set of doors, then on to the next. When she flipped the switch the fourth time, she tugged her lips back in a triumphant smile. A shiny plate read Estelle Capricorn. Centered beneath her name were the words: *Medium, Astrologer, Gold Bought and Sold.*

George pressed the buzzer and flicked off the flashlight, thinking that Estelle's dead spirits must be bearish or they wouldn't be advising her to tie up her assets in gold. She supposed it made sense in a way; being dead might make it difficult to be optimistic about anything, including the stock market.

"Who's there?" asked a shaky voice from the other side of the door.

"Georgette Richards."

A hand pulled aside the curtain gathered top and bottom on the French door. Estelle Capricorn's eyes appeared in the narrow opening. They looked wild, frightened.

Estelle admitted her with a nervous glance over George's shoulder. She hastily shut the door as though fearful an evil spirit might sneak through. "What do you want?" she asked, dragging trembling fingers over her sheep-kinked mane of curls.

"I need to talk to you."

"My broadcast—"

"I only need a few minutes of your time, I promise. And I will make it profitable."

Estelle fidgeted with an uncut crystal she carried in her hand and finally said, "This way."

She motioned George into a parlor that mixed fussy period furniture with unusual modernistic paintings. Some of the oils were striking blends of stark geometric shapes with colorful backgrounds, probably designed to be rife with symbolism. George sank into a chair opposite a rendering of a pyramid with outstretched wings fastened to its slopes. "Your art collection is intriguing," she said, meaning it.

"They explore metaphysical themes," Estelle responded in a chilly tone. "Do you care to change your opinion of them now?"

"Why should I?"

Estelle smiled in a calculating manner, revealing capped teeth. Could she and Harry have been lovers, George wondered? No, she thought, watching Estelle sweep into a wooden chair, her high-slit caftan settling around her in a ripple of aqua. Estelle preferred younger men, like Adam.

"When we first met, I immediately sensed your antagonism. Within minutes you called me a witch. Then you telephoned my show and accused me of being a vulture heartless enough to profit from Harry's death."

"Well, aren't you?" George asked, unable to help herself. Attacking Estelle's motives was not the way to win her cooperation, but damn, how she detested hypocrisy. "You promoted a package of séances, Mastercard and Visa accepted, right after dropping in all that lost soul business, the fascinating energy of the neighborhood, and sudden death, and you started the whole thing off with Harry's murder. What else would you call that kind of exploitation?"

She folded her hands. "My making a little money on innocent readings or séances will not harm Harry or his memory—or anyone else for that matter. I need to make a living, Miss Richards. Ruthless men made yours for you. You're in no position to judge me."

"Of course not. According to the Bible nobody is. Still, I don't pretend to be anything but what I am."

"Implying that I do. Consider this. If I were telling people they carried curses that I could remove for ten thousand dollars, I wouldn't have to work so hard to make ends meet, would I? I've never pressured anyone into coming back to me. My clients are pleased with the services I provide or they don't return. It's as simple as that. I give them what they want or need, and I wouldn't manipulate them to earn as much as a million or as little as a dollar. You've mistaken salesmanship for unethical behavior."

She lolled back in her chair, obviously satisfied that she had seized control of the conversation. Her smugness was infuriating. Thinking of Adam, George held back a retort. Whoever said that love didn't involve sacrifice was bluffing.

"My mother is virtually blind from cataract surgery she didn't need," Estelle said in a bitter tone. "The butcher who did it circulates brochures offering free limousine service to and from his office, free examinations, free surgery, free postoperative care for Medicare patients. On the day he ruined my mother's eyesight forever, he did over fifty operations. A review board recommended that his license to practice be revoked, but his peers gave him three years of probation." She spread her hands, palms-up. "Such outrages occur in every area of endeavor. Pick any profession and I'll show you rape, victimization, and callousness. But my profession, because of its mystical nature, is often targeted for ridicule."

George received the distinct impression that Estelle had dropped into an oft-repeated monologue, one that wasn't half bad either. It reminded her of the moving stories that politicians narrate to the strains of soft music and the laughter of children, one of those thirty-second-sound-bite minimelodramas that sometimes left her with the uneasy feeling that she was being manipulated. She wondered that same thing now.

George's jaw ached from being held closed. She hoped for speedy deliverance.

"We are all performers, Miss Richards, you, me, everyone. We all have a public face because we all have things to hide, whether they be innocent flaws and insecurities or things that are far more wicked. We are all performers, varying only in degree."

George released a huge breath and flexed weary muscles. She'd finally found something regarding Estelle's own self-promotion campaign that she could safely agree with. "Maybe that's so. Philosophy always put me to sleep, but I do remember hearing the saying that 'all the world is a stage.' I guess that's probably the same thing you're saying.

Anyway, that's all very interesting but that's not why I came. What do you think of Fiona?"

"She's a snooty woman with a very big mouth."

"Marvin Breathwaite?" she asked in a hopeful tone.

"Exactly like his mother, only better at hiding it."

George resettled herself in her chair. She was quickly exhausting her list of plausible reasons to beg for Estelle's help. "How about Adam Lawrence?"

"The gardener? He's a handsome man who appears out of place. He seems cultured, erudite. Why do you ask?"

"The police questioned him today. They suspect him of murdering Harry."

"That's odd that they would consider him."

"Why?"

"I don't think they even knew each other."

"Are you sure?"

"Not long after I first saw Adam Lawrence working on Fiona's yard, I happened to visit Harry." Estelle fixed George with a "just between us girls" look, her implication as clear as the outline of Adam's magnificent body. She'd likely spotted Adam and his biceps in Fiona's yard then rushed over to Harry's to get the skinny on the new hunk on the block. George couldn't fault her for that; she had been planning her own reconnaissance mission to Fiona's house.

"I asked Harry about the new gardener, and he said he hadn't noticed him. Harry seemed preoccupied that morning . . ." Estelle trailed off, absently fingering the crystal.

"The morning preceding Harry's murder?"

Estelle rubbed the stone like businessmen play with ink pens and women twirl their hair. "Yes, it was. I hadn't really thought about it before. It was very unlike him to be nervous, yet he was. He was out poking around his yard. He said he believed that his dog had stolen his dentures and hidden them outside. I remember asking Harry if he felt sick; he looked pale. He sort of laughed and said that it was nothing a little . . . what did he say? Oh, yes. He said nothing menudo wouldn't fix, whatever that meant. That seemed to make him think of something, and then he actually turned ashen."

"How do you say that word again?"

"Oh, it was something like men-new-doe or men-you-doe. I really can't remember. Anyway, that was the last time I saw him."

Menudo, she recalled suddenly, was Mexican tripe soup. No wonder Harry had turned ashen. She cocked her head and studied Estelle. "Do you believe that Harry had your gift and could really talk with spirits like Emperor Norton?"

Estelle rolled the crystal between her steepled hands. George found herself fascinated by the progression in the manner that Estelle had handled the stone, first aimlessly, then thoughtfully, finally purposefully. Her change in mood mirrored that progression exactly.

"I sensed that Harry had a talent for gauging the frailties and weakness of living souls far better than he empathized with dead ones. You see, the dead have no worldly possessions."

Estelle's eyelids sagged. Several minutes passed before she spoke again. "I sense that you have very strong feelings for Adam Lawrence and that you truly want to help him. Time is short and your motives are pure. The answer is yes, I will help you."

George scooted forward in her chair, clutching the arms. Estelle had virtually read her mind.

Estelle raised her head. The serenity she projected seemed to smooth her features, making them almost beautiful. "What is this thing that you want me to say tonight on my radio show?"

At the door, George thanked Estelle for her help and the marvelous herb tea that had completely removed the chill from her body. "I want to pay you for your time."

"I get one hundred dollars per hour for consultations."

George handed her a crisp bill. "What do you think about Agnes Clodfelter?"

"I don't think of her at all. I hardly know the biddy."

George decided to try the same ploy on Estelle that had worked with Agnes. "I really haven't met the Hoagsworths, but I was thinking of baking them a cake—"

"Don't," Estelle snapped, her eyes turning haunted again. "Just leave them alone. Stay away from them. Go home and stay there." With that, Estelle virtually shoved her out the door and slammed it shut.

George stared a moment into the darkness, allowing her eyes to adjust and trying to make sense out of another confusing conversation. Everybody on Scarlet Street spoke in riddles. Everybody had something to hide. Fiona was trying to protect Marvin, Agnes herself, Dwight a memory, and Estelle, who knew what? The Hoagsworths might as well have a moat around them, as inaccessible as they were. She made a mental note to quiz Elmo if she could ever find him sober, then Natasha and Joan LaRose.

She could hardly wait to see how everyone reacted to the message Estelle promised to relay to her listeners tonight. Of course her father was going to be furious, Adam stunned. But maybe the publicity would help the truth to surface.

Snuggling more deeply into her coat, she began her lonely trek back to her house, her bed, and Adam's arms. Her tennis shoes squeaked against the dew-glazed tiles. The wind had died, the night now still and silent and very dark. Even the stars had disappeared. She gave fleeting consideration to using the flashlight but decided instead to trail her hand against the side of the house to keep her bearings. No use in drawing attention to her presence.

She drew her first easy breath as her hand touched the panes of the fourth French door, knowing she was only a few steps away from the staircase and freedom from the omnipresent gloom of the Hoagsworth mansion. She dipped into her pocket for the flashlight, and plowed into a wall. A human wall.

Chapter
19

George recoiled and froze, her body inches from the looming hulk. Its hand pressed down on her head. Shock drained her mind of thought; the sudden void paralyzed her.

She smelled him, a sweaty, sticky-sweet odor that raised bile in her throat. The giant breathed in harsh, throaty rasps, sending moist wind eddying over her face. His hand slipped into her hair, grabbed and twisted, and jerked her head back.

Marshall Hoagsworth's eyes flamed like brilliant coals. A medieval-type metal helmet crowned his head, meshlike fabric framed his hard, angular face. A gruesome smile twisted his mouth. "It's no use to struggle," he spat, glowering insanely. "Your fate is in my hands now."

His words slithered up her spine like a clammy snake. He raised his arm, and she caught sight of the sword, heavy, double-edged, deadly. Her eyes flew wide. Openmouthed, unable to breathe, she plunged into an abyss of terror.

"Ruthless enemies! Did they tell you I was incapable of killing a woman? Fools!"

He lifted her by her hair, transforming her scalp into a cap of agony. Her hands flew to his massive hand, clawed at it. Her nails tore at his flesh, but he only raised her higher until all but the tips of her toes lost contact with the ground.

She heard screams. She swung her leg, kicking for his groin. Her head was on fire.

"Cease your struggling or I kill you now!" He hefted the sword to reinforce his threat.

She tried to force her body to go slack. Sobs gurgled in her throat.

"Thought you could breach my security, did you? Compromise my men? Tempt them? But I saw you. I know your kind. I'll show you and the evil ones who sent you how I deal with harlot spies."

"Brave warrior, I plead for your favor." Through the haze of pain she saw Elmo Burroughs drop to his knees at their feet.

"Speak, man," Hoagsworth growled.

Mercifully, his hold on her loosened. The soles of her shoes reached the ground. Her eyes watered from the pain.

Elmo scurried to his feet. "She is only a messenger, sent from your own scouts in the field to warn you of impending attack. It's time to prepare for battle. There isn't much time."

"Are you certain of this?"

"Positive. She is a loyal wife and mother."

Hoagsworth released her suddenly, pushing her away. She reeled into Elmo's outstretched arms.

"Then tell me, woman. Give me your message," Hoagsworth boomed.

Elmo's raspy voice whispered in her ear, "Say the baron is about to attack with three hundred men."

"The baron . . . he's going to . . ."

"Spit it out, woman!"

"She's weary from her journey," Elmo explained hurriedly. "Three hundred men," he prompted in a low tone, shaking her urgently.

"With three hundred men," she choked out.

"Brave warrior, they will be storming the fortress soon. You must go rally your men."

"I need to interrogate this woman further."

"There's no time now. She's fainted anyway."

"She's of the weak sex. You are right, old friend. Watch over her until the battle is over. Then I will deal with this woman."

She listened to his heavy footsteps as he retreated. When her reason returned, she found herself clinging to Elmo's spindly body as though her life depended on it. She shivered. A minute ago, it probably had.

"Can you walk?" he inquired.

"I . . . I think so." The pain in her head had lessened to a dull ache.

"Come this way." Elmo guided her down the stairs and tried to lead her toward his cottage.

"No," she protested, trying to pull away.

"He's watching." Elmo tilted his head over his shoulder. Her eyes followed his gesture to a downstairs window where Marshall, Jr. stood backlighted, dressed in full medieval garb, his arms behind his back, the outline of his sword clearly visible.

George looked at the wiry Elmo and back at the menacing form in the window. Elmo had saved her once; she really had no choice but to trust him anyway. With his long legs and athletic body, Marshall could catch her before she cleared the side of the house.

Reluctantly, she preceded Elmo into his unkempt little cottage. "You won't have to stay long," he assured. "In a few minutes he will have forgotten all about this."

He closed the door but left the deadbolt dangling. He flicked it and looked at her pointedly.

She swallowed the lump in her throat. Elmo was a perceptive man. After being totally dominated by Marshall Hoagsworth, Jr., Elmo obviously understood that any confinement might be frightening. Relieved, she collapsed in a wooden chair and cradled her aching head in her hands. "Do you have some aspirin?"

"Aspirin kicks up my ulcer. Tylenol okay?"

"Anything."

He returned, shook two tablets out of the bottle into her

hand and gave her a glass of cool water. She gobbled the pills and drained the glass. "Dear God," she breathed, closing her eyes. "I thought he was going to kill me." She opened a slit between her eyelids to watch his response.

"Aw, no." Elmo said, skittering around the room gathering up the empty glasses that littered the cigarette-scarred furniture. "He wouldn't have harmed you. He just gets a bit touchy when people come around at night, if he's in that type of mood, you understand."

"No, I don't. Not at all. He's dangerous. First, he nearly pulled my hair out, then he threatened me with a sword. Good grief, he as much as said that he planned to kill me."

Elmo flicked crumbs off an end table. They fell on a matted shag rug. "Games, you understand, always playing games. He's touched, but harmless. He never even breaks so much as a wooden soldier." Elmo disappeared into the kitchen with two handfuls of glasses. "You have to remember he's always been a bit afraid of women, never having been around them. Doesn't quite know how to treat a lady."

"That would have made a quaint inscription on my tombstone," George muttered, massaging her scalp searching for loose hanks of hair. No wonder Estelle had appeared frightened earlier this evening. She only had a flimsy wall separating her from a madman. At least Estelle wore a wig.

When Elmo returned from the kitchen, he asked, "What were you doing out behind the old manse this time of night?"

"I was leaving Estelle's apartment."

"Seems kind of late for a social call," he said, tipping a bottle of Old Granddad over a water glass. When it was half full of the brown liquor, he waved the mouth of the bottle in her direction.

"No, thank you." She decided to make a stab at diverting the conversation. "Estelle is terrified of Marshall, Jr. too."

"Like I say it's only because he's never had a regular girlfriend. 'Course I think it grates on her nerves Marsh calling her the mistress of Satan. He could stand to be more open-minded."

Elmo kicked back in his recliner and sipped his drink. "'Course everybody has their own little faults."

George rolled her eyes. She guessed that tolerance was a necessity or Elmo couldn't have remained in the employ of the Hoagsworths. She regarded the wiry man with growing interest. He was so calm now compared to the day after Harry's murder. At Fiona's party, he'd been paranoid bordering on the hysterical, seemingly in terror that he would be the next victim. Why? And Dwight Phillips had been so attentive and sympathetic toward him that afternoon.

Elmo was a direct link to the past, to Marshall, Sr. especially. Could Dwight be mining Elmo for clues to the identity of Marshall's former mistress, the mysterious Marie Antoinette? And what, if anything, did a forty-one-year-old unsolved murder have to do with the bogus Hangtown Harry Frye?

Gad, the whole thing was more puzzling than a government form.

"You know," Elmo said, "if strangeness was a crime, every last person on the entire street would be under lock and key. There's not a normal one of them in the bunch, except me, and maybe you. Then again," he said, scanning her with his shrewd little eyes, "I don't know you all that well."

"I'm the most normal person I know," George replied indignantly. She figured she'd better keep this conversation brief; the extreme heat coupled with the sour odor of Elmo's cottage was making her stomach contort. "What do you mean when you say everyone on the street is strange? Fiona and Dwight seem normal enough, and Estelle is just a medium which isn't too uncommon."

Elmo held up a stilling hand. "Think what society would've done to them in past times. Estelle would have been a pile of ashes before she ever needed a face-lift. Dwight might've ended that way, too, for worshiping a statue. Folks certainly would've slapped Natasha in the pillory for spreading gossip, probably Agnes also. The rest of the lot probably would've been committed or"—he squinted at her—"or maybe even hanged for their sins."

Thinking of what Dwight had said about Elmo and Zeb's wife, she wondered how he could omit himself from the ranks of the sinners. Saints certainly didn't have sex with their employer's wives. "What sins?"

"Oh, one hears talk, you know. In the old days there used to be a lot of servants and they talked. I listened. Over the years I realized that generally your vices fall into two basic categories, whoring and thieving. Now every family on this street had big money which they generally made in the usual way. That's thieving. Once everyone got the big houses, the cars, the power, they got bored. That's when the whoring came in. Every man on this street was known to dip a wick away from home, if you know what I mean."

She did. "You mean that moral decay has been a long-standing tradition on this street."

"Oh, yeah." He slapped his knee and drained his glass. "The women too," he said, in a deeper voice. "I always thought that Reed girl got exactly what she deserved."

"Agnes did say Harry's wife died suspiciously."

"Agnes," he snorted. "That Reed girl choked on an egg roll. Tell me what's suspicious about that? Naw, I mean the Reed girl deserved to get stuck with Harry for a husband. Nymphomania, they said. Family always said that gal took it after a fall from a horse, but she was just plain heartless, a real ball—"

"I get the picture," she interrupted. "Why did you think she deserved Harry?"

"He married her for her money and kept misses on the side. Old Harry always had a real taste for the ladies. I remember the look on Harry's face when he saw me the day of the wedding. I thought he was going to drop—"

"I get the picture," she interrupted, "vividly."

"But I kept his secret. It didn't matter to me what he called himself. He fit right into the neighborhood, being good at both thieving and whoring."

"Then you knew all along that Harry was a fraud?"

"Oh, sure. He was a second-class grifter, good friend of

Marsh's father. I'm sure that's how Harry came up with the idea to hit up the Reed girl when he got into trouble with the law. Of course, Marshall was long dead by then. Harry probably figured no one would remember him, but I sure did, even though it was a rough night." His expression grew pinched and sad. "A rough night."

"Do you mean you met Harry the night Marshall Hoagsworth, Sr. was murdered?"

"Who told you about that?" he asked without apparent surprise. "Natasha, Agnes?"

"Dwight."

His long sigh ended with a series of hacking coughs. The redness of his cheeks intensified. He tilted Old Granddad and gulped straight from the bottle. "Sorry, my cough." He lounged back in his chair, patted his chest pocket, and shrugged. "I quit smoking over a year ago. Guess I'll give up hoping the cigarettes are still there one of these dammed days."

George barely heard him. Miraculously, she'd finally ordered the facts into a semblance of logic. "Was Dr. Emerson there that night too?"

"Oh, sure. Practically every man on the block was there, all the young ones at least. Emerson was young in those days; barely forty, I'd guess."

She felt like cheering! Not only was her headache virtually gone, but she had figured out why Elmo had been so frightened the day of Fiona's party. He'd said something about death marching down the block and how he was next. Now she saw the link. Emerson, Harry, and Elmo had all been present the night Marshall Hoagsworth, Sr. was murdered! Dwight knew that too, which likely accounted for his tactful handling of the situation. On the day of Fiona's party Elmo thought he might be the next victim because of that shared event forty-one years ago, and now he felt safe because Agnes was poisoned that afternoon.

"You falling asleep?" Elmo inquired in a kind tone.

"Oh, no. I mean I'm fine. No, actually I mean I'm very tired and I have to go home now."

"It's probably safe enough now." Elmo hoisted himself with a grunt. "I'd better see you home though."

"Thank you, Elmo." When they got outside, she took his arm. Elmo Burroughs straightened, pushed out his chest, and strutted like a dignified gentleman squiring his lady down Scarlet Street.

The Chinese Chippendale clock chimed the half hour as George threw the deadbolt lock on her front door. Eager for a shower, she dashed upstairs, peeled to the skin, hopped beneath the warm spray, and began scrubbing.

Minutes later, her head and body each swathed in a towel, she checked on Adam and Mr. Moto. Satisfied that both were sleeping peacefully, she slipped back downstairs and into her study. She tuned the radio to the station that carried Estelle's broadcast then began the painstaking task of transcribing each clue she had unearthed on a separate three-by-five index card.

At 2:05 A.M., Estelle made the announcement in her clear, calm voice.

It has come to my attention that there was indeed a witness to the murder of Hangtown Harry Frye. Mr. Moto, who is currently a guest of Miss Georgette Richards, knows the identity of the murderer. A minor communication problem has rendered the Japanese-born Mr. Moto temporarily incommunicado. However, only this evening Miss Richards assured me that he will make his revelation to the police within the next twenty-four hours.

"Well done, Estelle." George toasted her performance with a glass of cranberry juice. "The murderer ought to be paying Mr. Moto and me a visit any time now."

Chapter
20

Adam awoke to the vision of the morning sunlight bathing Georgette as she lay asleep beside him. He brushed a curl from her forehead and wished selfishly that she would awaken.

Dark curls framed her fair-skinned face, another contrast in a woman of arresting contrast. Her background suggested that she might be a spoiled snob, yet she was not. Logic suggested that her father had influenced her to be like himself, a calculating, ruthless workaholic, yet she had somehow emerged from what surely must have been a difficult childhood as a sincere, caring, and vivacious woman.

He knew from his years at the bank the level of cruelty of which Harlan Richards was capable. His callousness was legendary; his reprehensible deeds had fueled watercooler gossip for decades. He ruined careers, crushed opponents, and leveled competitors with apparent nonchalance. If he had a conscience, he hid it well. Still, Richards must possess some redeeming virtue, some mercy. He had spared his daughter's spirit.

Georgette was a living miracle, and Adam figured that if

he had one bit of sense in his head, he'd stay the hell away from her.

He smiled. Maybe he was changing. In this same situation six months ago, he would have ignored Georgette's protests last night and done the wise, correct thing. It was in her best interests and possibly even his own that they stop seeing each other immediately. The simple truth was that he did not want to let her go.

He tugged the covers up over her creamy shoulders and began to carefully unpile the pillows stacked around him. He'd solved her riddle of the Italian Renaissance bed in the guest bedroom being too small for her. Fifty-plus pillows of every size, shape, and description, spilled over her king-size bed; her small body nested in a furrow between them.

He plucked up a maroon velvet pillow that carried a suspicious coating of dog hair, but when he rolled to his feet, he spotted the furry beast sacked out on a rug.

Mr. Moto peeled back an eyelid. His tail thumped.

Downstairs, Adam started a pot of coffee, let the dog out, and uncovered the dove's cage. "Ready to fly today, young lady?"

The bird cocked her head with seeming coyness.

"It's about time," Georgette answered over a yawn.

He straightened and took his lover into his arms. "Good morning." She had on a long, silky robe that revealed gentle curves. Judging by the way it clung, she wore nothing beneath the turquoise material. He settled his hands on her waist, and she stretched, tossing her head.

"I have something to show you," she murmured.

He toyed with the knot at the waist of the robe and raised a brow hopefully.

She plucked his hand away. "We can either have breakfast or release the dove, then I'll show you. Personally, I'm starved, but the dove's been waiting for so long, I think it's only fair she go first. What do you think?"

"I think," he said, his eyes tracing the outline of her small, upturned breasts, "that you had better put on a coat or risk immediate ravishment."

Her laughter swelled like a joyous melody. A smile danced

across her face and into her eyes. "You're only being salacious," she said, repeating the last word with obvious pride.

"Right," he said, with a warning pinch on her bottom.

With a merry shriek, she pinched him back and dashed away in a flurry of silk. She returned enveloped by a floor-length raincoat. Affecting a sultry pose, she peeled back the flaps and flashed him with what was underneath.

He heaved out a groan of exaggerated disappointment. "You're supposed to be naked when you do that."

She raised her chin a fraction. "That's the exact reason why you rarely see flashers anymore. They all died of pneumonia."

"Or ran for parts south," he added, lifting the cage and opening the back door.

Outside, the mist in the air seemed to hover undecided between light fog and drizzle. Adam filled his chest full of the moist vapors, remembering that along with the general atmosphere of the city, the often tangible presence of the air in San Francisco had intrigued him into staying here. Throughout his asthmatic childhood, he had wondered why his fight must be so different from the active, combative games his friends played. They fought for points and balls and yardage, things a boy could see and touch, and through their battles they attained measurable rewards, bruises of victory, cuts and other marks of valor, cheers of praise.

At the age of eight, he had asked God to grant him the opportunity to make his friends understand his struggle. He got his wish and nearly lost his life because of it.

During the bout with viral pneumonia, his classmates had covered the walls of his hospital room with large-lettered notes and colorful drawings. When he recovered, they begged in awed whispers for him to recount the details of his perilous adventure, especially the part about the tracheostomy. They huddled around him and studied the scar at the base of his neck with a mixture of fear and wonderment. He had finally earned his own visible mark of battle.

"What are you thinking about?" she asked, drawing her collar up against the morning chill.

"How often the most important things in life defy detection by the five senses." At her puzzled expression, he continued, holding up the caged bird. He unlatched the door. The dove viewed the sudden opening, her gray head wagging. "People walk around for years like this, inside cages that nobody else can even see, trapped because they are afraid to make a change."

"You felt trapped like that before you left the bank?"

"Absolutely." He watched the bird lean forward on her roost. She appeared tempted but still too wary to make a break from the known to the unknown. How long had he been like that? Too long. "It's going to be beautiful on the other side. I'm here and I know. Try it," he coaxed softly.

With a quick reach of her wings, the bird jumped. Her spindly toes grasped the bars of the cage near the door. She craned her long neck toward it, investigating cautiously.

"I spent about six months of my life doing exactly what she's doing now, poised near the edge of change, surveying the situation, assessing the pros and cons, but mostly wondering what life was like on the other side. After a while, I realized that I could end up mired in that position forever, close but never taking the risk. Finally, I knew that I had to make the break." He focused his eyes and energy on the dove, willing her to fly. "Come on. Go for it."

The dove bounced on the rim of the door. She hesitated. "Do it," he said. She bounded from the cage with a rustle of feathers. Wings fluttering in a gray blur, she swept across the narrow yard, over the tips of a row of pines, and out of sight. In his hand, the cage swayed from the recoil, deserted, almost transparent. He saw through it to the soft greens of the trees and shrubs beyond. The cage was as it should be—empty. He dropped the now meaningless object. It clattered against the porch.

Georgette's face raised to his, tears shimmering in her eyes. "When the dove flew out of her cage, for a second I could see what you meant by freedom so clearly, and you were right about it being beautiful on the other side. Then, suddenly, I was myself again, because I remembered all the complications. . . . Tell me, Adam, how did you make her well again?"

"I took care of her, provided her with food, water, and a safe place to rest." He watched her, wondering why she hovered on the verge of tears; this woman who seemed, in some respects, to embody freedom itself.

"No, Adam. I know that's not all of the truth. There's more. A magic. Why did you become a banker when you have such a special, calm way of healing things?"

"I tried it once in college when my great dream was to become a field biologist. My asthma had nearly disappeared, and I was ready to become the rugged outdoorsman. One summer I worked in a wildlife treatment center." He rested his hands on her shoulders and looked down into the warm blueness of her eyes. "Not all birds fly again, Georgette. Sometimes the wounds life deals are too damaging to overcome."

She nodded briskly.

"That fall, I changed my major to business and computer science. I needed the sense of security I derived from dealing with things as straightforward as numbers and with concepts as logical, mechanical, and concrete as the workings of a computer. That was my cage. I was obsessed with things I could deal with on a totally objective and rational basis."

"You've changed now, haven't you?" she asked in a small voice. Distress clouded her eyes. In them too, he saw her longing and understood it. She wanted him to say that he had changed completely, that like the dove he had escaped his cage and had achieved total freedom. He wished that was true. "I'm trying to change."

"Adam, you say that you want to find happiness and joy in life . . ." She paused and glanced downward, robbing him of even the muted brilliance of her eyes. She nibbled her lower lip, seemingly trying to arrive at some sort of decision.

Her uncharacteristic hesitation worried him. Concern tightened his grip on her shoulders. "You can tell me anything, Georgette. Anything."

Her head snapped up. "Don't you see that it's love that brings happiness and joy?"

Frustration bubbled up inside him. "God, that's what everyone says. We're indoctrinated with that message practically from the moment we're born. Businessmen use it to sell everything from perfume and diamonds to automobiles and mouthwash. But what is love? Define it for me."

She squirmed free of his grasp. "It's a feeling!" she exclaimed, lifting her hands and waving them in loops. "It makes you happy. It's like a warm thing that grows inside you when you hold a puppy or see a mare and her foal running through a field." She pointed toward the trees. "Like watching a dove fly free."

He closed the gap between them with one quick stride, somehow knowing, sensing she possessed the illusive piece to the puzzle of his life. "What depth of love enables people to make a commitment for a lifetime?"

"I didn't understand either until my cousin Shannon came to live with Daddy and me. After a while, I knew she loved me exactly the way I was, no matter what I did. I loved her back the same way. When she fell in love with Mark and married him, she moved and left me alone. But I was never really alone because the love we feel for each other is right here, always." She tapped her fist against her chest.

His hands circled her upper arms, capturing her, drawing her face close to his. "Love is only a word that's been designated to describe a mystery," he challenged. "I know a couple who have been through hell together, lost one child, had another that is hopelessly retarded. Still they make it. How? But it's like asking why the earth revolves around the sun. The answer is gravity, which is really no answer at all. We can describe the phenomena, write laws that predict it's behavior, use it, even defy it, but no one can explain why it even exists."

"Emotions aren't scientific. Love exists because we welcome it without reservation, and we welcome it because we want and need for it to happen."

"Dammit, I want it! I need it!"

She reached up, grabbed his arms, and held him fast. "People do love you."

"Not that way. Not like my parents loved each other, not in that all-consuming way it's supposed to be."

"You don't know. How can you know for sure how they felt?"

"I saw it." His thoughts raced back thirty years. "Nobody existed for them but each other."

Her expression smoothed to disbelief. "How do you know?"

"Because I didn't exist for them."

"Sending you away to Denver doesn't mean that. It was a sacrifice to help you get better."

"It was no sacrifice for them. I knew that before it ever happened." She prodded him silently with a soft, understanding look. He swallowed hard, realizing that the time had come for the entire truth, that he must now confess completely to his years-long, frustrating search. "My parents always ate supper together, and I felt left out. One evening I hid under the skirt of cook's rolling table and was wheeled into the dining room beneath dinner. I waited for my mother to tell my father about an important award I'd won."

He stopped, the memory stinging despite the passage of years. After an hour under that accursed table, his young arms aching from clutching the leg, he had pressed his face against the cold metal and began to cry. "They never even mentioned me," he whispered, his voice shot with tremors. "Not once. They only truly cared for each other, but God, I thought, someday—someday, I would share that kind of bond with someone. It never happened."

She ran the soft palms of her hands along his upper arms. "Adam, your parents were wrong. They sound just like my father only the wife that Daddy adores is his company. I don't think love is supposed to be some sort of obsession."

"Dammit, how can you say that? How do you know? Have you ever been in love with a man?"

"I was terribly in love!"

An emotion he couldn't name caused him to shout, "What became of this love then? Who was he?"

201

She twisted her face away. He shook her. "Look at me! Tell me what happened."

She raised watery eyes to his. A disturbing calmness settled over her features. In a flat, uninflected voice she answered, "He didn't love me back. He tricked me."

"Georgette, I—" he broke off, embarrassed, wrong, remorseful. "I shouldn't have forced you to tell me. I'm sorry."

"Listen to me, Adam," she said with surprising firmness. "I want to tell you how it was. I loved him so much that I felt empty when I was away from him. He made me feel valued and special, and I thought he loved me too, just for me. I thought he didn't know anything about me except who *I* was, only me, George—no Richards, no money, no aerospace industries, no trust funds. He sang me love songs; he painted my portrait, and when he told me that I was his life and his love he lied. He looked me right in the eye and lied, and I didn't know. *I never knew.* I never understood Michael and his scheme to marry my money until my father paid him to leave me alone."

A single tear escaped and became a shiny trail on her cheek. "So you're wrong when you say I've never been in love with a man. You don't know how wrong you are." Something flickered in her eyes, perhaps great sadness before her head sagged, and she buried her face in her open palms. "Oh, God . . ." she said, her voice quivering, "so wrong."

Her breaths sounded like strangled little gasps. Adam crushed her to him and carried her into the house, berating himself for asking her such a question. Of course, she had loved. How could he have doubted that?

He kicked the door closed, revulsion for this Michael churning inside him. Hadn't the bastard seen the treasure inside her, a treasure more valuable than a mountain of gold?

She cried silently against his chest. He ached with her pain and from the agony of her tears. He hated himself for hurting her, for bringing back the past. Clutching her to him, he sank into a chair and adjusted her on his lap. He began to stroke her hair and her back. "I'm sorry, Georgette. What I said was thoughtless. Only I get so frustrated because I've never been able to feel—" he broke off, ashamed. "I'm sorry."

She balled his sweater in two white-knuckled fists over his heart. She sniffed. "For ten years I've gone out with those men my father sends because they're all nothing but horrible, mercenary drudges after my money and a position in my father's company. None of them possesses an ounce of imagination. I know exactly who and what they are. They're safe!" she shouted with sudden savagery. "I could never fall in love with any of them. Now my father insists I marry one of them!"

Chapter
21

"What!" George's revelation struck Adam like a powerful blow to the solar plexus. He stared at her small body huddled in his arms, horrified at the thought of her being forced into intimacy with a man she disliked or distrusted. "This is the twentieth century. Your father can't pressure you into marrying someone you don't care for."

She pressed her clenched fists against his chest. "He'll try forever," she said in a miserable tone.

"And fail. There's nothing he could say or do that would make you even consider such a thing," he said, his resolve designed to pacify his own sanity as much as Georgette's.

He heard her drag in several deep breaths. "There's no time to dwell on that now. I'll figure something out."

"I know you will." He had faith in her. Anyone who had managed to shrug off the influence of a man as powerful as Harlan Richards for over thirty years could outmaneuver the old bear on an issue as ludicrous as arranged marriage.

"Freedom, that's what's important." She straightened in his lap, wiping her eyes with the backs of her hands. "Adam, we don't have much time left, and I'm determined to solve this murder. Last night I collected a whole new set of clues. It's coming together; I can feel it."

"Last night? You went out alone?"

"Don't be angry with me. It was crucial."

Creases appeared on her forehead. Her eyes searched his face, and, not for the first time, he sensed her desire for his approval. Her need might have been flattering if she didn't seem to seek it so desperately. Anger flooded him at the realization that Harlan Richards had left his mark on her after all. "I have great confidence in your judgment."

She beamed.

"But next time you get the urge to prowl for clues in the middle of the night, wake me."

"Okay." She nodded her head vigorously. "You were so tired and it was so important. Here," she said, tugging on his hand. "Let me show you."

He stalled her long enough to allow him time to let Mr. Moto back into the house and to grab them each a cup of coffee before she beckoned him into her office. He paused at the door and surveyed the room, astonished. "You did all this last night?"

She set down her coffee with a mischievous grin. In a whimsical parody of a game show hostess, she danced around the perimeter gesturing over her room-size collage. Dozens of index cards were scattered over the floor. Scores of lines crisscrossed between them. So much multicolored yarn connected the white cards that the entire thing appeared to be a giant, loose weaving.

"Each card has one clue on it or something that happened," she explained. "The lines connecting them are color coded by person. For instance, the yellow that I was going to use for Shannon's baby blankets is Agnes. Everything that relates to Agnes is connected with a butternut yellow line. My secretary's Christmas muffler is Hangtown Harry; he's the electric fuchsia and so on for everybody."

He lounged against the doorjamb, sipping his coffee. Her creativity, like her energy, seemed boundless. "What did all this tell you about the murder that's so crucial?"

"Well," she said, wending her way back to his side,

"actually nothing. I worked on it until four-thirty this morning and after I got done, I tried to follow one person after another through this maze, and you know I couldn't. I kept getting lost. Then I stepped back and stood exactly where you're standing. I was so frustrated thinking how I'd wasted all that time and ruined over fifty dollars worth of yarn that I'd run all over the city to find in the first place when it hit me." She swept her hand over the imaginative chart. "I thought to myself that the whole thing looks like a weaving. *That* is the real clue. Marie Antoinette, Marshall, Sr.'s murder forty-one years ago, Hangtown Harry's death, all those events are interwoven somehow, and everyone except you and I are involved in some way with nearly every incident.

"Look," she pointed, "you're competition orange. You're only tied two ways, one line for meeting Harry through the bank and another line for working for Fiona." She threw up her hands. "That's all. But everyone else is tied together all over the place."

He scanned the chart, the maze of lines that represented the myriad connections of these people through the decades. She was absolutely right, of course. "You're brilliant, you know."

She rewarded him with a dazzling smile. She wrapped her arms around his waist and nestled her softness against him. He found it impossible to resist running a hand over the curve of her back and lower.

"Adam, I'm convinced that the murders of Marshall, Sr., Dr. Emerson, and Hangtown Harry are all linked. Last night Elmo told me that Dr. Emerson, you know, the man who owned this house and supposedly got bonked by burglars a couple of months ago, was at the party the night that Marie appeared and Marshall died. So was Harry, even though he was Arthur then. Elmo was terrified the day after Harry was murdered, and he dismissed the police account of how the doctor died as irrelevant. Elmo also said that death was marching down the street, and that he was next. He must have thought that the deaths were connected to that forty-one-year-old crime. Last night he was calm because—"

"Because," he finished for her, "Agnes's poisoning relieved Elmo of his concern. It changed his mind about the motive because it didn't fit the pattern. If what you discovered yesterday about Agnes is correct and she poisoned herself, then Elmo might have been correct all along, that the murders of Marshall, Sr., Emerson, and Hangtown Harry are all connected. Still," he mused, "it doesn't make sense that someone would wait forty-one years to kill Emerson and Harry, unless . . ." He let out a long breath. Fiona had been away and living on the East Coast for over thirty years, returning to San Francisco only recently. But, if she was bent on murder, which he seriously doubted, why not do the nasty deeds after the election? Why would Fiona jeopardize her son Marvin's candidacy? After all this time, what were a few months more or less? What would be her motive in the first place?

And why would Agnes poison herself?

Georgette pressed her face against his chest. "Time is so short."

He set his coffee aside and caressed her tender skin, running his fingers over her delicate cheekbone. Time was short, barely two days and a night left before her father would attempt to force her to leave. In this instance, her father was probably right. She ought to get away from Watson, the murder, this street. A hollowness entered his heart at the thought of her going anywhere.

As soon as possible, he would look for another job and leave Scarlet Street. If she left, he would be gone by the time she returned. Continuing to see him would certainly endanger Georgette's reputation, perhaps even bring the full wrath of Harlan Richards to bear on his daughter.

Now, more than ever, it was imperative that he sever his ties with her forever. If her father discovered she was having an affair with a gardener, he might find some way to use it to his advantage. Coupled with her need for approval, a nasty scandal might give Richards a chance to sway her. Adam refused to become either a weapon or a cause of her being manipulated into marrying some fortune hunter.

The bell rang and Moto reacted with his trademark

earsplitting response. Georgette silenced him with a sharp no, and peeked around the corner into the foyer. "Adam, I can't see well through the stained glass, but I think it's that Detective Hernandez I met when he was searching your apartment. None of my friends have mustaches. Besides, he said yesterday he wanted to question me. And of course, he's probably heard about last night . . ." she added cryptically.

Adam made a mental note to question her in detail about the previous evening. He'd meant to do it earlier, but getting Georgette to stick to one subject always presented a colossal challenge. "You'd better get dressed." Shielding her from the view of the door with his body, he walked her to the staircase.

For some unknown reason, she called the dog and demanded that he accompany her. When the two of them reached the top stair, he crossed the foyer and opened the door.

Detective Dan Hernandez and a middle-aged Oriental man with round glasses and a black umbrella over his head stood on the porch. Hernandez appeared determined. "Where's Georgette Richards?" he growled.

"Upstairs. Whom shall I say is calling?"

"You know damned well *whom* I am, Lawrence." He hitched up his pants and strutted into the foyer. After lowering his umbrella, the Oriental man followed. Adam repeated his name and shook the man's hand.

Georgette bounded into the room, dressed in record time. "Good morning, Detective." Without giving the detective a second glance, she approached the Oriental gentleman. "I don't believe we've met," she said, extending a hand.

"Sidney Sakura, and I am very pleased to make your acquaintance." He grasped her hand with a slight bow. His English carried a moderately heavy accent. Nattily dressed in a dark suit, tie, and starched white shirt, he looked more like a professor than a police officer.

The detective marched up to the pair. "Miss Richards, what do you mean withholding evidence in a murder investigation?" His dark mustache quivered.

"What do you mean?" she asked, her face carefully blank.

Adam had heard that tone of voice before. She knew exactly what the detective meant. He cringed. He should have chained her to the bedpost last night. No telling what she'd done.

"Where is this Moto character? I intend to question him now." He thrust a pointed finger at the ground.

Relieved, Adam located a chair with a good view and relaxed. The pieces had fallen into place, the detective's accusation about withholding evidence, Mr. Moto, and a nonpolice type with a Japanese name. He had no idea how she'd managed to alert Hernandez to her oft-repeated theory about Mr. Moto, but he wanted a front row seat for this show. Detective Hernandez was about to go up like a Roman candle.

"Mr. Moto," Georgette caroled, her eyes never leaving the face of the determined-looking detective.

The Japanese man cleaned his wire-rimmed glasses and watched the stairs, an expectant look on his face. "Ah," he cooed as Mr. Moto barreled into the living room. "Akita."

Oddly enough, Sakura appeared overjoyed.

Hernandez reddened.

"This," the detective bellowed, "is Mr. Moto, witness to murder!"

"Yes, and if you'll only give me a chance to explain—"

"Don't do that!" Hernandez commanded Sakura who was bowing extravagantly to the bewildered-looking dog.

"Akita is a national monument in Japan," Sakura said with a mischievous smile. "Also known as *Matagiinu,* esteemed hunter dog."

"What the hell is going on here?" Hernandez shouted.

"Really a national monument?" Georgette asked Sakura, completely ignoring the detective.

"Oh, yes." Sakura replied. "In old past, Akitas hunted the Yezo, a very fierce bear. They are fearless warriors and, in my culture, symbolize health, happiness, and long life. This Mr. Moto is also very noble. He protects you, yes?"

"He's very protective," she said, stroking the dog's stiff,

alert ears. "That's the whole point. He always patrolled Harry's yard, every single night. He still does, and he only barks at strangers."

Hernandez started to raise his hand, then dropped it with a groan.

Adam laced his arms behind his neck. He found himself identifying with the detective for the first time. The man's obvious frustration reminded him of his initial attempt to make logic out of a conversation with Georgette. Hernandez should count his blessings that he wasn't enduring this ordeal hog-tied and gagging.

Sidney Sakura continued to nod at Georgette in an understanding manner. "The Akita is very intelligent and loyal, also obedient. Hachiko, faithful pet of professor at Tokyo University kept vigil for master until his own death."

"Really?" she prodded. "Oh, this could definitely be important. What kind of vigil did Hachiko keep?"

"What the hell does this Hachiko have to do with anything?" Hernandez blustered. Adam sensed the starch ebbing out of the detective. Georgette's unusual approach to logic had a way of wearing a man down.

Sakura freed his glasses and began polishing them again with his handkerchief. "Hachiko see master off every morning at Shibuya railroad station, return every night to meet. When his master die at university and does not come back, Hachiko visit station every night to wait until midnight for nine years. Throughout Japan, people heard of Hachiko and give money to build fine statue in train station."

Georgette's eyes narrowed. "No wonder Mr. Moto acts the way he does. It's natural."

"You can't mean to tell me that a dog is actually capable of . . . that you could believe that he . . . I mean it would be impossible for . . ." The detective trailed off, stroking his mustache.

"It's a grave mistake to keep slim mind," Sakura announced.

"Mr. Sakura is right. You shouldn't be so narrow-minded." She glared pointedly at the detective.

Evidently, the detective's curiosity was taking over now.

He drilled Mr. Moto with an intent gaze. Moto cocked his head in return. They both appeared to be sizing the other up. "Miss Richards, this dog may or may not know who murdered Frye. He may or may not be able to help us identify the murderer. Those points considered, it was still totally irresponsible of you to insinuate that a dog was going to reveal the identity of the murderer to the public. Totally irresponsible."

Georgette recoiled as though Hernandez had slapped her. Adam jumped to his feet and strode to her side. Defending her would be a hell of a lot easier if he knew exactly what she'd done. "Miss Richards has suffered a great deal at the hands of the press. Surely you've heard that she's being sued by Don Dick Watson, and as a witness to that incident, I can tell you he deserved to have far more cracked than a bone. Anything the press says at this point is suspect where she's concerned, and I suggest that you keep that in mind."

Adam felt a stirring at his side. "He's right, Adam," she confessed in a small voice. "I told Estelle to say those things about Mr. Moto on her radio show."

She *had* been busy last night. "To say what?" he asked.

"Oh," she began in a forced little singsong, "that Mr. Moto witnessed the murder, that he was staying here incommunicado, and that he was going to reveal the identity of Harry's murderer within the next twenty-four hours."

Adam tried to speak; he really tried. But every time he started, he choked on a chuckle. Everyone stared at him strangely, including Mr. Moto, and Adam was left wondering why they all weren't howling with laughter.

"What's so damned funny, Lawrence?"

"Detective Hernandez," he managed, "do you mean to tell me that you fail to see the humor in dragging this Japanese interpreter here in the rain"—he swallowed hard to compose himself—"because a woman who does a talk show at two in the morning and mutters constantly about the orgiastic cosmos and perpends said on the air that Mr. Moto, the name incidentally of a fictional detective played in the movies by Peter Lorre and in this case, a dog, knows the identity of the murderer?"

He dissolved into a gale of laughter. Georgette tugged on his sweater. "I think you ought to try to take this all more seriously. Detective, he's really been under a great strain lately."

Adam staggered to a chair and collapsed, gripped by spasms of laughter.

"They don't fill the gas chamber with laughing gas, Lawrence."

"Oh, he's innocent. I'm absolutely positive. Both of you sit down, and I'll get you some coffee." Georgette herded the two men to the sofa. "You see, Detective," she began, placing two trivets in front of them, "the night that Harry was murdered Mr. Moto didn't bark because . . ."

Chapter
22

"So you see, Detective Hernandez, Adam couldn't have murdered Harry because Mr. Moto didn't bark." George punctuated her statement by folding her hands in her lap resolutely. Adam could have made her recitation of the facts far easier if he had controlled himself. His incessant chuckling had made it difficult to concentrate.

Sidney Sakura winked at her again. "Very interesting explanation for behavior of esteemed guard pet."

"Thank you," she replied automatically, her attention focused on the detective. He massaged the bridge of his nose, his eyes closed, filling her with hope that he was seriously mulling over her conclusions. Somehow sensing that victory was hers if only she continued her calm, clear presentation of the facts, she invited him to come into her study. "Adam, please talk to Mr. Sakura."

Adam gave her a jaunty salute.

George opened the door to her soon-to-be office and waved the detective inside. She closed the door behind them.

"I'll be damned," Hernandez said, circling her clue weaving.

"Adam has very little connection with any of these people, yet they're all involved one way or the other with an unsolved murder in 1949. I can't believe that it's an accident of fate that Dr. Emerson was killed under suspicious circumstances two months ago, then Hangtown Harry, when both of them were present the evening Marshall Hoagsworth was murdered forty-one years ago."

George went on to tell him about Elmo's fear the day after Harry's murder, describing only what drew suspicion away from Adam. Hernandez dropped to one knee, apparently studying her clue weaving, his expression inscrutable. Still, from his stance she sensed a grudging shift in his point of view, swayed by too many coincidences and too many links between the residents of Scarlet Street.

"Herlihy," Hernandez muttered. Abruptly, he jerked up and began to fidget. "Miss Richards, thank you for your cooperation. And don't plant any more tidbits on Estelle Capricorn's show or anybody else's. Amateur detectives can end up dead citizens, and personally I'd hate to get a homicide call for Twelve Scarlet."

"The press will find me totally incommunicado." She added what she hoped was a totally guileless smile.

As soon as Hernandez and Sakura departed, George sprinted past Adam toward the kitchen and the telephone. She rifled through the directory, found Elmo's number, and punched it into the keypad.

"What are you up to now?"

She waved off Adam's question. Elmo drawled a hello. "Elmo, this is Georgette Richards. What was the name of the detective who investigated the murder of Marshall Hoagsworth, Sr.?"

Elmo hacked for a minute then wheezed, "Irishman name of Herlihy."

"Thanks, Elmo." Replacing the receiver, she said, "I've convinced Detective Hernandez to at least keep an open mind. After we talked for a while he finally said, 'Herlihy,' thinking out loud. Elmo says that's the name of the detective who investigated the Hoagsworth murder."

Adam only sighed. The laughter that had so recently transformed his face into smiles had disappeared—and just when things were looking up.

"I suppose that is good news."

"What's wrong?"

"While you were in talking with Hernandez, my friend Lois called from the bank computer center." He shoved his hands in his pants pockets and leaned against the counter.

"And?" she coaxed, hoping for the entire explanation sometime before she keeled over from starvation.

"Several large accounts at Pacific West have been drained. Natasha Velour's was the first, presumably tying the thievery directly to Scarlet Street."

"Oh, no. How do you feel about waffles? They're frozen but good."

"They'd need maple syrup."

"Fresh from Vermont." She clicked on the oven on her way to the freezer, her mouth watering at the thought of two thick Belgian waffles smothered with syrup and melted butter.

"Why do they think that any of this implicates you?"

"Mainly the fact that I left the bank so abruptly, I suppose. Someone inside the bank was required to execute the scheme. It was a simple, straightforward plan. In this age of computer theft Harry relied on old-fashioned fraud."

"Did Lois tell you how the thieves did it?"

"They have a pretty good idea. The insider located a very large, inactive savings account, then substituted the signature card on file with a phony one. When their accomplice arrived at the bank armed with false identification to withdraw the money, the unsuspecting teller verified the identity of the depositor by comparing the accomplice's signature to the fake signature card and, of course, saw a match. After the withdrawal, the phony card was replaced with the real card, tidying up and leaving behind no clues."

"Wow." George stuffed the waffles into the oven.

"Inactive accounts are most vulnerable to this type of fraud. The absence of transactions allows months to go by before the bank is alerted by the depositor. It gave the thieves time to loot a number of accounts."

"How can they be sure that Harry was involved?"

"The police discovered that he made several trips to Switzerland presumably to deposit the pilfered money. He also wired a large amount of money through the Cayman Islands."

Arranging the flatware on the table, she asked, "How did Lois find out about that?"

"Troy Hasselbush has been suspended but not before one of Lois's data entry operators coerced some inside information out of the talkative young man. Apparently the majority of Harry's trips were to Reno and Las Vegas where he gambled heavily. A woman always accompanied him."

"Humm, I'll bet that's Joan LaRose. Did he say anything else?"

"Only that on paper, at least in this country, Harry was flat broke. Oh, and he also said that the police are having trouble locating Joan LaRose."

She pinched her lower lip. After a moment, she said, "Adam, I have a plan."

George opened her front door, caught one glimpse of Scarlet Street, and slammed it shut. She darted to the window and swept the drape aside. "I can't believe it!"

Outraged, she followed the progress of a plump woman in a garish straw hat leading a brace of camera-toting tourists back to an idling bus. "What on earth!"

Adam touched her gently on the shoulder. "I have a feeling that once the election is over, this sort of thing will cease. The Smith campaign is blaming virtually everything from the great earthquake of 1906 to the last heat wave on the residents of Scarlet Street. Given such billing, people are naturally curious."

"I suppose you're right," she grumbled, watching the bus lurch away with a puff of black smoke. "How is Marvin doing in the polls?"

"Surprisingly enough, he's neck and neck with Smith."

"He'll win if we straighten this mess out in time." She reached and ran her fingertips over the side of Adam's face. He deserved happiness and joy, not suspicion and innuendos. "Let's go," she said, brightening. "We have three murders to solve."

Her hand tucked in Adam's, she locked the front door and marched alongside him across Scarlet Street.

"You see, Adam, other than Ina Hoagsworth herself, only one woman involved in all this cannot be Marie Antoinette."

"Natasha Velour," he agreed, pressing the bell of the author's Moorish mansion.

"Fiona said that she's been heavy all her life."

"I was thinking of another reason."

"You mean Miss Tierra del Fuego."

"I also find it difficult to conceive of any man being held in thrall by Miss Velour for forty-one years."

The heavy double doors burst inward as if swept aside by a hurricane wind. "Georgette Richards," Natasha boomed. "And you." She shot Adam a glare most women reserve for things like smelly fish and the *Sports Illustrated* swimsuit issue.

George scanned her portly body covered neck to toe with a black leather floor-length cape and winced.

Natasha motioned them inside. "Like my new coat?" she asked, pirouetting in the mammoth foyer. She grabbed a slouch hat with a purple ostrich plume and plopped it on her head. She looked like a black mountain with a bizarre flag planted on top. "Had it made for my next promotional tour."

"It's lovely and so unusual," George managed. Adam managed nothing at all. His tight smile and frozen expression told her he was on the verge of hysterics.

"Natasha, I really need to ask a favor," she said hurriedly, hoping to stave off another of Adam's laughing fits by getting right down to business.

"What can I do you for?" she said, bumping into a living room that could have easily accommodated a fully inflated

217

hot air balloon. The ceiling soared so high, she wondered if Natasha was forced to hire professional window cleaners to dust the wrought-iron chandeliers.

Natasha shooed several cats away and flopped down on a zebra-skin couch. George sat next to Adam opposite Natasha on a couch made of some sort of brown hide, maybe impala. The hairs tickled the backs of George's legs through her hose. A particularly large black cat crouched on the arm of the sofa, glaring at her, tail swishing. "Uh, Natasha, I know that you are a real authority on Scarlet Street and its history."

With a wave of her plump hand, she signaled a yes.

"Well, as you know, I'm having a Halloween party this Saturday night for the neighborhood. I thought it might be fun to use the scarlet scandals angle as a theme but I need some more information on them."

"Great idea, Richards. Planning to invite any reporters?"

"If you think—"

"Why sure," she drawled. "Great publicity. I've got a book out right now, you know. *Open Wide, My Darling.*"

George felt Adam stiffen beside her. His face appeared masklike, like a time bomb waiting to explode into smiles.

Natasha handed George a copy of the novel. The cover featured a dental chair with a lab coat sprawled across one end. Near the name tag, the coat was impaled with a knife. She flipped to the first page.

Mary Terry sized up the messenger Igor with her gorgeous baby-blues. Igor reminded her of Los Angeles: big, sprawling, and ugly.

"Great spy novel about love, betrayal, and dentistry," Natasha interjected, "with a plucky little dental hygienist who tries to thwart an international scheme to kill our nation's top leaders with a phony home plaque removal system. Nearly worked too. You know those guys in Washington can't afford to let their teeth go. You won't see the voters electing anyone with wooden choppers these days."

Natasha's eyes leveled on Adam. "Lawrence, you look like a man about to split a gut. Bathroom's out that way, room with the suede door. Watch you don't scare any of the cats."

Adam rose and strode away, a strangled cough trailing behind.

"Ain't only the women with weak bladders," she remarked. "Only men won't admit it."

George scratched the back of her legs, wondering if the couch had fleas. In this room alone, she counted a dozen cats and a few feline statues that looked suspiciously real. A smallish Persian tried to scrabble up Natasha's slick coat but slid back, paws flailing. Natasha ignored them all. "As for my theme party, I decided after talking to Dwight that I might come up with something relating to the unsolved murder of Marshall Hoagsworth, Sr."

Natasha scooted her bulk forward. "Great idea."

"Dwight told me about that evening and Marie—"

Natasha guffawed. "Dwight has forty-one-year-old stardust in his eyes. Told you that woman was innocent, did he? Didn't tell you about the note they found near Marshall, Sr.'s body? Here," she said, lifting a tabby and rifling through a stack of books and papers. "I was just doing some research for an article for *Truly Bloody* . . . ah, here it is." She shoved a paper across the table. "That's a photocopy of the original handwritten note, lyrics to a song found only inches from the bleeding corpse of Marshall Hoagsworth."

George reached for the paper. "How did you get it?"

Natasha lounged back, both of her chins framing a smug grin. "Connections. This publicity about Hangtown Harry is too good to pass up. Gotta strike while the iron is hot and I will. You can count on it."

"I'm sure," George said, hoping she sounded sincere rather than condemning. "You seem to have an absolute sixth sense about working with the media."

Natasha's smile broadened, clearly savoring the compliment. The older woman's gloating would pay off with extra information, George thought as she bent to examine the note. The handwriting was rounded and embellished with loops:

I was pure and lily-white,
Just a baby from the clover in the house of Casanova on
   a dark and stormy night.
Oh sisters weep for me,
There ain't no sleep for me,
There ain't no peace of mind till I find that double-
   crossing son-of-a-gun of the lowest kind.
The dirty dog.
If he doesn't do what's right,
He'll be quickly executed for the gal he disreputed on
   this dark and stormy night.

"Holy heaven!"

"What does that tell you?"

George opened her mouth. "That—"

"I'll tell you what it tells you," Natasha interrupted. "That lyric says that the woman dressed as Marie Antoinette did the nasty deed. Hoagsworth deflowered more virgins than the Roman army. I bet Estelle was one of 'em."

"Really?"

"I think she was Marie Antoinette even though I can't prove it. I expect she killed Marshall—executin' for disreputin' like the note says—then came back years later to live in his house, hoping to get close to his dead spirit or his son, whatever worked out best. Did you listen the night I was on her broadcast?"

"Yes."

"Remember that guy who telephoned and called Estelle the mistress of Satan? That was Marshall, Jr. sure as I'm sitting here. It's common knowledge that young Marshall thinks his dad was the old ring-tailed demon himself, and Estelle turned white as chalk at his pointing out her former habit of hitting the sheets with his old man. Junior sounds just like his father too. I figure her guilty conscience acts up a bit from time to time. Feel sorry for her, you know. I only went on her show to help her out. Lousy ratings."

"Couldn't one of the men have killed Marshall? They were all there, Dwight, Elmo, Dr. Emerson . . ." She trailed off, hopeful that Natasha would bite on the last goodie.

"Ummm, I see what you mean. As far as Dwight goes, there's a chance that his obsession is some kind of blind. I always did think that statue routine was a bit forced. But did Elmo or Emerson kill Marshall? Hell no. Elmo thought the world of him, and Marshall was the cornerstone of Emerson's practice."

"What do you mean? I thought Dr. Emerson was a gynecologist?"

Natasha heaved out a throaty sigh. "Gad, girl, where have you been? *A-b-o-r-t-i-o-n.* That's what he did. He couldn't have made the kind of money he did delivering babies. Emerson did most of his practicing in his basement, ridding little society belles of unwanted baggage."

A shiver crept up George's spine. "My God, no wonder they call this place the street of a thousand miseries." She swallowed hard, hoping to quell the queasy feeling rising in her stomach. "Natasha, who do you think killed Hangtown Harry?"

"Somebody with good sense."

George grudgingly unlocked her front door. "Adam, I can't believe it! Abortions in my own basement! No wonder the realtor called this house charming. It's probably their jargon for the place being haunted, evil, or having termites. Murder was one thing, but this—" she sputtered. "I'm putting it up for sale immediately. Oh, why did I buy this pink elephant?"

"It's really a nice house," he said reassuringly as he bent to scratch Mr. Moto's ears. The dog moaned his pleasure at Adam's ministrations.

She understood the feeling. "At least we know now how Marshall, Sr.'s murder and Emerson's are linked. Marshall got Marie pregnant, and Emerson performed the abortion —maybe. It's a breakthrough. The only problem now is that we don't know how Harry fits into all this and if the theft of money at the bank has to do with either of the other murders. Natasha refused to talk about Hangtown Harry, except to say that she didn't give a damn that someone killed him. We simply have to find Joan LaRose. But how?" She paced the room nibbling on her lip.

"I've got it! What was the name of the man who accompanied her on the guitar? Maybe we can find him."

"The speaker introduced him as Ricardo Pena." Adam paused, clearly thoughtful. "I'm certain that a call to the musician's union will reveal where he's playing."

"That's it!" Five minutes on the telephone and she had the information plus the costume she needed lined up with Marfa. "Adam," she said, returning to the living room. "I need your help. Pena is playing at Rosa's Restaurante y Cantina."

"That's interesting. LaRose, Rosa's."

"You're getting so brilliant." She reached on tiptoe and kissed the tip of his nose. "I have a plan. Marfa is going to lend us a costume that is sure to be a big help. I thought we could go in a couple of hours, after the lunch rush and before the dinner crowd, and see if we can prove that Rosa and Joan are one and the same."

"Great. Fiona has been generous to suspend my duties, but now the rain has stopped, the ground is damp, and I should use the next two hours or so to weed the back flower beds."

"Are you sure you really want to do that?" she asked, snaking her arms around his narrow hips and pressing against him.

"No."

From the hard feel of him she knew he told the absolute truth. "You're going to do it anyway, because it's the right thing to do."

"Still," he said huskily, his mouth descending to hers, "I can't be expected to deny myself completely."

Wondrous, George decided after searching for the right word. Adam's lovemaking had propelled her to rapture so quickly. Of course, his touch seemed to instantly transform her from normal woman to wanton savage which definitely saved a lot of time. Though he had been gone now for more than fifteen minutes, she could still feel the warmth of him covering her skin and flushing her cheeks. At the chime of the bell, she glided to answer the door, humming off-key.

The looming presence of her father's chauffeur instantly broke the spell.

"Good afternoon, Miss Richards. I have a message from your father," he droned, offering her the note with his gloved hand. "A reply is requested."

She steeled herself for the message. Undoubtedly, her father had heard about Estelle's radio broadcast and was likely on the verge of threatening to banish her to the island he owned off the coast of Alaska where the only contact with the outside world came once a week with the mail and supply plane. She ripped open the envelope.

Georgette: I have canceled your trip to Baja. Adam Lawrence seems a suitable marriage candidate if cleared of suspicion of murder. Proceed as I instructed.

H.R.

Numb, she read the note over four times before she lifted her eyes to the waiting chauffeur. "Mr. Richards asked for your assurance that you would comply with his requests."

Alaska had to be better than this, better than her father approving of Adam. She had wanted to marry him, and this made it such a tempting prospect.

But she couldn't marry Adam—not after hearing his words when he released the dove. He deserved better than year after year of being badgered by her father. Adam deserved freedom.

"Tell him, yes, I understand," she replied, pain closing around her heart. She waited until the chauffeur pulled away, then stuffed the note in the pocket of her skirt and rushed next door.

Adam kneeled in the flower bed, Mr. Moto stretched out on the lawn nearby. "Adam?"

He rolled back on his heels, straightening his back. His smile was so broad and beautiful, it made her want to cry. She forced words out in a rush. "I have to stop seeing you."

His smile vanished. "What's wrong?" He jumped to his

feet, held out his muddy hands, and shouted, "What would make you say such a thing?" Anger reddened his tanned skin.

"I can't do it to you! I have to give you up now before it's too late!" she yelled, dashing for her house. Inside, she threw the bolt and turned up the radio until it blared.

But it was already too late.

Upstairs, she filled the claw-footed bathtub, stripped to the skin, and descended into the steaming water, covering her ears. Still, the words Adam had shouted at her back reverberated in her head.

"Not now! Not yet!"

Chapter
23

George lifted one side of the fuzzy white earmuffs. Only the telephone again, she thought, and probably Adam. It had been ringing incessantly for the four hours since she had told Adam she couldn't see him anymore.

She let the muff snap back against the side of her head. Arms akimbo, she surveyed the living room. One ugly moving crate marred the appearance of the spacious area, but from the soaring white walls to the sprawling area rugs, the place finally looked passable.

She glanced at her watch in triumph. She had unpacked the knickknacks, hung the pictures, and arranged the glasses in the bar, all in only three hours flat. She raised the muff again. The ringing of the telephone was now joined by the chime of the doorbell. She popped the muff back into place. The moving company at last.

"Oh!" she cried, startled to find Fiona Breathwaite standing on her front porch in an emerald green velvet jogging suit, her red hair barely contained in a loose bun. "I thought you were the movers."

Fiona appeared horror-stricken. Her mouth began to

work rapidly. George stripped off the earmuffs in time to hear her exclaim, "Surely you can't mean that you're leaving here today!"

"No," she said, waving her inside. Mercifully, the telephone had finally stopped ringing. "At least not until I have my pre–Halloween housewarming party tomorrow night and unmask the murderer. Then I'm putting the house on the market. I can't live in this horrible place anymore."

"But, George, you have it looking so lovely." Fiona's athletic shoes squeaked on the hardwood floor as she drifted through the various furniture groupings on her way to the carved stone and marble fireplace. "I like the way you've rearranged the furniture."

George rubbed her aching back. "Thank you. It's the fourth way I've tried this week. I never thought my life could get so complicated that I'd need casters."

Fiona spun. "You aren't going to move out until the house sells, are you?"

George pointed at the lone packing crate in the corner. "These bleached cow skulls were delivered here instead of to my office. One of our clients likes bones."

A gleam came into Fiona's eyes. "How does your client feel about dead, furry trophies?"

George stiffened at the shrill blare from the kitchen telephone. She sank into a chair with a groan. "I wish he'd stop calling."

"You must mean Adam. Saying you wouldn't see him again has devastated him. He's pacing his apartment. Even Mr. Moto looks upset." Fiona took the chair beside her. "Adam doesn't understand and neither do I. I thought you'd truly come to care for him."

She flexed the stiff semicircle connecting the furry ear warmers, counting telephone rings. Five. Six. Seven. Eight. Nine. Flinging the muffs on the floor, she moaned, "I do care for him."

"Then call him."

"I don't have his number."

"It's—"

George clapped her hands over her ears. "I don't want to hear!"

With a shrug, Fiona reached for her purse and retrieved her checkbook. She wrote something on a bank deposit slip and laid the paper on the table between them.

George lowered her hands.

"You'll change your mind," Fiona promised, "then be frustrated. I wrote the number down. It's unlisted."

"Fiona, I can't call Adam. Don't you understand? My father approves of him!"

"I know Harlan Richards is supposed to be an old stinker, but frankly, George, you've finally baffled me."

She slid down in the chair, her arms dangling over the arms. "I was right in the first place, Adam Lawrence must have a criminal streak. Maybe not burglary but larceny. And not petty—otherwise my father wouldn't like him. He only likes men who are large-scale plunderers. Fiona," she exhaled, her chin sagging to her chest, "I was wrong—wrong again. I have no sense where men are concerned."

"Ah, I see the point you're trying to make. However, I disagree completely. When I was a young woman, I hadn't your good judgment. I was attracted to the flashy, pretentious type of man, the more dangerous the better. It caused me a great deal of pain. I'd be willing to bet that like me, you wouldn't be fooled now by whoever hurt you before."

"Michael tricked me so easily. It wasn't until my father—"

"Stop. Excuse my mixed metaphor, but the cream of the scum are the ones who pursue women with our kind of money. Michael whoever was probably as smooth as eel skin and twice as tough. I suppose he was terribly handsome?"

"Like Adonis."

"How old were you when this happened?"

"Twenty."

"How old was your father?"

"Fifty-seven."

"Ah! And your father has held this mistake up to you all these years?"

"Yes, I suppose he has. I always thought that if I could be so naive—"

"Believe me," she said dryly, "if you were a fifty-seven-year-old self-made millionaire assessing your daughter's young suitor, you could spot a fortune hunter too."

She swiveled in her chair and rested her forearm across the padded arm. "Listen, the only people who never make mistakes are dead." She waved her finger at George. "Remember that. I finally learned to turn my disastrous affair into a memory I could live with, a memory of excitement, of reckless foolishness. Love will make fools of us all if we're lucky enough. After my affair, I married an understanding and forgiving man. Now you've found Adam. You know he's a fine man. Don't bother to deny it."

"He stood on my very own back porch and told me that he doesn't know what love is. When I tried to tell him that people love him, meaning me, he said that nobody loves him enough. He has some fairy-tale notion about love and marriage."

"Possibly the world's greatest delusion is that men are more pragmatic than women. George, ask yourself, isn't a relationship with a wonderful man worth fighting for?"

George moaned dismally, feeling worse than ever. "I know you're right, Fiona—about Adam's character, I mean. It took me four hours to work myself up to doubting him." She squirmed in her chair, too depressed to sit still. "Don't you see that if he actually is what he says he is, it only makes things absolutely impossible? A part of me wants to believe he's ruthless. If he's like my father then I can have him."

Fiona rested her chin on her fist. "Heaven help me, there is something more complicated than the new math."

"If Adam is ruthless, then I could marry him. He would go to work with my father, and they'd both be happy. Adam would be the man of my dreams in every other way and maybe I could be fairly happy too. On the other hand, if Adam is exactly the person I think he is, the man who is searching for joy, freedom, and happiness, I can't marry him. He would be miserable working for my father."

"Why should he have to work for your father?"

"Because my father says so. Even if Adam said no at first, he would keep pressuring him, and believe me that can be worse than doing what he wants in the first place. He would make Adam absolutely miserable." She toyed with the piece of paper with Adam's telephone number, her chest strangely hollow and her breaths long and shaky. "I do love him, Fiona. That's why I have to let him go."

George picked up the paper to tear the temptation in half and stopped, flabbergasted.

She thrust her face closer to examine the careful handwriting. True the letters were less rounded and more streamlined, but the bull's-eye loop on the tail of the M in Adam matched the ones in the murder note. The truth blinked like screaming-red neon on a black night.

"Marie Antoinette," George breathed, slowly raising her head. Her eyes fixed Fiona's, the pieces of a forty-one-year-old puzzle falling magically into place. "I saw a copy of the song lyrics at Natasha's. They're in your handwriting. You wrote them, didn't you?"

Fiona met her gaze. The older woman's eyes telegraphed shock then fear. She twisted her head away.

"You said you had a tragic affair with a flashy, dangerous man. That was Marshall Hoagsworth, Sr. Then, later, you married the understanding, forgiving man. All along I knew that you were trying to protect your son. Now, it's easy to see why. Gracious, Marvin is Marshall's son, isn't he? That's the big, horrible secret you were so afraid Smith or someone else would uncover."

Fiona straightened her shoulders and rose, her face oddly composed. Transfixed, George followed her progress as she crossed to the window and drew aside the curtain. A pale spike of sunlight outlined her profile. She was still lovely, even in her early sixties, and radiated a regal presence. Holy merciful heavens, no wonder Dwight had remained bewitched for nearly half a century.

"Marie Antoinette?" Fiona whispered.

"Hold that thought," George commanded, dashing to answer the door. She swung it wide. "Adam! You're here just in time." She grabbed his arm and dragged him inside.

229

"Ugh, I brought you—"

"Thank you," she jabbered, snatching the potted dandelion from his hands. Contorting her face at him, she muttered for his benefit alone, "Fiona was just telling me about Marie Antoinette."

Adam transformed his startled expression into a benevolent if somewhat bewildered smile. He slipped into the living room and took a seat.

George dropped the dandelion off on an end table and returned to her chair. Fiona appeared frozen in place—as still and serene as Dwight's marble statue. George took a deep, steadying breath and prayed that when she opened her mouth this time that the right words would pour out. The stakes loomed monumental. Fiona was the key to saving Adam. "Fiona, the day after Harry's murder you arranged to have the gathering at your house, hoping that the murderer would make a mistake and betray his or her identity. You hoped to somehow stop the investigation before Marvin was harmed. That's why you felt so guilty when Agnes was poisoned."

Fiona laced her fingers as though in prayer. "You are a clever girl."

"That afternoon at your house you realized that what happened to Hangtown Harry and to Dr. Emerson is tied to Marshall Hoagsworth, Sr.'s murder in the forties. You can't go on protecting people forever. Don't you see that the quicker these murders are solved the better off everyone will be, especially Marvin? No one needs to find out his real father is Marshall, Sr., and once this mess is cleared up, he'll easily beat Smith in the election. Adam and I need your help. Please."

Fiona stood still, seemingly oblivious to every word. George searched her mind for a way to pry forty-one-year-old secrets from this proud, stubborn lady.

"You've read that Hangtown Harry was a fraud. What you don't know is that Harry found a way to cheat people out of their savings accounts and that's why the police suspect Adam. The police think that Adam killed Harry. He needs your help." She paused, waiting, overcome by helplessness. Her pleas seemed as futile as rain beating on stone. "It's not fair to put Adam through this—not fair at all!"

Without looking at him, George sensed Adam's silent encouragement from across the room. His confidence in her seemed to stream through her like a warm flow of blood, replacing numb resignation with renewed strength. Suddenly she felt invincible. *Oh, Adam, how I love you.* She scooted to the edge of her chair, determined. "Fiona, you said yourself what a fine man Adam is. He doesn't deserve this, especially when we both know he can't be guilty."

Nothing penetrated. Damn her! How could she stand there, as cold as a diamond and twice as hard. George dug her nails into the arms of the chair to keep herself from rushing to the window and slapping the serenity from the older woman's face. "Think of Adam!" she cried. "He needs your help!"

The words echoed throughout the house. When they died, George screamed them again.

Fiona slowly angled her head toward George. Her face revealed no clue to her thoughts, but her eyes sparkled as though with a strange detachment, her bearing odd and spell-like. "I suppose that Adam has a right to know the truth," she said without conviction.

George steadied herself and glanced at Adam. His feet were planted apart, his hands gripping his knees. His blanched knuckles contrasted sharply with his tanned skin. He flashed her a tight, thumbs-up type of smile.

Fiona spoke to the window, her tone wistful. "Marshall smiled at me one day. It all seemed rather innocent at the time. I had just returned from my first year at college, and I was rushing to the front curb to get my mother's prescription from the delivery boy. Marshall tipped his hat and smiled. I remembered thinking that a wanton impulse stirred to life inside my body, a desire for dangerous knowledge. Marshall sensed it. He courted me slyly and deftly, feeding me great doses of excitement and intrigue. He kept a lavish apartment in Pacific Heights, a secret, shuttered place with a sparkling crystal chandelier and soft, soft furniture.

"I knew it was wrong; he was married." She lowered her head. Her voice shook. "But I was only nineteen. Just nineteen. I had no idea what price we'd all pay. My mother couldn't bear it. She . . . died."

With a sharply indrawn breath, she threw her head back, and once again returned to the composed, regal lady. "Right before I was to return East to school, he asked me when my period had come. When I told him I was overdue, he told me to go to Emerson to 'get fixed up.' I had to make him explain, which he did, quite clearly. You see," she said bitterly, "he was very experienced in dealing with that sort of thing.

"Still, I clung to his lies. When I learned about the plans for the birthday party at his club, I remembered that his wife, Ina, had performed on stage. I thought that maybe if I . . . Nineteen," she repeated, "and foolish enough to dream that a man like him would seek a divorce and marry his teenage mistress.

"The night I was to take the train back to school, I copied the words to a song from a movie. I took my bag and waited in the dark behind the club, hoping to bribe one of the women into letting me take her place. Taking great care to hide my face, I approached one who was reeling drunk and struck a bargain without any idea of what I was in for. Inside I discovered my costume and dressed. The instant before he pushed me on stage this horrible man rasped, 'Remember to take it all off and do it slow.'

"I was trapped, terrified. I could never recall much about what happened on stage. I do remember Dwight appearing like a gift from heaven. Then I heard shouts. Marshall shoved Dwight aside. Marshall's face was red and ugly, his anger incredible. He grabbed me and carried me into the dressing room, slamming the door behind him. He shoved a towel in my mouth and beat me. His eyes were unfocused, insane. He must have hit me on the chin because I blacked out.

"When I came to, I was dressed in my own clothes and slumped in the backseat of a taxi approaching the train station. When I questioned the driver, he told me that a man dressed like a stevedore had dropped me in back and a woman had paid the fare. I couldn't be sure if the driver was being truthful; he seemed edgy. I assumed that someone from the club had arranged for one of the female performers to handle the situation to avoid a scandal and to protect Marshall. It seemed logical that when she dressed me, she had gone through my things and run across my ticket."

Fiona began clasping and unclasping her hands. She continued, speaking quickly. "I got on the train that night. I was back East before I even knew that Marshall had been murdered. To this day, I don't know who killed him or why."

George hopped to her feet, knowing she must challenge her story now. "You can't go on protecting her any longer. I know Agnes poisoned herself, and I know why." She swallowed and bluffed, "I also know that Agnes had an affair with Marshall, too, and that Dr. Emerson performed her abortion."

Fiona whirled around. "You're guessing."

"The basement, I mean my basement. Dr. Emerson kept records. Adam found them when he went to get the pump." She prayed Adam would back her in this small hoax and he did, remaining silent.

Fiona began wringing her hands, her skin pale. George seized on Fiona's indecision, hoping to beat it into abject submission.

"You told me that Agnes was your childhood friend. She followed you that night to the club, saw Marshall beat you, then shot him dead. It's the only way it makes any sense. Only a friend would go to all the trouble to search for your ticket and hire a stevedore to carry you away from there."

"Dr. Emerson blackmailed Agnes for years," Adam interjected. His fingers closed reassuringly over her arm. George leaned against him, grateful for his touch. She drank in the sight of his strong profile, his quiet power. He was going to be safe.

He continued, "Only this afternoon, I found out that Agnes is virtually penniless. Her savings account clearly indicates that she'd been withdrawing large sums of money in cash once a month for years. Her balance dwindled to virtually nothing about the time Emerson died mysteriously. Enter Hangtown Harry Frye.

"Harry had an inside contact at Pacific West Bank and Trust searching for a sizable account to raid. Harry evidently checked his neighbors first, and Harry was probably surprised to learn that Agnes had so little money in the bank. When Emerson died about the same time that Agnes's account was closed, Harry, well aware of Emerson's basement business, put the two events together. Harry's accomplice inside the bank had only to check Dr. Emerson's account and spot the deposit and withdrawal patterns to confirm the link.

"Then Harry, ever the con man, decided to blackmail Agnes hoping that she had some additional lucrative assets. Her house alone is worth a fortune. Harry became her third victim."

George decided the moment had arrived for the final telling clue. "Adam and I found Agnes's herb garden. She poisoned herself with a plant to divert suspicion."

Fiona pressed her hands over her cheeks, tears glimmering in her eyes. "Oh, Lord," she cried. "I've been afraid of this."

George rushed to her and hugged the sobbing woman. Her towering body seemed frail and bony. She wept silently. "Fiona, I know she's sweet, but try to keep in mind that she's also dangerous. She has killed three people, after all."

"Poor Aggie," she sniffed. "She must have been such an easy target for Marshall. Nobody ever showed her any affection. Isn't there some way that we can help her?"

"She has to be stopped, Fiona," Adam added sensibly. "We can't just let her continue to run around murdering men."

George smoothed back the riot of red hairs escaping from Fiona's untidy bun. "Marvin knows a wonderful lawyer. She can probably plead insanity. She's lived on Scarlet Street all her life; that ought to help her convince the judge."

"I suppose you're right. Grandmother always said that Aggie's oars barely skimmed the water."

George gave Fiona a reassuring squeeze. Fiona's attitude heartened her. They needed her help to trap Agnes. George didn't have a bit of confidence that the police could wrap this murder up before the election. "It's just there's so little time left until Election Day. At my party tomorrow night we could all dress up—"

"I'll give it. It's the least I can do for Aggie. After all, it will be her last—" Fiona's voice broke. "I can hardly believe it. Aggie."

Adam raised a brow. "Your punch certainly can't hurt our cause," he remarked dryly.

Hearing scratching and crying, George swiveled.

Adam strode to the door and freed the lock. Mr. Moto galloped into the room sending rugs flying. He slid to a halt at George's feet. Leaning over, he spat a large piece of bloody meat out of his mouth with a shudder and a retch. A watery flow of saliva streamed from his jowls. He coughed.

"Poison!" George shrieked. "It must be! Agnes got home from the hospital today. This is no coincidence."

Fiona crouched next to the drooling dog. "Poor boy. We have to get him to a veterinarian immediately."

Adam appeared at her side and dropped to his knees. "Look, he didn't eat it. Good boy," he soothed, scratching the dog's furry neck. "There's no sign of the meat being torn."

Fiona ripped off her jacket, wrapped it around the meat, and tied the arms. "Adam, go get my car and pull it around front. I'll drive him. George, go dial the emergency animal clinic and warn them that we're coming. They're in the book. I expect the two of you to stay here and work things out. If poor Aggie can't be saved from an institution and Mr. Moto has to be sick, the least you two can do is make me happy by salvaging your relationship."

Several minutes later, George watched through the window as Adam loaded Mr. Moto into the backseat of Fiona's Cadillac. Thank heavens the veterinarian had been encouraging on the telephone.

She paced the floor, knowing she needed to rehearse or she would certainly blow her farewell speech to Adam.

235

She stopped and extended a stiff hand into empty air. "Thank you for the dandelion, but I still can't see you anymore." Too trite, she decided.

She extended both hands. "We can never be together. It's fate." Too melodramatic.

She rolled her shoulder. "It was fun while it lasted but . . ." Oh, mercy, too flippant.

The second Adam stepped into the foyer, she whirled around and panicked. He looked so tall and gorgeous and lovable that her resolve evaporated. She blurted, "Forget what I said before. I take it back. Why don't we go down to the basement and see if Dr. Emerson's files are really there?"

Chapter
24

Adam shouldered open George's basement door and stood aside.

"Why do I have to go first?" George asked, straining to penetrate the darkness. "It's black as pitch down there."

He held up the flashlight. "Then follow me."

"What if we get separated?"

"It's only your basement, not a cave."

"No one could tell that by looking," she grumbled, lifting the back of his corduroy sport coat and lacing her fingers through one of the belt loops on his jeans. "An illegal abortion mill in my own basement. So much for the hidden joys of home ownership!"

She crept along behind Adam down a steep flight of rickety wooden stairs. An eerie chorus of creaks and moans marked their descent into the dismal depths of the house. The dust on the rail combined with the sweat on her palm and coated her hand with a thin layer of mud. She wondered how many trembling hands had touched the rough rail, how many faltering footfalls had sounded on these awful stairs bringing heaven knew how many frightened young women and girls one step closer to a gruesome appointment.

Finally, mercifully, she heard the soles of Adam's shoes rasp against concrete.

"Last step," he coached, training the light at her feet. When both her tennis shoes were firmly planted on the hard floor, Adam pointed the flashlight at a wooden pallet nearby. "That's where I found the pump. I didn't have to search much at all."

His voice sounded strangely hollow in the damp gloom. She snuggled closer to his warmth, still clutching the belt loop. "I can't imagine why I suggested this."

"Because you want to know whether or not you told Fiona the truth."

"I always tell the truth or—"

"Or a reasonable facsimile thereof. You definitely told a white lie this afternoon. You said that when I came down here several days ago for the pump, I had discovered Emerson's records and proof that Agnes had an abortion."

"Somehow I just had to convince Fiona to help us, and you see that my bluff worked. She suspected Agnes all along; she simply refused to admit it."

"I must confess to a white lie myself. I had Lois check on Dr. Emerson. He didn't bank at Pacific West." Adam began slowly panning the room with the light. "Still, an old con artist like Harry with a suspicious nature and access to Agnes's financial records could have deduced the link between Agnes exhausting her savings and Emerson dying mysteriously. Did you hear something?"

"Only the sound of my heart jumping into my throat."

"There." The beam illuminated miscellaneous gardening implements, their narrow shadows spilling over the edges of a door frame.

"Let's try that door," Adam suggested. She gripped his belt even tighter as they picked their way through a welter of paint cans, clay flowerpots, and rusty tools. He ran the light over the handles of a rake and shovel that were propped against the door. "Look," he said, repeating the same procedure with a nearby hoe. "The cobwebs on the hoe are undisturbed while some on the rake and shovel are broken."

"Someone beat us here."

Adam set the tools aside. "Or Emerson came here himself from time to time. There's quite a bit of dust on the doorknob. I doubt it's been tampered with in several months." He drew his handkerchief out of his pocket and turned the knob. "It won't budge. Hand me your keys."

She obliged, watching intently as he tried several in the lock. A slender gold key rotated the tumblers with a *thump*. Taking a deep breath of dank, stale air, she followed Adam into an examining room. A narrow table centered the cubicle, the walls outfitted with a metal cabinet and a matching credenza, their glass doors hazy with grime. "This must be where he did those . . . things." She glanced back at the sheet-draped table. "Think how desperate those poor women must have been to come into this hole and—ugh. That table makes my skin crawl."

"There's a filing cabinet in the corner."

They padded toward it together. Her eyes darted over the shadowy recesses, alert for rats or mice or disgruntled ghosts. "No wonder I have trouble sleeping in this house," she said with a shudder, "with all this under my bed."

Adam repeated the tedious process with keys, trying several before the filing cabinet yielded. The ancient mechanism squealed as he rolled out the top drawer. He angled the light and ran it over the file labels.

"My God," he muttered.

George reached on tiptoe and scanned the names, her amazement growing with every entry. "Holy heaven! I've heard of these people! Most of them are famous, and this drawer only goes as far as the letter G."

"It's a blackmailer's gold mine."

She studied his face in the dim light. "Surely Dr. Emerson couldn't have been blackmailing all these women."

"Not this one," he said, flipping one of the tabs with his index finger. "She married a man in organized crime who plants his problems six feet under."

She ran her thumb over several charts then stopped. "This woman used to be a social reporter for the paper. She's an absolute shark. She said all sorts of awful things about my mother once at a party. Here's Agnes's chart." She extracted it from the file. "It has an orange clip sticking up on top, and the crime wife and reporter charts don't."

"I think you may have something there. Here's another orange clip. Didn't she marry the Higgins fortune?"

George nodded. "There're only a few orange clips in this drawer."

"With the kind of money these folks have, it doesn't take many to turn a tidy profit."

George blew the dust off Agnes's chart. "Shine the light here." She peeled back the flap and shuffled through the pages. "She had her abortion in July 1949."

"That means that Agnes was probably Fiona's predecessor in Marshall's bed. If Fiona returned to school in the fall, she must have become pregnant by late August or early September. Hoagsworth didn't waste much time. God, you'd think a guy seducing young, inexperienced girls would have at least used some protection."

"He was a totally reprehensible man. I'm convinced of that. Oh! Oh! Here it is! Proof!" She pointed to the nearly illegible writing.

Adam rested his chin on her shoulder. "I can't read it."

"That's because the entry is as messy as one of your notes. It says 'convulsions, unconsciousness, breathing shallow and irregular' which was the exact way Agnes reacted when she drank the tainted punch. Here it says, 'Later the patient admitted to locating grandmother's cache of home remedies and taking a teaspoon of oil of tansy hoping to induce abortion.'" She snapped the file shut. "No wonder Agnes used tansy. She'd used it before."

"That makes sense. It's definite then; Agnes is a murderess. Hell, I certainly wouldn't have picked her." He straightened slowly. "Maybe while we're down here, we ought to take a quick run through the names. Didn't Fiona say that Natasha's real name was Trimmer?"

George tucked Agnes's file back in its place between a

movie star who spent most of the fifties wilting in the arms of brawny cowboys and a current and highly respected state representative. "I'll look down here. Do we have any idea what Estelle Capricorn's real name is?"

"Not a clue."

"No Trimmer. No LaRose. Adam, it may not work, but let's scan the files for the first name Rosa."

"A through Z and no Rosa," Adam said minutes later.

"Still," George mused, "Harry knew about Emerson's illegal business. . . . I've got it. His wife! Elmo said she was a nymphomaniac!"

"He did? Did I miss something here? I think I would have remembered that sort of revelation."

"Reed, Reed, Reed. Here it is! Gracious, this is a fat one." She thumbed through her chart. "Several, the last in 1968 and the one before that was in . . ." She ran her finger over the yellowed paper. "It was 1966 and both of those were after her marriage to Harry twenty-five years ago. I guess that settles it. That's how Harry knew about Dr. Emerson and guessed about Agnes."

"Maybe Mr. Moto didn't bark the night of Emerson's murder either. That would've certainly focused Harry's attention on the neighbors, just as it did yours." Adam wiped his forehead with the back of his hand. "I can't understand why a woman like Agnes would pay blackmail for a forty-one-year-old abortion."

"Pride, I suppose."

"It would make more sense to me if Agnes paid Emerson because he had some bit of convincing evidence that she murdered Marshall. There's no statute of limitations on murder. Maybe Emerson did have evidence that Agnes killed Marshall."

"If it ever existed, Agnes surely would have destroyed it the night she killed Emerson."

"A blackmailer as skillful as this," he gestured toward the packed files, "would have kept a hidden ace in the hole to prevent just such a thing. I wonder if we could convince Agnes that we had found it."

"And trap her! Oh, Adam Lawrence, you do have a

devious mind." She paused, nibbling on her lip. "The only trouble is that none of this will clear you of conspiring with Harry to defraud the bank. I still think that we have to question Joan LaRose, or Rosa, or whatever her name is. Surely, she must know the identity of his contact."

"Getting her to part with that information might be a little tricky."

George put her arm through his. "Not for a man in uniform."

She only raised her chin at his quizzical expression.

"I feel silly in this uniform," Adam grumbled. "Everyone is staring at me."

"That's because you look devastatingly handsome." George gripped his arm more tightly as they dashed off the bus on Valencia Street. "Rosa's should be about a block over on Mission near 21st Street. If Marfa hadn't babbled so much I would have had plenty of time to show you my favorite Victorian house on Guerrero Street, but as it is we'll just beat the dinner crowd." She picked up her pace, her heels clicking on the pavement. "I'm so happy that Mr. Moto is going to be all right."

"I fail to see how a forestry service uniform is going to be of help in questioning Joan LaRose, assuming she's even there."

"No one will be able to read the insignia in the dim light. Trust me. Joan won't be focusing her attention on your pocket if I'm any judge of character. Besides, we only need it as an excuse to get past her help."

"I'll be lucky to avoid arrest for impersonating Smokey Bear."

"Absolutely not," she said, angling her head. "Without that funny round hat, you don't look a thing like him. Here it is." She pulled up in front of a hole-in-the-wall with blackened windows and a gaily painted sign that spelled out Rosa's Restaurante y Cantina in green vines accented with red roses. On an easel near the door, a photograph of Ricardo Pena holding his guitar was mounted on a black cardboard sign sprinkled with silver glitter.

As she had predicted, the interior was dark and deserted except for two waiters setting tables and a plump man behind the bar pouring brown liquid from a mason jar into a funnel stuck in the neck of a Chivas bottle. As they approached, he snatched up the funnel and swept both it and the jar under the bar. "We don't open for another twenty minutes," he informed them, regarding Adam with a cool, appraising stare.

"I'm Georgette Richards and this is Adam Lawrence. We need to speak to the proprietress regarding an immigration problem."

"You got ID?"

George raised her chin with an imperturbable air. "I'm flattered, but I assure you that I have been over twenty-one for quite some time now."

"ID as in badges, lady," he hissed, revealing white teeth.

"Show him, Adam."

Adam tugged out his wallet and flipped it open and closed in virtually one smooth movement—a good thing, since Marfa had lent them a badge belonging to the hunk of a fireman who was currently spending his "three-off" in Marfa's bed. Thank heavens she'd switched from professional athletes to men with badges in the nick of time.

The bartender dropped the bottle of phony Chivas into a slot beneath the bar and shuffled toward the rear of the restaurant. With a flip of his head he motioned for them to follow. The young waiters fled from their path like frightened deer.

At the end of a hallway adjacent to a kitchen that smelled very strongly of chili peppers and pine cleaner, the bartender rolled his knuckles against a door and muttered, "Unwelcome guests from immigration, Senora Velasquez."

Damn, she thought, hearing the name. Where in daylights was Joan LaRose?

"Show them in, Pietro."

The clear voice sounding from inside the office renewed her hopes. The phrase vibrated with the melodic lilt of a singer.

"You!" Joan LaRose exclaimed, shock registering on her

perfectly made-up face. During the instant of first sight, George decided that the woman appeared different somehow. With a quick movement, Joan clicked off the light on her desk, plunging the room into near-gloom and effectively thwarting any opportunity for George to study her to figure out why.

"This is Adam Lawrence. I don't believe you met at the funeral."

"What brings you down to the Mission? Slumming?" she asked in a mocking tone.

In the soft lamplight, George spotted Adam gesturing toward a worn leather couch. She took a seat. Surprisingly, Adam remained standing, his expression strange and unreadable.

George folded her hands in her lap knowing good and well she wouldn't be able to contain them there for long. Swaying the wary Joan LaRose might require a performance. "Miss LaRose, I know that this is a difficult time for you, but after I've explained why we've come, I know you'll agree that our talk is absolutely essential."

"We'll see," she said dryly.

"I certainly admire your devotion to Hangtown Harry and the lengths you went to so that he received a wonderful send-off according to the traditions he believed in. I know what a rough time Mr. Brill gave you, and after all you did for Harry it really hurts me to have to tell you this."

Joan propped her elbow on her desk and ran her thumb over exceptionally long, blood-red nails.

George took a deep breath and said, "Harry probably told you that he wasn't Harry at all, but Arthur Mossbeck, and now of course, everyone knows. But one thing the police have withheld from the press is Harry's scheme to defraud Pacific West Bank and Trust." She paused, noting that what she could see of Joan's expression betrayed absolutely no hint of emotion.

"Harry managed to raid huge accounts at the bank, and the strange thing is that all that money has disappeared."

"We never discussed money," she said, her tone containing a trace of bitterness.

George let Joan's denial hang a minute. Of course Joan and Harry hadn't discussed money, George mused. Joan only went to Reno and Tahoe and watched him gamble heavily while her bartender served fake Chivas to stretch the profits.

"You see—oh, dear, how shall I put this? I guess there's just no other way but to spit this out. I know you and Harry were close, but . . ." she sighed heavily for dramatic effect and lied, "he was having an affair with another woman."

Joan froze, her fist clenched.

"He took her on numerous trips to Switzerland," she exaggerated, "and the police can only guess that he deposited all that money over there." Her bluff worked; anger seemed to storm out of Joan with the speed of a grass fire. So Harry had not taken Joan to Europe, probably not even once in the several times he'd gone.

Joan rasped, "What do you want from me?"

"Help. We want Marvin Breathwaite to defeat that odious Jack Smith in the race for city supervisor. If the scandal surrounding Harry's death isn't cleared up soon, he's going to lose and so will San Francisco. We think that the woman who went with Harry to Switzerland murdered Harry after he transferred all the money overseas, and we need your help to trap her. If we don't, she's probably going to spend the rest of her life lounging in a villa in the south of France, living like royalty off poor Harry's ill-gotten gains." She lounged back into the soft depths of the sofa pleased with herself for adding the last bit. Joan was livid.

Nor hell a fury like a woman scorned, George thought happily, inwardly reciting Congreve's famous line.

Joan's voice shook. "Who is this woman?"

"The woman who helped him with the bank scheme."

This time Joan was silent. Adam roamed the room, glancing at her. Once again, she began running a thumb over her nails, almost idly.

"Either that," George blurted, scrambling for a way to compensate for her mistake and pressure her again, "or he simply used some poor soul at the bank, discarded her, then ran off to Switzerland with the woman Adam and I have been watching for some time."

Joan's thumb swished quickly back and forth. "Who might that be?"

"One of our neighbors. Would you like to meet her?" she inquired casually.

Joan nodded very slowly.

"Come join us at eight tomorrow night at Fiona Breathwaite's home at Sixteen Scarlet. It's a costume party."

George mustered exceptional willpower and contained herself until they left the restaurant and hiked a safe distance down the street. She wanted to run down the sidewalk cheering. "Adam, everything is going to be all right. Joan LaRose must've been Harry's plant in the bank. She seemed so relieved when I said that the plant was the woman I made up."

"Joan LaRose seemed familiar to me at the funeral, but I couldn't place her. Not with that blond wig and all that stage makeup."

"When we first went in I wondered why she said 'You!' but she actually meant you not me, and she switched off the light because she was afraid you'd recognize her. We make quite a team," she caroled. Adam's arm stiffened beneath her hand, jarring the optimism right out of her.

On the long bus trip toward home, she clung to his arm. He said nothing. His silent tension reminded her that once the murders were solved, Adam would be off again chasing the joy and happiness he only *thought* he'd glimpsed once before. He believed in a thirty-year-old fairy tale taught by parents who actually couldn't have loved each other very deeply or they would have loved the product of that love—their son.

Of course she understood that situation perfectly; her father didn't love her either. But she could name a few people who did so the flaw must be in him, not her. Anyway, that's what her cousin Shannon always said.

Adam helped her alight from the bus. The long shadows of early evening followed their slow progress. She gazed up at his handsome face wanting to memorize the crinkles around his eyes, the faint lines along his cheeks that only accented the hard angles of his jaw, and the slight dimple, now ominously absent.

They turned the corner onto Scarlet Street and walked in silence.

Finally he said, "What you said this afternoon was correct. We shouldn't be seeing each other. We're only delaying the inevitable."

"I agree." But, Adam, she thought sadly, not for the reason you think.

She hesitated on her porch, still holding his arm possessively. "Mr. Moto won't be back until tomorrow. I'm frightened to be alone here. Will you stay with me just for tonight?"

"Georgette, promise me that you won't marry some fortune hunter."

"I'll promise on one condition."

"Name it."

She paused, collecting her thoughts, rounding them up and trying to put words to an emotion so deep that it seemed to defy expression. Once she labeled it as love, the rest of her feelings clarified instantly. She thought, I love Adam and I can't let my father destroy his dreams. She looked into Adam's gray-blue eyes and said, "Promise me that you won't ever give up your dreams for anyone."

He promised and she believed him. The weight inside her seemed to lift a little. She could bear this sacrifice—her heart for his dreams.

Chapter 25

"Daddy!" George recoiled in shock. She fumbled with the ties on her bathrobe, pulling them so tight that pain circled her waist. She tugged the flaps of her robe against the base of her throat, mortified by her father's surprise visit.

Upstairs only a moment before, Adam had ducked from under the spray of his morning shower to give her a kiss. The moistness still clung to her lips.

But this was *her* house!

"Daddy, you really should have called first. That's the polite thing to do."

"Invite me in," her father demanded.

"Come in," she replied with an exasperated wave of her hand. "I'll just be a minute getting dressed." She turned, intending to run upstairs.

His cane blocked her way. "What I have to say won't take long."

"What do you want?"

"For you to sit down and stop fidgeting with that damned bathrobe."

She walked into the living room and slid into the deep

recesses of a wing chair, her bare feet dangling off the ground. She watched her father cross the floor with a muted *tap-tap* of his cane. He selected the matching chair and twisted it around to face hers with an easy swing of his good arm. He lowered himself into the chair and set his cane across his knees. He seemed determined to sit in silence.

Dear heaven, what if Adam finished his shower and came downstairs? Thinking of the prospect of that awful scene, she repeated, this time more forcefully, "What do you want?"

"Are you going to marry this Adam Lawrence that you're having an affair with?"

She raised her chin. "What on earth do you mean?"

He lifted the cane and pointed to Adam's corduroy sport coat draped over the edge of one of the sofas.

"So?"

He pointed to a pair of shoes nearby. "I'm not blind."

"I'm not going to marry him."

"That's fine. Just fine," he said, his tone hinting malice. His head shot up, and he boomed, "You're only going to sleep with the man!"

"You've slept with women that you didn't marry. Lots of them."

"Appetite is not the focus of this discussion."

"That's right. What I do with Adam has less to do with appetite than with caring and giving."

"If you care for this man, what's stopping you from marrying him?"

"You."

"I told you he was acceptable."

"Because you think you can manipulate him into working for you. Adam left that life behind forever. He's looking for important things that you don't understand, things like self-fulfillment and happiness—"

Her father stopped her dead in midsentence, his laughter chilling her to the bone. Suddenly her hands and feet grew icy as if all the blood had run away to beat hard in her temples and swim behind her eyes. She rubbed her hands against her thighs, forcing the blood back into her fingers. "You have no right to laugh at me."

Her father raised his heavy-lidded eyes and studied her. "Did Lawrence tell you that he was ambitious enough to become a millionaire through side investments by the time he was thirty? Or did he happen to mention that in years past, I've tried to get him to come to work for me?"

A woozy sensation spun through her head, sending a chorus of wild, horrible conclusions reeling through her brain. Had Adam used her, tricked her?

He paused, undoubtedly preparing to shoot the ruinous barb. "Did he tell you that he hasn't a cent to his name now?"

Her heart fluttered in her chest. Adam had admitted openly that he hadn't any money. What was her father getting at? Why was he prolonging this agony?

"What do those three facts about Lawrence suggest to you?"

"I don't know. But I wish you'd go ahead and tell me because I know you're going to eventually anyway."

"Think about it."

"I know Adam doesn't have any money; he already told me. What difference does it make that he was a millionaire and lost it?"

"It reveals the reason he chose to position himself in your sight. He's down on his luck, but smart. You are a wealthy woman who has a reputation for shunning men of finance so he became a gardener. He courted you with fine words that appeal to your idealistic mind. Undoubtedly his plan is to marry you to assure himself a fortune and a position with my company. So much for caring and giving."

She dug stiff fingers into the arms of the chair. "Those are assumptions, not facts. I don't believe you."

"No? Open your eyes wide for once. This world is full of users. The challenge is to recognize them and turn the tables to one's own advantage. Marrying Lawrence will give him and me what we both want. He can't outwit me. He knew I'd approve or he wouldn't have tried this scheme."

She forced herself to straighten her fingers, to sit back in the chair, to fold her hands in her lap, all the while longing to scream at her father. Instead, with quiet composure she asked, "What about what I want?"

"You have no earthly idea what you want and probably never will. I've introduced you to numerous suitable men and you have refused categorically to keep an open mind. Instead, you waited to take up with another stranger and once again proved your lack of judgment. You've been deceived a second time."

"You actually want me to marry someone who's deceived me?" she squeaked.

"Lawrence is as close as we've come to a mutually beneficial match. You must see by now that you are incapable of choosing a man on your own."

"How could you say such a thing?" she stammered. She glanced away, tears filling her eyes. She ordered herself not to cry and blinking, focused on her father. The words spilled out of her. "Why don't you love me?"

"That's a foolish question. I've always safeguarded your interests."

"Is it because you hated my mother?"

"What gave you that idiotic idea?"

"You don't have a single picture of her. You never mention her. You didn't even let me mourn her. You made me hide my sadness."

"There's nothing wrong with that. I didn't want you to go around hang-faced and moping."

Her hands flew out of her lap. "I'm not going to hide my feelings anymore, not behind my business or my possessions or my friendships. I love you, Daddy, but I don't like you."

Her father stared at her blankly and at last, after years of ceaseless wondering and frustration, she understood that her mother must have left her father for a very simple reason. Harlan Richards was completely incapable of loving anyone. Actually, she had known for years that the capacity for strong emotion was strangely absent in him, but had always held the hope that deep inside him lived the seeds of compassion and understanding. The master of disguising emotion actually had no need of a disguise after all. He was hard as steel right down to the marrow.

"I've never expected you to like me, only respect me."

He'd omitted the word *love*. For him, the word must be empty and meaningless. She tilted her head, regarding him with great sadness. *Have I actually tried to please you all these years because deep in my soul I've always felt sorry for you?*

Maybe.

"Daddy," she said, strangely more calm and composed than ever before in her father's presence, for years you've used my mistake with Michael as an excuse to pair me with every stodgy businessman in this city, and I went along with you because I doubted myself. This time I can't rely on your assumptions; I just can't. I have to have faith in my own judgment."

"And carrying on an affair with a gardener is your idea of good judgment," he mocked. "Don Dick Watson and his cronies are going to smear your name all over the papers to generate publicity for his damned lawsuit and attack me in the process. He's done this kind of thing before."

"I know. That's why I'm going to make a deal with you."

Her father started. "Deal?"

George pinched her tongue between her teeth, her mind clicking. "Yes, a deal."

He shrugged. "State your terms."

She gripped her hands tightly in her lap, knowing she was about to say the most important words of her life. She took a deep, steadying breath and fixed her father's eyes levelly. "Tonight I'll ask Adam Lawrence to marry me providing he agrees to work for you. If he says yes, you'll be right about him. I'll be wrong, but I'll marry him anyway.

"If he says no, I'll be right. In that case, I'll never see him again. In return, you'll stop pressuring me to marry."

Her father planted his cane and raised himself slowly to his feet. "You're a foolish woman. You'll likely end up married to a man who deceived you."

"I think you're wrong about Adam."

"On the other hand, if you happen to be correct, you'll be

giving up the only man who's truly interested you in the past thirteen years. Either way you lose."

"Somehow I knew you'd see it exactly that way."

As dusk yielded to night, George ran downstairs, her glittering blue heels in one hand, her large sapphire earrings, hat, and shepherd's crook in the other. In her newly ordered office, she arranged Agnes's yellowed medical chart on her desk, centering it beneath a small pharmacy lamp. She flipped on the light and surveyed the room. The clue weaving was gone, replaced by tonight's trap for a murderer.

The telephone jangled beside her. She jumped, startled, then pounced on it. "Mark?"

Instead Shannon's voice trembled over the wire. "He's gone to get the car to take me to the hospital. George, I'm scared."

George could hear her cousin weeping into the receiver. "Gracie Shannon," she began firmly, banishing her concern from her voice, "I want you to remember why all this happened in the first place. I know you're hurting from the contractions and it's all Mark's fault. After all, he forced you to fall in love with him, then had the absolute gall to make you outrageously happy and pregnant with two babies. So when he comes for you, I want you to give him a reassuring hug because he called me after he talked to the doctor and admitted that he's terrified. But he's always strong and knows exactly what to do when it really counts so when he says breathe—do it!"

"Thank you, George," Shannon answered softly, her tone steady.

"I love you, Gracie Shannon." The room swam through her misty eyes.

Mark came on the telephone. "She says she loves you too. We have to go."

"Hold her head between your hands," George shouted. "It always makes her feel better."

"I'll take care of her," he said and hung up.

"Why tonight?" she cried.

"Maybe you ought to go to the hospital."

She whirled around at Adam's words. He stood just inside the room, tall and confident, resplendent in his classic black tuxedo. His reassuring presence seemed to jolt half of her fear right out of her. "It's no use." She hung up the telephone and reached into a drawer and pulled out a tissue. She wiped her eyes, the tissue coming away smeared with mascara and shadow. "I'd just have to sit in the waiting room with nothing to do but worry. Mark is going to be with her all through it, and Shannon is very strong. But twins—" She choked on her words.

Adam closed the distance between them and enfolded her in his arms. He ran his hand over the lacy back of her dress, caressing her with his soothing touch.

"If you like, I'll take you to the hospital as soon as this is over."

"Okay." She nestled against him, her hand flat against the studs on his shirt.

"You look lovely in that blue dress. Let me see."

She backed away. His eyes roamed with obvious appreciation over the saucy couture dress she and Marfa had finally agreed on: a scandalously sheer lace mini with a full, fluffy skirt. A dark blue velvet apron draped the front and swept to a loose bow in back at the waist; her shoulders and back were bare beneath a single layer of lace. She slipped into her three-inch heels, put on her small net hat, and picked up the shepherd's crook.

"Wow," he breathed, hands on hips looking lean, dashing, and altogether devastating, "you certainly have made Little Bo Peep sexy as hell."

She set aside the crook and reached for her earrings. She scooted onto the desk and crossed her stockinged legs over the side. The moment of truth had arrived. She clipped on her earrings. "Adam," she said, lowering her arms and straightening the ruffled lace over the crest of her knee, "will you marry me?"

"Good God," he murmured, clearly stunned. "Do you mean that?"

"Of course I mean it. I wouldn't have asked otherwise."

He shoved his hands into his pockets and moved his head slowly side to side. She thought he might be in shock.

Oh, Adam, she prayed, please be the wonderful man I think you are.

"There's a condition attached. You'd have to work for my father, at least for a while." She picked at the lace with her fingernail, willing herself to think of this as an experiment, telling herself that no matter what he said she would survive and not disintegrate into a million shattered pieces. She stared at her knee, waiting.

"Dammit, Georgette! You can't walk into my life and expect to take over."

She snapped her head up and said indignantly, "You could use a job."

"I have a job!" he shouted, throwing up a hand.

"You can't honestly expect Fiona to go on letting you ruin her yard. Then where will you be? You'll be out on the street, maybe even destitute."

"I'm not destitute and never will be."

"But you don't have any—"

"I'm determined to change, Georgette, so determined that I tied my money up so tightly even I won't have access to it for a long time. I wanted the challenge without that temptation and now—" he broke off and paced. "Temptation, hell!" He stopped, spun, and confronted her, red tinting his tanned skin. "Why are you asking me this?" he demanded.

"I . . . I . . ." she stammered. She searched his face, suddenly full of hope at the frustration she saw written there. "Will you marry me?"

"Hell, no! Not under these conditions. Don't you believe the things I say to you?"

George bounded off the desk, tripped on her high heels and fell against him, throwing her arms around his neck. "Oh, Adam, I do believe you, and I love you." She stretched on tiptoe to plant a kiss on lips parted in obvious consternation. "You don't know how I prayed that you'd say no!"

Chapter
26

"Let's hurry," Georgette suggested. "Fiona may need our help with something before the party."

Adam strained to make her out in the dense, dark fog. Logic told him that Fiona's house was about ten feet ahead but with the air as opaque as frosted glass, he was navigating virtually blind. "Georgette, will you slow down. I can't see a blessed thing."

"I'm right in front of you, Adam."

He tramped onward. *Whaap!*

"Damn!" he howled. He thrust away the tree branch and massaged his stinging face.

"Are you all right?" she asked.

"I think it's my pride that's wounded."

She touched his arm. "Why?" she asked in a completely innocent tone.

"You could show a little disappointment that I turned down your marriage proposal instead of acting so damned gleeful about the whole thing."

"I don't understand why you're so upset. You want to be free and because I love you that's what I want for you."

"Don't you feel any . . . any feeling about it?"

"Oh, yes! It's the most wonderful thing that anyone ever did for me!"

He clapped his hand to his forehead. She was ecstatic. He felt like hell. Typical, he thought, cursing inwardly. Typical. "I swear I will never understand you, Georgette."

"Air of mystery, you know." She danced ahead.

Mr. Moto and Fiona greeted them at the front entrance. Dressed as a white-robed Helen of Troy, Fiona's hair was stacked into an impressive mountain of red curls. "See, Mr. Moto's fine, George," she said, hugging her. "Although he seems a bit agitated all of a sudden."

The dog pranced at Georgette's feet. "You know you're going to help us trap your master's murderer tonight, don't you, fella?"

Fiona said, "You look pained, Adam."

"It's only his pride," Georgette said with an infuriatingly casual toss of her head. "He'll get over it. Is everything ready?"

Adam grumbled as he trailed them into the cavernous great hall in the center of the house.

"The hand-delivered invitations worked. Everyone gave the messenger an affirmative reply. Apparently all of them had saved the date for your party despite the Bay Bridge World Series."

"Not the Hoagsworths?"

"I'm afraid so." Fiona spread her hands in an expansive shrug. "But it's too late to change our plan now. Aggie is already upstairs getting ready. She seemed absolutely delighted with her costume. Poor Aggie," she mumbled, lines creasing her forehead. She snapped back to herself. "Anyway, Estelle's in the side parlor working herself into some kind of trance. How did you get her to give up one of her pre–Halloween séances and cooperate with us?"

"I talked to a reputable psychic who belongs to a parapsychology association with a strict code of ethics. When I confronted Estelle, I sort of implied that I would let San Francisco know that she, on the other hand, considers ethics a matter of multiple choice . . ."

"You are brilliant!" Fiona exclaimed.

Now Fiona seemed ecstatic. Adam still felt like hell.

Georgette stepped close and smoothed the tuxedo over his shoulders. Dammit, he wondered, why did she have to look so happy?

On impulse he lifted her and kissed her hard, long, and potently. He set her down, her lipstick smeared, her mouth agape. She appeared dumbfounded.

"After this, we talk," he stated flatly. He stalked past her and marched upstairs to wait for his cue.

Half an hour later, Fiona telephoned to signal that all stood ready. Adam knocked on one of the bedroom doors. Extending his bent arm to Agnes Clodfelter, he waited for her gloved hand then guided the murderess to the head of the staircase.

The lights in the great hall dimmed and died. Darkness descended like a stifling cloak. From below came the rasp of a match. A murmur swept over the assembled guests as a wavering light touched the tip of a candle. When thirteen tiny flames burned in the omnipresent dark, Estelle Capricorn blew out the match. Draped in some sort of flowing black garment emblazoned with geometric symbols, she posed on the last stair beside the candelabra. The candles flickered as she raised her arms.

"Tonight and every night, the dead walk among us, restless spirits doomed by fate to wander, searching but never finding peace through the gloom of Scarlet Street. They died in all matter of ways: razed by the bullet of a dueling pistol, hanged by their own hand, or murdered by club or gun—or knife. And we the living, here tonight, pay tribute to their immortal souls.

"The most infamous murder in Scarlet Street history took place forty-one years ago on a night much like tonight, when revelers journeyed through the fog, gathering to celebrate the birthday of Marshall Hoagsworth, Sr. A mysterious lady mingled with the entertainers, some say, intent on murder.

"During the performance of a masked Marie Antoinette, Marshall leaped to the stage, some say, to subdue his paramour. She disappeared forever that night. He died. But after a touch of magic—"

She flipped both arms. Light flashed. A puff of smoke expanded with a pop. "Here they are."

A chorus of "Ahs" accompanied Adam and Agnes's descent down the stairs. Although it was difficult to believe that this ploy was going to work, Adam had to concede that a strange aura now surrounded Agnes. She moved with studied grace, a calm assurance. The mystical gleam in her eye made him wonder if she actually believed that she had become the bewitching Marie Antoinette.

By the time they reached the foot of the stairs, someone had lit the other candles and raised the numerous Gothic chandeliers. "Shall we dance?" Agnes asked shyly.

"Of course." Adam guided her into the area near the small orchestra. They trod the floor, her scarlet silk dress swaying and rustling, the other dancers staring. Reminding himself of the task at hand, he waltzed Agnes aside. "Marie?" he asked, hoping to maintain her mood. The eyes she raised to his were hazy and unfocused.

"Yes, Marshall," she murmured.

"Dr. Emerson's journals have been located."

Beneath the mask, the color drained from Agnes's parchment skin. She searched his face as though pleading for help. He swallowed deliberately and forced himself to increase the pressure. He repeated his rehearsed line. "The documents were discovered in a secret room adjacent to Miss Richards's study late this afternoon, but because the paper was damaged and is now so brittle, the police are sending for an expert to remove them in the morning."

Her stricken expression made him want to recant his lies. He easily strengthened his resolve by reminding himself that this woman had ruthlessly murdered three men. This scared rabbit act of hers was only a ruse to disguise an evil soul capable of three bloody killings.

"We must stop now. We must," she said in a shaky little voice. Gingerly, she tapped her hands against his chest, as though begging for freedom. He refused to be swayed by her convincing act.

"Once the police see Dr. Emerson's records they are certain to realize that the murders of Hangtown Harry, Dr. Emerson, and the most famous crime of all are linked. Won't they, Marie?"

Agnes shook as though gripped by spasms, her head bowed, her shoulders slumped. He thought he heard a tiny whimpering sound escape from her throat. What a performance.

A hand fell heavily on Adam's shoulder. Dwight Phillips, dressed as Davy Crockett, said, "May I cut in?"

His question sounded more like a demand than a request.

Adam slid his hand from Agnes's waist and relinquished the trembling woman. Agnes extended a beseeching hand to him, a strange gesture considering the way he'd tormented her.

With a swish of scarlet silk and the slap of buckskin fringe, the mismatched pair waltzed jerkily away.

He scanned the eerie old room. Even in the scanty illumination, he picked Georgette out of the group of costumed people. She smiled at him, and he marveled at her ability to enliven his spirit with a single glance. Is that what happens when you love someone?

He elbowed his way toward her. She poured so much into the look she gave him—encouragement, admiration, pride to be his lover—and conveyed the messages with such clarity, he could imagine her words. Her praise quickened the life that beat inside him until he felt ebullient and invincible. *Do I love you, Georgette?*

He signaled her to meet him near one of the trophy alcoves.

"How did it go?" she asked in a conspiratorial whisper, directing a quick glance at the dance floor.

He closed his hand on her arm. "We'll have to wait and see. Where did all the people come from?"

"They're just a lot of acquaintances to fill out the party and make everyone feel less conspicuous. Do you know that Don Dick Watson had the gall to crash as Julius Caesar? What an insult! If he'd come as Ivan the Terrible, well . . .

Do you know he's over there trying to get Marfa to do the Dance of the Seven Veils?"

Adam tightened his grip on her arm and lowered his face to hers. "Forget Watson. You telephone Hernandez the instant Agnes bolts. I'll follow her. You do nothing. Understood?"

"Understood. I have to tell you I talked to Marshall, Jr. and Joan LaRose and—"

Earsplitting barks shattered conversation and silenced the orchestra. Adam saw Mr. Moto charge out of the kitchen, teeth bared, fur hackles raised. He barreled across the stone floor, scattering the guests as bulls do the boys of Pamplona.

He stopped and whirled. He raised his nose to the huddled people with an ominous-sounding growl.

"Moto!" Adam shouted. "Mr. Moto."

He swung his massive body around, his ears angled forward. His eyes gleamed like green fire.

"Come!" Adam commanded.

The dog hesitated, obviously in turmoil. He snapped his head back toward the people then toward Adam, apparently torn between loyalty and some primal instinct.

Chapter 27

George gaped at the snarling Mr. Moto. Now with his ears laid back, his body hunkered low to the ground, he looked ready to kill. But who? Agnes?

She quickly skimmed her eyes over the crowd. No Marie Antoinette. Did that explain the dog's hesitation? Had Agnes fled?

"Adam, she's gone!" she cried. Too late. He had already released her arm and was approaching the dog.

Mr. Moto growled a warning that Adam refused to heed. He stopped several feet away and extended his hand palm-up inches below the flickering lips of the enraged dog.

Mr. Moto's stance seemed to relax. His tail twitched tightly over his back.

In one smooth motion, Adam rotated his hand over the furry head and snagged Mr. Moto's collar at the crest of his neck. A collective sigh rippled through the crowd as he began leading the reluctant dog toward the kitchen.

George rushed toward the dance floor, scanning the area, hoping to glimpse the scarlet costume. A sinking feeling entered her stomach. She ran into Elmo Burroughs, his bony body covered in a saggy body stocking, his torso draped in leopardskin. "Tarzan," he announced, flexing a skinny arm.

"Elmo, have you seen Marie?"

"Marie?"

"Agnes Clodfelter, full dress, mask, the one who came downstairs with Adam."

"Ahhhh," he drawled. "I can't say as though—"

She darted away before he could finish, desperately searching the gloom, suddenly certain that Agnes had availed herself of Mr. Moto's outburst to escape next door to locate Dr. Emerson's journals. Agnes had murdered Hangtown Harry. She must have been terrified that Mr. Moto would find her despite the crowd.

George hesitated. Shall I get Adam? No, she decided. No time. Agnes could have her chart and disappear in minutes, the opportunity to trap her gone—perhaps forever.

She walked quickly toward the front of the house, trying to appear calm, inconspicuous. She spied Fiona's tranquilizer gun that she'd seen Dwight use earlier to complete his Davy Crockett costume. She hoped it was loaded. She glanced around her, assured herself that no one was watching, and angled next to the gun. After one more hasty check, she snatched up the unwieldy weapon and headed out the front door.

Fog blanketed every landmark. She followed the porch railing, then the side of the house. In the distance a door slammed. She strained to get a bearing on the sound, but it seemed to ricochet through the heavy haze, mingling with the faint noise of traffic until it melted into oblivion. Had Agnes reached her destination?

George crept along the side of Fiona's house, her steps silent against the dewy grass. At the hedge she turned, hoping that if she struck out at a dead right angle to the wall, she'd eventually encounter one of her own.

Clutching the gun to her side, she began to pick her way toward her house. The chill penetrated her lacy dress and crept up her legs. She shivered.

She walked blindly forward, straining to discern the undertones of this eerie night. Her footfalls now squished against soggy grass, creating an echo around her and forming an infuriating cocoon that robbed her of the ability to identify the chorus of soft and potentially dangerous rustles, sighs, and whispers.

Hold the gun on Agnes and call Detective Hernandez, she repeated to herself with every step. Adam would miss her soon and follow with help.

Agnes would confess. Earlier when she had descended the stairs with Adam, her eyes had held a desperate, haunted look. She was near the breaking point. Hernandez would catch his murderer. Adam would be safe and free.

She sensed the house, reached a tentative hand, and touched it. The stucco had trapped the night's damp cold. She trailed her fingertips along the sandpaperlike wall, stumbling at the porch. Now confident of her bearings, she darted up the stairs and eased open the front door.

A triangle of light escaped from the study, spilling a meager glow over the foyer floor. Suddenly the light flickered as though someone had passed in front of it.

George sucked in a breath and plastered her back against a wall, inwardly repeating her mission. Hold Agnes. Call Hernandez. She held her breath. Silence.

The clock chimed the quarter hour.

Again, silence.

Hugging the shadows, she edged toward the study, her knees bumping with every step. Her icy fingers fumbled with the gun, trying to position it to point and cover Agnes in one swift movement. She said a quick prayer.

She jumped into the doorway and lowered the gun. "Put up your hands!"

Agnes jerked her head up from her chart on the desk, her face an inscrutable mask in the dim light.

"Put your hands up then back toward the wall," George shrilled. What if Agnes said no?

Mercifully, she didn't. Agnes inched backward, raising her hands.

George inched toward the telephone.

"Why . . . why?" Agnes stammered.

"You came here to cover your tracks—"

"No, you're wrong!" she cried out in an anguished tone. "I went to see him that night, but I didn't mean to kill him. It was an accident. It was all a terrible mistake."

"So you were there that night." Joan LaRose's harsh voice sounded from somewhere behind her.

George started. What was she doing here?

"How did you know Dr. Emerson?" Agnes shrilled at Joan.

George gripped the gun more tightly, determined to stay calm. "Call the police, Miss LaRose," she instructed.

Joan advanced on Agnes in a swirl of black lace. "Why did you go to see Harry that night?"

"Oh!" Agnes took a shaky step backward. "You mean *that* night. Why, he insisted that I come. I certainly wouldn't have paid Harry a visit otherwise. I hardly knew the man."

"Ha!"

"Really," she pleaded. "When I left, he was fine." Agnes turned to George and extended her hands. "Someone else came later. A woman. I hid in the shrubbery so she wouldn't see me but I heard the sound of her high heels and smelled her perfume. Georgette, please believe me! I've never actually murdered anyone, not on purpose. I simply couldn't."

"You lying hussy!" Joan shrieked, pouncing on Agnes and grabbing her by the throat. "Harlot!"

Agnes flailed at Joan's arms, her eyes wide with terror.

"Stop that!" George screamed.

With a throaty growl, Mr. Moto bounded into the room. He charged toward the struggling women, clamped down on Joan's long dress and tugged, rending the fabric. He spat out the piece and locked his jaws higher on the dress. He pulled her backward and held fast, growls rumbling deep in his chest.

Joan shrank from him crying, "Get him off me!"

Agnes recovered her footing. Her hand flew to her throat. "You," she exhaled in a hoarse whisper. "You were the one. The perfume . . . you went to see Harry after I did." She panted, wheezing loudly. "Why did you attack me? You know I didn't kill Harry."

George lowered the gun, groaning in frustration. "I don't

believe this. Agnes, if you're telling the truth then Joan couldn't have killed Harry either. Mr. Moto didn't bark that night, and he obviously hates Joan so . . ." George levelled the gun on Joan. "Unless Mr. Moto didn't hate you until you gave him poisoned meat! You thought he was dead or you wouldn't have come tonight!"

Fury seemed to bubble from Joan's eyes. "Harry used me!" she spat. "I helped him steal all that money, then he hid it from me. He was going to leave me for that." She shot a shriveling glance at Agnes.

"Oh, my goodness," Agnes twittered. "He never mentioned wanting my body, only my brain."

"Your brain?" George asked, incredulous. "That does it. It's going to take a professor of logic to sort this out." She crept toward the desk, gun pointed, doing the best imitation of a tough guy that she could manage in heels and a miniskirt.

She slid her hand over the desk and closed her fingers around the telephone. It rang in her hand. She brought it slowly to her ear, focusing intently at both women.

"This is Georgette Richards and—"

"Twin girls!" Mark exclaimed. "Shannon's fine."

"That's wonderful! I'm an aunt—" She broke off and dropped the telephone. Horror was written on Agnes's face.

A *whoosh* of air whined in George's ears a second before a hard object hit her back. The wind rushed from her lungs. The gun flew. Instinctively, she curled her body and rolled head over heels over the floor. She landed sitting up, shaken but whole.

Marshall Hoagsworth, Jr. stood in full medieval garb, legs spread, sword raised, a giant of a man whose eyes held the glint of insanity. He wielded the sword with the skill of a master, slicing the air with savage gusto.

George gulped.

"Marshall," Agnes began shakily. "I really think it's time you realized that there's a difference between these games of yours and real life."

Marshall cocked his head and his sword. "Silence!" he

bellowed. "I'll hear nothing of your cunning words. I shall not save you this time!"

George hugged the corner drawers of the desk, amazed to see Agnes groping beneath it with a dainty foot. Her shoe touched the gun.

Out of the corner of her eye, George caught movement. Behind Marshall, a curtain fluttered. Someone was coming in the window. Holy heavens! It must be Adam!

Marshall swished his sword.

"You saved Marie Antoinette?" George squeaked from the floor, hoping to distract him.

"I rescued her from the evil baron," he announced, "vile devil and defiler of women."

Marshall killed his own father? But there had been a woman there too. A woman had paid the taxi driver to send Fiona away. Agnes?

Slowly, calmly, Agnes started to crouch and reach for the gun. Did she mean to attempt to kill Marshall, Jr. to prevent him from talking?

George babbled, "Why did you kill the baron, brave warrior? For Marie Antoinette?"

He shook his head. "For my queen."

Agnes's fingers closed on the gun. If she fired it—empty or not—Marshall might kill Agnes. Damn them! They might murder each other before they confessed!

George positioned her hand just below the lip of the desk directly even with a heavy bubble of Baccarat crystal on its surface. "Queen?" she asked.

The curtain bulged. Adam was inside. His feet were visible.

Agnes raised the gun.

Marshall made a growling sound and charged toward the desk, sword raised.

Joan screamed.

George grabbed the massive paperweight and heaved it. It sailed by Marshall's head and slammed into the stereo amplifier.

Agnes fired the gun and missed.

The figure behind the curtain moaned.

Inexplicably Marshall grunted, hesitated, then keeled over like a felled redwood.

"Adam!" George screamed, jumping to her feet and rushing toward the window. She tore back the curtain.

Don Dick Watson hugged the wall, a dart protruding from his arm. He was pale and sinking fast, limp as a mackerel. "Sue me, will you! How does breaking and entering sound to you?"

"I'm over here, Georgette."

She spun around and sighed her relief. Adam kneeled over Marshall, Jr., holding the sword aloft. Marshall sprawled on the floor, impassive and somehow dignified, even in defeat.

"Nice move, Lawrence," Hernandez said, strolling into the room, followed by several uniformed officers. "Great flying open field tackle on the knight here, but the referees would've gotten you for clipping. What do we have here?" he asked, touring the carnage.

"Oh, Adam," George murmured, dropping to her knees and hugging him.

Fiona sprinted into the room. "Thank God you got here in time," she said to Hernandez. "It seemed like the dispatcher asked me a thousand questions."

Ina Hoagsworth rushed past Fiona to her son's side and cradled his head in her lap. She rocked him, sobbing.

"Don't cry, my queen," he implored her.

"Son, your father wasn't worth this."

George groaned. "Adam, we were wrong about everything."

"We certainly were," he managed before being drowned out by Mr. Moto's barks.

Chapter
28

"Some detective I am," George said, flopping onto her sofa next to Adam. The clock struck the last chime of midnight as she sank into the cushions, weary from the parade of policemen and the furor of hauling away two murderers and an accomplice. Joan LaRose, Marshall, Jr., and Ina Hoagsworth all had gone quietly. "How on earth am I going to explain to the insurance company that I broke a Baccarat crystal paperweight, totaled the amplifier on my stereo, and didn't even hit a murderer when there were so many in the room?"

"Poor Marshall, Jr.," Agnes replied. "That LaRose woman deserves whatever she gets for murdering Harry, I don't care if he was going to leave her. But I can't see how anyone could prosecute Marshall, Jr. for murdering his father. Ina never said as much as a cross word to anyone, especially her husband. I guess seeing his mother mistreated by such a cruel man made Marshall snap." She glanced nervously around the house as if to assure herself that the three of them were finally alone, then took a chair opposite them, her teacup poised on her lap. "Marshall, Jr. was always infatuated with Fiona too. Now I see that he must have trailed her to the club, killed his father, and called his mother to help him cover up."

"You knew all these years that Fiona was Marie Antoinette?" Adam asked.

"I certainly guessed. Who else would have the audacity to go on stage and impersonate a stripper!"

"I couldn't even sneak over here without being followed," George muttered dismally.

"Don't blame yourself, Georgette. That Joan woman followed me, though I thought I'd lost her in the fog. Who knows how Marshall, Jr. found us? He was always prowling around."

Adam leaned forward. "If you weren't involved in Hangtown Harry's or Marshall, Sr.'s murder, then why did you poison yourself at Fiona's party? And why did you take our bait tonight and come for your chart?"

"Well, I—" Agnes fluttered her hanky back and forth. "You two are certainly better detectives that you're giving yourselves credit for. Dr. Emerson did have a nasty habit of blackmailing his old patients. You see, he thought that I was Marie Antoinette and that I killed Marshall. It was easier to pay—"

"You paid all those years to protect Fiona!" George exclaimed.

"Of course. She was always my dearest friend, and I had nothing to hide, really. I paid rather than risk him looking elsewhere for the mysterious Marie. After Marvin returned, I was afraid the doctor would deduce his parentage. Marvin and Marshall do share some similarities, and evil minds do put things together quickly." Her eyes darted over the living room. "I must say, I'm surprised that his presence has somehow been exorcised from this house."

"Thank heavens. Emerson was an odious man," George said. "I can't say that I feel a twinge of remorse that he met his end at the hands of thugs. He deserved worse."

"I'm glad you agree," Agnes said. "Thugs."

"Thugs," George repeated, firmly ending her first stab at detecting. If the police were happy with the thug theory, why should she worry? Besides, Agnes claimed Emerson's death had been accidental, and George believed her.

Agnes set aside her cup of tea and got up. "Will you escort me home, Adam?"

"Certainly—that is, after you answer my two questions."

"This much I will say." She raised the scarlet mask to her face. "Harry thought I knew where Emerson kept his records. We argued about that very thing the night he was murdered. I felt endangered. When Harry's bank scheme was revealed, I realized that he didn't need blackmail money for himself. Now we know why he pressured me, don't we? Harry intended to leave those charts as a lucrative legacy to pacify his jilted lover Joan."

Agnes lowered the mask and plucked up her own chart.

Adam stalked toward her. "Still, you were afraid the police would connect the depletion of your savings account with Emerson's death."

"Thugs, you remember. But I could have shown the police my rows of mason jars. Those preserves may be labeled 'golden delicious,' but what's inside them has more to do with bullion than preserves." Agnes took his arm with a giggle.

He escorted her into the foyer while George marveled at the glow of youth in the older woman's cheeks. Neither Agnes nor any other of Dr. Emerson's patients would ever have to worry again. She planned to burn every last file personally.

Adam raised his brows at Agnes and inquired, "Did you happen to visit Dr. Emerson the night he died?"

As they slipped outside, she heard Agnes say, "We women must 'preserve' our secrets." She chuckled heartily at her pun.

George collected Agnes's teacup and wandered into the kitchen, relief washing over her. The money in the mason jars removed the last doubt; Agnes had had no motive to harm Emerson. She could have simply continued paying him until one of them died. So Marshall, Jr., had murdered his father. Joan LaRose had killed Hangtown Harry, and Agnes had accidentally done in Dr. Emerson. Everything was settled perfectly, perfectly at least for everyone except her.

The excitement that had carried her through the last six hours ebbed from her body. She hugged herself, suddenly feeling tired, empty, and desolate. Adam had proven himself to be the man of her dreams, and she had promised her father to give him up.

Mr. Moto barked. She dragged herself into the living room and found her father snarling back at the dog.

"The door was open," he stated flatly, thumping past a stunned-looking Mr. Moto. The esteemed hunter dog had finally encountered a bear impossible to hold at bay. "I just left the hospital. Mark Ryerson said there was some sort of hullabaloo going on when he called you regarding the deliveries. What happened?"

She tilted her chin up a notch. "Adam turned down my proposal. I was right; you were wrong."

"He said no without any form of trickery on your part?"

"If you don't believe me, ask him yourself."

Adam closed the front door and crossed to stand beside her. "Richards," he said curtly.

"My daughter tells me that you refused her offer of marriage."

"She attached a condition that I find impossible to fulfill. I turned down a position with your company, not your daughter."

George gripped the arm of the strong, unflappable man she loved so much. Hope surged through her. *Maybe he has grown to care for me*, she thought.

"My daughter made a deal, Lawrence, and I expect her to stick to it."

Her desperation deal. Her meager hopes flagged.

Oh, God, I've made it all impossible.

Adam stiffened. He tilted his head, and his eyes fixed on hers. His gaze relayed his doubt, his puzzlement.

"That's why I was so happy when you turned me down, Adam. My father said that because you were broke you were after my money and a position with his company. I didn't believe him so I made a bargain. I knew that if you were the man I thought you were, you'd turn me down."

"What if I had said yes?"

"I told him that I would marry you."

His expression grew stricken, lines and tightness everywhere. "And because I said no?"

Harlan Richards thundered, "She promised to terminate your affair and never see you again. That alleviates the possibility of you freeloading married or not."

Anger flashed in her, blinding as sun on a mirror. "That wasn't the reason I agreed to that!" she snapped. "I knew you'd never leave Adam alone. You'd make him just as miserable as you've always made me!"

Her father scowled and continued in a steely tone, "Be that as it may—"

"You've lost, Richards," Adam said calmly, clearly relieved. "Georgette may have agreed to stop seeing me, but I struck no such bargain. I love your daughter, and I intend to see her."

George clutched Adam's arm. Her anger dissolved as quickly as it came. Adam believed her, not her father. He believed without reservation or explanation. Tears swam in her eyes. *Adam loves me!*

Her father glared at her. "You're disappointing me."

Dear Lord, how do I say this? She bit her lip, praying she could make the words come out right. "I know, Daddy," she said softly. "You've always disappointed me because you couldn't love. Now I'm disappointing you because I can."

Her father turned abruptly and limped away. She trailed him outside and watched his progress through the lifting fog, knowing with absolute certainty that his flaw had nothing to do with her. She was worthy of love. Adam had taught her that.

She gripped his hand, hard.

As the Rolls-Royce sped away, she noticed a sticker on the bumper. "It can't be," she muttered, rushing down the walk and into the street. "He's never put one on that car, not even for Richard Nixon."

"What did you think of the bumper sticker?" Adam asked, capturing her in his arms, swinging her off her feet, and setting her down.

"I couldn't quite read—"

"It says I Drive Nude."

"You put that on his car?" she asked, incredulous.

"I was just waiting for the right moment."

She started to giggle. "Oh, dear, he's going to be furious, absolutely furious. But then my father can't intimidate you, can he?"

"That's right. He can't make either of us miserable unless we let him, and I won't let him."

"Do you realize that you've freed me just as completely as you did that dove?"

"Not that free," he said, pulling her close. "I have no intention of letting you get away."

"You really do love me? You weren't just saying that to make my father angry?"

"Don't you believe the things I say to you?" he mocked, parroting his earlier words. "Believe me, I love you. When I saw Marshall with that sword . . ."

"You had to save me, my Sir Walter Raleigh, because you're always brave and true."

"Now that you understand me completely and I've laid all your concerns to rest once and for all, you're going to say yes when I ask you to marry me."

She averted her eyes, toying with the stud on his shirt. "We've only known each other a few days. Maybe we ought to wait to discuss—"

"We could wait until tomorrow. Think that's long enough?"

George reached on tiptoes and slid her arms around his neck. "I think so," she said, breathing against his lips, and Adam kissed her passionately and shamelessly, a gardener embracing an heiress right in the middle of Scarlet Street.

Scandalous!

FROM
THE BESTSELLING AUTHOR
OF *TOO DEEP FOR TEARS*

CHILD OF AWE

Kathryn Lynn Davis

*C*HILD OF AWE, a hauntingly beautiful story of passion, courage and love.

Muriella Calder is a young Scots beauty and the sole heir to a castle and fabled fortune. She was stolen from her family and betrothed against her will to the second son of a rival clan.

John Campbell is a proud young warrior and hero but his bloodlust dismays his stolen bride.

Every corner of Muriella's new world is locked in a violent struggle, but none so fierce as the passion that rages in her heart.

COMING IN OCTOBER
FROM POCKET BOOKS

POCKET
B O O K S